"They're going to dive into the lake? The water's got to be freezing," Noelle said.

She studied the Santas crossing the road in front of the town car, the crowd trailing behind them. There was one noticeable Santa, taller than the rest, strolling in the middle of the pack. He had his chin up, his shoulders back and he moved with a relaxed, loose-limbed stride that drew attention.

This was no traditional ho-ho-ho, lap-sitting Santa Claus. He was ripped, his biceps bulging at the seams of his red and white Santa suit.

Oh Santa, you can come down my chimney any old time.

Goodness, how brave they were. Not only to plunge into the icy waters, but to publicly embarrass themselves. Tall Santa took off his top, revealing that indeed, he performed physical labor regularly. His abs were taut and toned and she could make out every striation of well-honed muscles. Tall Santa laughed and said something to the Santa next to him. His fake beard slipped a little and in the sunlight, Noelle caught a glimpse of light blue eyes just as the double dimple in his right cheek deepened.

Goodness! Thirteen years might have passed, but she would know those lively blue eyes and that fetching dimple anywhere.

Gil Thomas.

The Christmas Brides of Twilight

A TWILIGHT, TEXAS NOVEL

LORI WILDE

AVON

An Imprint of HarperCollinsPublishers

THE CHRISTMAS BRIDES OF TWILIGHT. Copyright © 2023 by Laurie Vanzura. All rights reserved. Printed in the United States of America. No part of this book may be used or reproduced in any manner whatsoever without written permission except in the case of brief quotations embodied in critical articles and reviews. For information, address HarperCollins Publishers, 195 Broadway, New York, NY 10007.

First Avon Books mass market printing: October 2023

Print Edition ISBN: 978-0-06-313803-2
Digital Edition ISBN: 978-0-06-313802-5

Cover illustration by Reginald Polynice
Cover images © iStock/Getty Images; © Shutterstock

Avon, Avon & logo, and Avon Books & logo are registered trademarks of HarperCollins Publishers in the United States of America and other countries.

HarperCollins is a registered trademark of HarperCollins Publishers in the United States of America and other countries.

FIRST EDITION

23 24 25 26 27 BVGM 10 9 8 7 6 5 4 3 2 1

To Michelle, thank you for your friendship and your love of Chuck. We never knew we needed you until you appeared. Keep shining your sweet light!

The
Christmas Brides
of Twilight

CHAPTER 1

WELCOME TO TWILIGHT, TEXAS.

The freshly painted billboard glimmered glossy in the sunlight beaming off Lake Twilight as the town car Noelle Curry hired at DFW Airport motored past.

Elbow-deep in business emails, Noelle barely noticed. Her job came first, and she was on a mission to orchestrate the most spectacular double wedding this little burg had ever seen.

Successfully pulling off her assignment was her path to independence from the shadow of her illustrious family. Everything else was secondary. Including her nostalgic past with this darling place.

"Are you famous?"

She glanced up from her cell phone to see the Uber driver who'd picked her up at DFW Airport and had been surreptitiously peeking at her in the rearview mirror for the last forty minutes.

Ugh.

She didn't get recognized nearly as often as her movie star mother or documentary filmmaker father, but unlike Crescenda and Clint, she didn't welcome the attention. With attention came scrutiny and with scrutiny came criticism and more expectations for her to live up to. She preferred to stay behind the scenes. It was where she felt safest.

"No," she said, because in her mind she wasn't.

"Yeah, yeah, you are. I saw you on that daytime talk show, *The Klatch*. You're her. You're the Wedding Whisperer."

One show. She'd been on one measly morning talk show and now she couldn't check her emails in peace. At this rate, she'd have to hire bodyguards like dear old Mom and Dad.

Eek. Her worst nightmare.

"You have a sharp eye," she said.

The guy beamed. "That's a big compliment coming from you. According to the talk show host, you're the queen of intricate detail."

That was a kind way of putting it. Her mother called it anal. Dad didn't comment on her personality. He globe-trotted, usually with women half his age, and had barely been an influence in her life. Crescenda and Clint had divorced when she was three and she'd seen her father maybe a dozen times in the twenty-five years since then.

"You live in LA?" he asked.

"I do."

"And your mother is Crescenda Hardwick?"

Noelle sighed. Here it came. "She is."

"That's how you got a leg up in the biz."

"Yes."

If her mother hadn't been married five times and had lots of friends who also got married and divorced as often as some people changed their hair color, Noelle wouldn't have had the opportunity to plan celebrity weddings at such a young age. But while Crescenda might have given her the opportunity, it was Noelle's efficient organizational skills and calm aplomb in the face of overwrought drama that caused her successful business, Once Upon a Wedding, to flourish.

"I love your mom's movies."

"Thanks."

Sweet Summer Sunshine is my fave."

"That was her first blockbuster."

"I'm a bit of an actor myself. I was in a dinner theatre production of *Annie Get Your Gun*."

"That's nice."

The driver, named Knox, was fortyish, on the scrawny side, and reminded her of the bumbling deputy on the TV program her maternal grandparents had watched in endless reruns when, from the ages of eight to fifteen, she visited them every summer right here in Twilight, Texas.

A wisp of sadness slipped through her. Grammie and Grampie had been gone thirteen years now, and she hadn't been back to Twilight since. But fond memories of the small lakeside community, where her beloved grandparents had retired after Grampie left a lifelong career as a pilot with Delta Air Lines, had stayed with her.

Because of Noelle's talk show appearance and her connection to celebrity, a media and technology company called The Tie, which paired engaged couples to wedding planning services across the United States, had invited her to be their official wedding planner for this year's Christmas Bride Contest.

It was the first gig she'd gotten solely on her own merit, and it was her breakout opportunity if she didn't blow it.

Couples, vying to have their wedding completely paid for by The Tie, had sent in essays about their love stories and Noelle had been the final round judge. Among the contenders, she'd been thrilled to discover a composition penned by identical twin sisters who'd fallen in love with identical twin brothers.

Icing on the cake? Sierra and Sienna Buckhorn were from Twilight.

Now Noelle would be spending the next six weeks in the small tourist town that had been her only source of stability during her chaotic childhood.

This trip was, in effect, a homecoming.

Noelle's heart skipped a beat as the car drove down the main thoroughfare, headed toward the charming town square that was listed in the National Historic Register. To the right, the lake glistened silvery blue in the rising sun. A rippling banner stretching across Ruby Street announced: Santa Claus Polar Plunge, Friday, November 17.

That was today.

"Isn't it a little early for Christmas events?"

"Not for Twilight," Knox said. "We get into the spirit right after Halloween."

"Aah, the Christmas creep."

"Yeah, it comes earlier every year."

Noelle wasn't an enthusiastic fan of the holiday, not since her grandparents had died, anyway, and taken her Christmas spirit with them.

As the signal light turned red, Knox halted at the intersection directly underneath the banner. The marina overflow parking was on one side of the road, the lake on the other. From the jam-packed lot, a thick crowd milled, many with cell phones out, snapping pictures as a white delivery van pulled to a stop.

The back door flew opened . . .

And a passel of Santas tumbled out.

Passel. Was that the right word?

Curious, Noelle Googled it and learned, to her delight, that a group of Santas was called a sleigh. There were at least two dozen of them—youthful, aged, slender, plump, Black, White, Brown, male, female—a diversity of Santas.

"What's going on here?"

"It's the annual Polar Plunge benefiting the Special Olympics," Knox told her. "Twilight puts their unique twist on the event by having participants dress up as Santa Claus."

"They're going to dive into the lake?"

"Yep."

"The water's got to be freezing."

"That's the point."

Noelle herself had once plunged into those dazzling blue waters, but only in the swelter of a hot Texas summer as her grandparents watched from a blanket spread over the sandy beach. Even then, a poor swimmer, she'd never ventured far from shore.

She studied the Santas crossing the road in front of the town car, the crowd trailing behind them. There was one noticeable Santa, taller than the rest, strolling in the middle of the pack. He had his chin up, his shoulders back, and he moved with a relaxed, loose-limbed stride that drew attention.

This was no traditional ho-ho-ho, lap-sitting Santa Claus. For one thing, he was young, near her own age, no older than thirty, and he was ripped, his biceps bulging at the seams of his red-and-white Santa suit.

And she forgot all about her emails.

Even beneath the faux white beard, she could see his angular jaw was chiseled and his cheekbones high. His jingle bell hat was cocked rakishly to one side, and he'd hitched his thick black belt low on lean hips.

Oh Santa, you can come down my chimney any old time.

As the Santas hit the curb on the lake side of the street, they started taking off their clothing—doffing caps, unbuckling belts, slipping off their fur-trimmed jackets.

Goodness, how brave they were. Not only to plunge into the icy waters, but to publicly embarrass themselves. Onlookers were laughing, pointing, and snapping pictures. Humiliation by proxy washed over Noelle. She could never do something like that. Not in a million years.

Tall Santa took off his top, revealing that indeed, he performed physical labor regularly. His abs were taut and toned and she could make out every striation of well-honed muscles. Gawking at his chest, her jaw unhinged. There was something so familiar about him.

Did she know this Santa Claus?

But how could she? She hadn't been in Twilight for thirteen years. Surely, anyone she'd known as a teen would be almost unrecognizable by now. She had certainly altered her appearance—dropping twenty pounds, exchanging glasses for contact lenses, straightening and lightening her unruly curls.

Keeping it tight in Hollywood.

Tall Santa laughed and said something to the Santa next to him. He angled his head toward the person. His fake beard slipped a little and in the sunlight, Noelle caught a glimpse of light blue eyes just as the double dimple in his right cheek deepened.

Goodness! Thirteen years might have passed, but she would know those lively blue eyes and that fetching dimple anywhere.

Gil Thomas.

The light turned green.

"Could you pull over?" she asked Knox. "I want to watch the Polar Plunge."

"I'll slide into the marina's loading zone. Since we'll only be here a few minutes, we won't block anyone, and that way we won't have to compete with the overflow parking lot crowd."

"Oh, great idea." Moving over to the lake side of the road would give her a much better view. "We can leave if someone needs the space."

Knox parked in the loading zone, engine idling. The Santas were kicking off their boots, shucking their pants, and revealing their swimsuits, which were also Christmas themed.

Noelle felt a bit guilty sitting in the comfort of the warm vehicle in this primo location, while the Polar Plunge participants shivered in the wintry morning air. She was privileged and she knew it. She should donate to their cause. She did an internet search for the Twilight Chamber of Commerce website, found the event page, and scrolled through the names of participants.

Sure enough, Gil Thomas was listed.

Her breathing quickened illogically. She hit the pledge button beside his name and sent a thousand dollars via a popular payment app.

While she was doing that, her phone rang, chiming "Here Comes the Bride," letting her know that dear old Mom was calling.

Her gaze searched the sleigh of Santas. Gil wasn't hard to find. The man towered above the rest. When she'd last seen him, he'd been seventeen and six-foot-one. He was at least two inches taller than that now. And currently strutting in nothing but Rudolph the Red-Nosed Reindeer swimwear.

"Halloo," Crescenda said in an affected British accent. Her mother was in London, shooting a film about Agatha Christie's life and she sounded fully immersed in her character. "How is my favorite offspring?"

"I'm your only offspring."

"You forget I have a cadre of stepchildren."

"I forget nothing, Crescenda," she said, calling her by her first name out of habit. Her mother disliked people knowing that she was old enough to have a daughter Noelle's age—as if the internet didn't exist—and she'd coached Noelle to use her first name in public.

"Are we in a mood?"

"Did you know Gil Thomas still lived in Twilight?"

"Who?"

"The boy I had a mad crush on when I was a teenager."

"Why would I know that?"

"He lived across the street from your parents. You *did* come back here just last year to finally sell their house when the market shot up. Didn't you talk to anyone while you were here?"

"I did sell at a fortuitous time, didn't I? I was smart to hold on to it and rent the place out. Made a mint on that hovel." Mom was as sentimental as a bulldozer.

"Yes," Noelle said, giving Crescenda the ego stroke she was looking for. "You did a fabulous job, but why didn't you mention Gil?"

"I try not to think too much about the past. Besides, none of those die-hard Twilightites ever leave town. Why are you so surprised?"

Because Gil once had big dreams about becoming a country music star. Noelle used to sleep upstairs in her grandparents' house with the windows open, listening to him play the guitar on his back porch as she daydreamed about kissing him.

Now she watched him saunter languidly toward the water, unlike his fellow Santas, who scurried past him, heads down against the wind and shoulders hunched. His Rudolph swim trunks clung to his burly thighs, showing off an eye-popping amount of flesh. Her mouth watered and her pulse galloped as her mind flew to illicit places.

To steamy North Pole fantasies.

Objectifying his rock-hard body felt wrong in nine hundred different ways, but she stared at him anyway.

She tried to focus on something else, but she simply couldn't pry her gaze off him. Truth be told, it wasn't the first time she'd ogled the guy. More than once, she'd peered over her grandparents' privacy fence while he mowed his parents' front lawn, shirt stripped off, bare skin covered in sweat.

Back during those long, hot summers, she'd been a shy loner, seeking refuge from her mother's star-studded lifestyle between the pages of romance novels. She doubted Gil Thomas even remembered she existed. He might have waved at her a few times and chatted with her once or twice at a neighborhood block party barbecue, but for sure he had no idea her silly teenage heart had desperately pined for him from one vacation to the next.

Shouting "Hoo-rah!" in unison, the Santas ran toward the water, their feet kicking up beach sand as they plunged into the frigid lake.

Noelle sucked in her breath, empathy sending

her mind into the water with them. She shivered as an imaginary chill gripped her body.

But Gil?

He looked as comfortable as if he were stepping into a sauna. Unlike most of the others, whose mouths were pinched and pained, this easygoing Santa actually smiled as the water lapped at a waist that didn't possess a drop of fat. Damn, if her California girl lungs didn't clutch as she admired his cool, unruffled badassery.

He didn't care what anyone thought of him.

"Noelle, you still there? Did we get disconnected?"

Oh Mom, we've been disconnected for so long it's normal. "I'm still here."

"Now that you mention it," Crescenda said. "I do remember Gil. Tall, dark, stunning blue eyes, dimples galore. Don't feel bad that he barely noticed you. You didn't stand a chance. Gil was a ten."

Yeah. She knew that. Noelle eyeballed the man bathing in the lake. "He's an eleven now. Way out of my league."

"There's nothing wrong with being a solid seven, darling," her mother said, still hamming it up with the British accent. "Everyone can't be a ten like me. They really had to ugly me up to play Agatha. Besides, you could easily be an eight if you just followed through with the nose job."

Noelle fingered the hump in the bridge of her nose. When she was sixteen, Crescenda made an appointment for her with a plastic surgeon, but she hadn't kept it. She liked that her nose wasn't perfectly straight. It gave her character.

"Is there a reason you called?" Noelle watched the Santas flee the lake, blue-faced and teeth chattering as they raced to the beach, helpers waiting with oversized towels to envelop them.

But not Gil. His head was thrown back, his eyes closed, the sun glistening like gold off the water sluicing down his chest.

"Yes, I called to tell you I'll be stuck in London over Christmas. I'm unable to come to Twilight for your wedding thingy."

"I'm pretty sure Agatha Christie wouldn't say *thingy*," Noelle said. So, she would be spending yet another Christmas without Crescenda. What else was new?

"Ack! You're right. Although Agatha probably wouldn't say *ack* either."

"Who knows? She did have a book called *The Murder of Roger Ackroyd*."

"Did she?"

"Yes."

"You're the reader, I'll trust you. Listen, darling, the reason I shan't be able to spend Christmas with you is that I've met someone, and he's invited me to his family's celebration in Kent. It's an opportunity I simply can't pass up."

Noelle groaned.

"Don't make that noise. Be happy for me."

"The ink isn't even dry on your fifth set of divorce papers."

"Who cares?"

"You should."

"Why?"

"People will talk."

"And that's a *bad* thing?"

"The tabloids will say mean things." Noelle bit her bottom lip, as a montage of memories blasted through her mind—paparazzi camped on the street outside their house, kids at school laughing at Noelle and shunning her because of her mother's flamboyant lifestyle, hate mail from fans calling Crescenda a slut because she'd broken up another celebrity marriage, the time that Noelle—

She shook her head. No, she wasn't going to remember that.

"You care too much about what other people think. You always have."

"Because it matters."

"The only thing that matters is what *you* think of yourself. And I think I deserve to have all the love I can find."

For of course Crescenda believed that. She thought the entire world revolved around her. "Mom, I—"

"Mum. That's what they say in England."

"You're not from England."

"No, but Dame Agatha was."

"I gotta go."

"You're not the least bit curious about Basil?"

"Nope."

"But I listened to you talk about Gil Thomas."

"Fine. Tell me about Basil. Does he have a brother named Dill? A sister called Rosemary?"

"What? Oh. Ha-ha. No. He doesn't have any siblings. He's an only child . . . like moi."

"That's splendid, Miss Piggy."

"Are you mocking me?"

"You totally asked for it with the pretentious use of *moi*."

"Agatha said *moi*. She spoke French, you know."

"Goodbye, Agatha. I've got an appointment. Have fun making your movie and hanging out with Thyme."

"Now you're just being tacky. FYI Basil means king."

"And is he a king?"

"In bed he is."

"Okay, I do not need to hear this. Bye, Crescenda. Hanging up now."

"In England we say—"

"Bye." Noelle ended the call. Sometimes, Mom could be a handful. She blew out her breath and glanced back at the water.

At some point, while she'd quipped with her mother, Gil had walked back to the beach. He was the last Santa out of the water. His nipples beaded tight. It was the only evidence that he was chilled. Someone handed him a towel.

Rubbing his hair dry, he stared across the stretch of sand, peering straight through the window of the town car.

He sauntered toward the vehicle, naked except for the swim trunks plastered to his body and revealing the outline of an impressive package.

Noelle jumped and her pulse fluttered. Holy crap! Had he caught her ogling him? Had he recognized her? But that was silly. The windows were tinted.

"Put the vehicle in gear," Noelle told Knox, her voice coming out exceptionally high. "And let's get out of here. Quick."

"On it," he said.

As they sped away, Noelle turned to look over her shoulder, but Gil had already vanished from view.

CHAPTER 2

Banner after banner adorned the road, announcing various upcoming events. The Harvest Craft Fair was this weekend, the Turkey Trot was happening the morning before Thanksgiving, and the last banner, just as they reached the square, read: Christmas Tree Lighting Festival, Thanksgiving Day, November 23!

Overwhelmed, Noelle took it all in, her objective momentarily sidetracked by a barrage of memories.

Noelle recalled another tree lighting festival the year she'd turned thirteen. It seemed the entire town had shown up for the event. The atmosphere was festive. Her grandparents arrived early to stake out a spot near the tree, but once the mayor threw the switch to light up the thirty-foot pine, it was a free-for-all as people surged forward to decorate the branches.

In their enthusiasm, the crowd stampeded, and Noelle, who'd been clutching a manger ornament, got shoved to the ground. She was face down in the dirt, terrified and struggling to get up, certain she was about to die.

And then, a miraculous hand reached down, grabbed her by the hood of her coat, and lifted her to her feet.

"Are you okay?"

It was only then that she realized she had her eyes tightly closed. Her lashes fluttered opened, and she stared up into Gil Thomas's gorgeous blue eyes. That might have been the moment she tumbled madly into her first crush.

He reached out to brush debris from her coat, and his casual touch electrified her entire body. She couldn't speak. Couldn't move her tongue.

"Noelle? Are you all right?"

He knew her name! Gil Thomas knew her name! Her teenage heart throbbed.

She'd squeezed her hand tightly around the manger ornament, the tail of the small plastic donkey poking into her palm. She looked down and felt a tear slip over her cheek.

"What's wrong? Are you hurt?" Gently, Gil steered her out of the way of the throng.

"Not me." She shook her head and held the ornament out to him. "Baby Jesus fell from his crib. We'll never find him in this crowd."

Instead of laughing at her tender tears or pooh-poohing her upset as overly sensitive as Crescenda would have done, Gil shook his head, clicked his tongue, and said with an earnest expression, "Why, that's a downright shame."

"We can't put the manger on the tree without Baby Jesus in his crib."

"Sure we can," Gil said. "We'll pretend it's just before Jesus has been born and everyone has gathered around the crib to await his arrival."

"Oh!" Noelle loved the way he thought. "That could work."

"C'mon, I'll clear a path so you can put up your ornament."

"Thank you."

He shooed people aside and escorted her to the tree. She spent time looking for just the right branch and once she found it, she turned to see if Gil approved.

But he'd already disappeared, just as he had at the Polar Plunge. The man was nothing if not consistent.

Noelle bit her bottom lip. She'd forgotten all about that memory. Staring out the tinted window of the town car as Knox passed the courthouse lawn where the town Christmas tree would soon stand, Noelle wistfully pressed her fingertips against the window glass. In her mind's eye, she saw the girl she used to be, standing with Gil beneath the sheltering branches of that long-ago pine.

Yikes! Why couldn't she stop thinking about him? This was nonsense. She was here to plan a double wedding, not light a flame where there had never even been a spark. *Eyes on the prize, Curry.* If she made a splash with The Tie, she could stop planning weddings for her mother and her friends and focus on forging her own way.

Knox left the square and turned down a residential street. Here, the homes were all sprawling Victorians. This was Twilight's richest area of town. It was unimposing compared to the vast wealth of Beverly Hills, but she loved the quaint little neighborhood and restored homes. And just ahead stood the Merry Cherub B&B.

Once upon a time, whenever she visited her grandparents in Twilight, she babysat the four Cantrell children who'd lived at the Merry Cherub. They were toddlers then and must be teenagers by now. Her spirits leaped at the possibility of seeing them again.

Like the town billboard, the Victorian had been given a fresh coat of paint. It was no longer the sweet pink of a cherry Slurpee. Instead, it sported sunny yellow siding with white trim. New outdoor furniture sat on the wraparound veranda, including a porch swing and two rocking chairs.

Knox took Noelle's luggage from the trunk. "Do you need help inside with your bags?"

"I can manage, thank you." She tipped him a hundred-dollar bill.

"Thanks!" He gave a wave, got back into the town car, and drove off.

Pulling the two wheeled suitcases behind her, Noelle turned toward the house. The yard and porch were decorated for Thanksgiving with wreaths, pumpkins, gourds, cornstalks, and dried red chili pepper garlands.

She went up the sidewalk, the wheels of her luggage click-clacking merrily against the concrete. A bright orange leaf broke free of a branch and drifted down from the big oak on the front lawn.

There was that dangerous feeling of belonging again.

Home.

It felt like she'd come home.

But that was absurd, wasn't it? She'd never lived in this town. She'd only been an occasional visitor.

Inside the B&B, the foyer opened up into a small reception area. Behind it, an attractive woman in her sixties was humming "It's Beginning to Look a Lot Like Christmas" and watering poinsettias with a cute little watering can patterned with a chubby angel and the Merry Cherub logo.

Noelle had been inside the bed-and-breakfast many times, so she was not overwhelmed by the home's excessive angelic decor, which was composed of angel-themed wallpaper, mobiles, wind chimes, statues, candles, and more.

The woman spied her and set down her watering can. "Hello! You must be Noelle. Welcome!"

"I am." Noelle glanced around, looking for Jenny Cantrell. She wanted to give her a big hug but didn't see her. "Is Jenny here?"

"Jenny?" The woman frowned, and then a knowing expression came over her face. "Oh, you mean the previous owner. The Cantrells left town a few years ago. I'm sorry. I didn't know them. My husband and I recently retired to Twilight, and I needed a part-time job to keep from getting bored and this suits me just fine. I'm Delphine, by the way."

"Hello, Delphine. It's nice to meet you." Noelle shook the woman's hand.

"You'll be in the Roost." Delphine reached for a key on the pegboard mounted on the wall behind the desk.

"The Roost?"

"Pamela Landry, the representative from The Tie who made your reservations, thought you'd like privacy, so we suggested the garage apartment out back." Delphine handed Noelle the key.

"Do I need to sign in or give you my credit card or—"

"Nope. You're all set." Delphine waved a hand. "The Tie is paying for everything. I would lead you to your room, but my arthritis is acting up and the stairs are a challenge, but if you need help with your luggage, I can text my hubs, Luther. We live just down the block."

"I'm good." Noelle wrapped her hand around the angel keychain. "Thank you, Delphine."

"In your room, you'll find a welcome packet and contact info for the local restaurants. We only serve breakfast, zoning laws and all that. We stop service at ten thirty. You're . . ." Delphine looked at her watch. "Over an hour past that."

"It's eleven thirty?" Noelle asked. Time had gotten away from her. She was supposed to meet the Buckhorn twins and their mother at noon for lunch, and it would take her at least ten minutes to walk back to the town square.

"It's eleven thirty-seven precisely."

"Thanks, Delphine. I need to get a move on."

"Let us know if you need anything."

Noelle went outside again with her luggage. A wooden sign was staked in the ground with an arrow pointing the way to the Roost. A charming white picket fence enclosed the huge backyard filled with trees, including apple and pear trees bearing ripe fruit. At the back of the property sat a cozy little cottage.

Could this place be any more on-the-nose adorable?

The wooden staircase led to a deck. Noelle picked up her suitcases and scaled the sixteen steps to the top. She counted them. Counting was something she did to keep herself grounded in her body whenever anxiety crept in.

Positioned on either side of the door of the upstairs living quarters were two potted pine trees decorated with orange garlands and Thanksgiving-themed ornaments. Over-the-top for sure, but at least the pumpkins, cornucopia, and turkeys provided some relief from the relentless angel theme.

Noelle let herself into the small apartment. Without looking around, she dumped her bags at the door and rushed back outside. She couldn't be late. She was determined to make a good impression on the Buckhorns. If she did well with this wedding, she'd be in good with The Tie and her business would skyrocket.

Preparing to count her way back downstairs, she caught sight of a man closing the side gate.

He had his back to her, so she couldn't see his face, but that imposing height and those broad shoulders looked awfully familiar.

Gone was the Santa costume and in its place were faded Wranglers, cowboy boots, and a black hooded sweatshirt with WINDMILL MUSIC HALL emblazoned on the back in red lettering. Below the words was a logo of an old-fashioned windmill featuring musical notes being generated from the spinning blades.

What was Gil Thomas doing here? Did he rent a room at the B&B? If so, why?

Feeling fifteen all over again, Noelle ducked behind one of the potted pines. She held her breath. Maybe he wouldn't see her.

She crossed her fingers. *Please.*

The gate hinges creaked.

Seconds passed. She heard nothing but the soft whisper of the wind shaking the autumn leaves on a nearby cottonwood tree. Slowly, Noelle peeked around the pine branches . . .

And her gaze crashed headlong into Gil Thomas's azure-eyed stare as he stood at the bottom of the steps looking up.

Ulp.

He'd seen her. Now she looked like an idiot for trying to hide from him.

Noelle swallowed and exhaled at the same time, making an indelicate noise that sounded like a burp. A wall of heat spread from the center of her belly, across her chest, and up her neck to burn her cheeks with red-hot intensity.

Maybe her embarrassment wouldn't show on her face. Maybe her skin wasn't blistered crimson.

What *did* she look like?

Knowing that she'd be meeting with the Buckhorn twins and their mother as soon as she arrived in Twilight, she'd dressed to impress instead of for comfort. Image mattered. She wore a navy blue pencil skirt, matching navy blazer, and a ruffled white blouse along with three-inch stacked high heels.

Ugh.

In aiming for a professional image, she'd ended up looking like a flight attendant.

Noelle stabbed her fingers through her long whiskey-brown hair streaked with golden highlights. She had ironed her hair perfectly straight, so there shouldn't have been flyaways sticking out all over the place the way they used to do when she was a sad sack teen drooling over her grandparents' sexy across-the-street neighbor.

"Hello there," he called.

She readjusted a pumpkin ornament on the pine tree as if realigning decorations had been her intention all along, not avoiding this potent man.

Gil came closer and craned his neck back.

She moved to the railing and peered down. Those stunning blue eyes narrowed in amusement.

"Can I help you with something?" he asked.

"Y-you don't recognize me." *Way to play it cool, Curry.*

"Should I?"

"Not really, no." She came down the stairs . . . *one, two, three, four, five* . . . to join him on the sidewalk, disappointment a soggy wet sponge in the center of her stomach.

"We've met?" He arched his eyebrows. "I don't see how that's possible. I wouldn't have forgotten someone like *you*."

Her pulse fluttered at his flattery. "It was a long time ago. Before contact lenses and braces and hair-straightening tools. I don't blame you for not remembering me. I was pretty blah back then, and you were a rodeo star and had your own band. The girls swarmed you like honeybees."

He squinted as if trying to see into the past and then suddenly his eyes popped wide. "Holy moly, Noelle Curry! As I live and breathe. Is that really you?"

She lifted her shoulders, feeling shy and invisible all over again. She thought she'd buried that awkward teenage wallflower. Apparently, she had not.

"Why," he said, "you're gorgeous."

The flush returned to her cheeks, and she ducked her head.

"N-not that you weren't cute before. I mean . . . oh hell, I've got my size eleven boot wedged in my mouth, don't I?"

"It's okay. I've changed a lot."

"You haven't been back to Twilight since your grandparents died."

"No. I've been so busy building my business and there was nothing left for me here once Grammie and Grampie were gone."

"Yeah, I heard that your mom came back to sell your grandparents' house last year. You chose not to come with her?"

"I couldn't. I had a wedding in Aruba."

His gaze went to her left hand. "You're married?"

"No, no. I'm a wedding planner."

"Aah, you're the one The Tie sent to plan the Buckhorn/Maxwell wedding."

"I am."

"So we'll be working together." A pleased smile tipped up his lips.

"How's that?"

He showed her his back, pointing a thumb over his shoulder at the logo. "I run the Windmill."

"The Windmill?"

"It used to be the old Twilight Live music hall."

When they were kids, the old music theatre on the square had been boarded up and vacant for years.

"Yep, I renovated the place and renamed it. My wife and I did it together."

His wife.

He was married.

Her silly hopes fell. Of course he was married. The man was hotter than a smoking gun with dreamy blue eyes and dimples that wouldn't quit. It was her turn to stare at the ring finger of his left hand. It was bare.

But that didn't mean anything. A lot of guys who worked with their hands didn't wear wedding bands for safety reasons.

"So you live here now? At the B&B?"

"Yes." His eyelids lowered and his voice took on a languid quality. "My seven-year-old daughter, Josie, and I moved into the carriage house." He waved at the small cottage behind him. "After my wife died."

He was a widower.

Her heart ached for him. "That must have been so very hard to lose a spouse."

"It was right after my sister, Gretchen, bought the B&B from the Cantrells. She needed help running the bed-and-breakfast and I needed help raising Josie. Moving in was a win-win."

Noelle remembered his older sister, Gretchen, as

a lively girl who told ghost stories around beach campfires to the neighborhood kids, who delighted in being scared. She'd attended a few of those neighborhood events.

"What about your parents?"

"Mom and Dad retired to Costa Rica the year before Tammy Jo died."

"Tammy Jo was your wife?"

He nodded. "She was killed in a plane crash with her parents. Her dad had just gotten his pilot's license and he had taken them out for a flight. I'd stayed behind to watch Josie, who was still a toddler. Wind shear. Her dad was too inexperienced to handle it."

"That's so tragic. I'm so sorry that happened to you, Gil." She reached out and touched his wrist.

That brief contact took her breath away and she quickly dropped her hand.

He gave a sad smile. "Life is hard sometimes, but at least I have Josie and Gretchen and the support of my community. We make it through with a little help from our friends."

What a lovely attitude. She wanted to keep on talking to him, but she was already cutting it close and risked being late for her meeting with the Buckhorns. She didn't want that relationship getting off to a rocky start.

"Listen," she said. "I have to go. I have a meeting with the Buckhorns, but please let's catch up later?"

"Sure, sure, I won't hold you back." He gave her a casual salute, then turned and moseyed toward the carriage house.

She watched him walk away, her gaze locking on his amazing tush, admiring just how fantastic he looked in those tight-fitting jeans.

It was only after she hurried toward the town square that Noelle realized she hadn't asked him how or why they'd be working together, but the idea of being around Gil and his magnificent butt didn't disturb her.

Not one little bit.

But she had to be careful. He was definitely a distraction. She'd have to stay on her toes and keep on task. She wasn't here for her romance but for other people's love affairs. Work came first.

Especially with this job, where she had so much riding on the outcome.

CHAPTER 3

His family claimed that Gil was born with a guitar in his hand and there was some truth to it.

Music had seen him through highs and lows, from the band he'd formed in high school that earned him local fame, to buying and renovating the old town square music hall that gave him a living, to sorting through the grief of losing his wife and in-laws. There weren't many experiences he didn't distill and convert into song.

Transmuting his life into art.

So he shouldn't have been surprised when a tune about Noelle Curry started running through his head as he listened to his student strumming basic chords. He and his pupil were in the cottage's garage, directly underneath the Roost, which he'd converted into a sound studio so he could make money for Josie's college fund by giving guitar lessons at home.

He mentally pushed aside the unfolding lyrics about an awkward girl-next-door who'd blossomed into a confident drop-dead beauty.

Noelle was so far out of his orbit he couldn't reach her by spaceship.

Gil forced himself to focus on his protégé, one Derrick Driscoll, a certified public accountant who had rock star dreams and more money than talent. Derrick took lessons from Gil every Friday at noon on his lunch break. He had also participated in the Polar Plunge with Gil, and he was bundled up in so many layers now it hampered his guitar playing.

"I can turn up the heat," Gil said. "So you can take off your ski jacket."

Derrick shuddered. "How about you turn it up and I keep the jacket on anyway?"

"Sure thing." Gil pressed his palm against the sweat gathering on his forehead. He strolled to the thermostat on the wall and dialed it up to seventy-eight degrees.

"I'll never do that Polar Plunge again." Derrick shuddered. "How are you not frozen to the bone?"

"I'm used to it. I've been taking cold showers every morning for the last ten years."

Derrick's jaw dropped. "On purpose?"

"Cold showers increase endorphins, improve circulation, and heighten immune response. Didn't you feel wildly invigorated after the plunge?"

"I felt like an icicle is what I felt," Derrick muttered and fumbled his guitar pick.

"A lot of successful musicians swear by ice-cold showers."

"Yeah?" Derrick eyed him as he scooped the pick off the floor. The man was willing to do just about anything to make it in the music business except practice regularly. "Maybe if you had a girlfriend you wouldn't have to take cold showers."

"How about we don't talk about my love life?"

"Or lack thereof." Derrick chortled.

"Warm enough to take off the ski jacket yet?"

"Sure, sure." Derrick removed his jacket and draped it over a nearby music stand.

The stand toppled from the weight of his garment and fell onto Josie's drum set with a clattering *bang, bam, boom.* Good thing his upstairs neighbor was out.

"Oops, sorry." Derrick lifted his shoulders to his ears.

"Go ahead and practice your scales." Gil moved to pick up the stand and transfer Derrick's jacket to the coat tree by the door.

Derrick obligingly massacred the major scale.

Suppressing a sigh, Gil pulled up a stool beside Derrick, picked up his own guitar, and demonstrated how it was done. "You should be able to do this exercise in your sleep."

"Yeah, yeah, but I'm aching to get to the good stuff. When can I play 'Free Bird'?"

"All in good time. Gotta crawl before you can run." What was it about the Skynyrd ballad that so entranced novices? Perhaps it was the endless quality of the song.

He showed Derrick a few tricks and tips, then let the accountant repeat them back to him. As he listened, Gil's mind wandered back to Noelle Curry.

Their brief encounter at the bottom of the stairs

had been a bright spot in his week. This past Saturday had been the anniversary of Tammy Jo's death and Josie had been cranky ever since, although Gil wasn't sure why. His daughter had only been two when her mom died. She didn't even remember Tammy Jo.

Picking up on your vibes, most likely, Dad.

To be honest, he'd actually forgotten what day it was, and Gretchen had to remind him it was the fifth-year anniversary of the plane crash.

He'd felt guilty as hell, and he'd taken Josie to put flowers on the graves of her mother and grandparents. Josie got clingy afterward and every night this week, she'd asked to sleep with him. The kid was all elbows and knees and sprawled all over the bed when she slept. He'd gotten precious little sleep.

Was it time to stop marking her mother's passing? That felt wrong somehow, yet it disturbed him how much the trip to the cemetery had affected his daughter's emotional well-being.

And Gil's only goal in life was to provide a calm, safe environment for his daughter. Raising Josie was all that mattered. He let nothing get in the way of that.

An hour later, with Derrick's lesson complete, Gil headed over to the B&B. Gretchen had asked him to fix the leaky kitchen faucet and he was hoping she would make him a sandwich in exchange for plumbing services.

His sister had read his mind.

He stepped through the back door to see two plates with ham-and-cheese sandwiches cut diagonally, dill pickle slices, and ridged potato chips, along with two glasses of chocolate milk. It didn't pass his notice that this was Tammy Jo's favorite lunch menu.

"Hey," he said. "What's this?"

"Have a seat and let's eat before you tackle the plumbing."

Gil washed up at the leaky faucet, dried his hands on a kitchen towel embroidered with angels, and joined his older sister at the table.

She raised her glass of chocolate milk. "To Tammy Jo."

"To Tammy Jo," he echoed and clinked glasses with his sister. "What for?"

"To letting her go." Gretchen hoisted her glass again.

Gil lowered his. "Okay, what's going on?"

"You buried Tammy Jo five years ago today and Josie's been out of sorts since you guys went to the cemetery."

"I know."

"Five years is a long time. Especially for Josie. It's two-thirds of her life. Or maybe three-fourths. Whatever. I'm bad at math."

"Your point?"

"You've been holding on to survivor's guilt for too long, little brother. It's time to let Tammy Jo be part of the past."

"So you made Tammy Jo's favorite lunch?"

"Yes. Our final communion with her. Our good-bye meal."

"Is that ghoulish?"

"Only if you make it so."

"What if I'm not ready to let go?"

"It's been five freaking years. That's long enough. Besides, I saw the way you were looking at Noelle Curry this morning."

"Huh?"

"I was laundering the sheets and I looked out the washroom window and there you were at the bottom of the stairs, staring up at her like she was some long-lost treasure."

"I wasn't."

"You were."

The song he'd started writing about Noelle skipped through his head again. "Okay, maybe I was, but that doesn't mean anything."

"Maybe not, but it sure is a sign you're ready to move forward. I haven't seen you look at a woman like that since Tammy Jo."

"Noelle's from Los Angeles. She's here to plan the Buckhorn/Maxwell wedding and then she'll be gone. Nothing's happening there."

"I'm not saying you need to get anything serious cooking with Noelle, just that it's time to live again. What's wrong with casual sex?"

"I'm a dad. Josie is my sole obligation."

"You're a human being."

"Look, I'm just too busy—"

"That's an excuse."

"I'm raising a seven-year-old. I have to set an example."

"Of what? Stoic self-sacrifice?"

"Gretch, I look around and see other single parents so desperate for partners, any partners just so they're not alone, and then getting in over their heads with problematic relationships. I see their children suffer as a result and I'm sure as Hades not doing that to my kid."

"She's a kid who would be much happier if her dad was happy too."

"I'm not unhappy."

"Maybe not, but are you living to your full potential? I don't think so."

"Said the woman who hasn't had a date in two years."

Two years ago, his sister had been left at the altar and Gretchen had taken the rejection hard, even as she'd realized that ultimately it was for the best.

"About that . . ."

"You're seeing someone?"

She lowered her lashes, then peered at him. "I am."

"Well, hey, that's great. Who is it?"

"A cutter from Jubilee," she said, referring to the town thirty miles north of Twilight that was known as the cutting horse capital of the world. "You don't know him."

"Well, I hope to meet him."

"Not yet. It's still new and we're taking it slow."

"Good luck."

Gretchen winked. "You too."

"Don't start matchmaking."

His sister held up both palms. "The way you and Noelle were ogling each other I don't think my matchmaking is needed."

"We weren't ogling each other."

"Please, who are you trying to kid? Yourself? Because you sure aren't fooling me."

"I was just being nice."

"Uh-huh."

"I was."

"Noelle used to have a mad crush on you when we were kids."

Gil snorted. "No, she didn't."

"Oh yes, she did. You were just too full of swagger to notice."

Had Noelle been crushing on him? She'd been a quiet girl who mostly kept to herself, spending the summers and holidays when she visited her grandparents sitting on the front porch swing reading a book. He teased her about it a few times, calling her a bookworm.

He wouldn't lie to himself. He liked hearing that Noelle had once been interested in him. He might not have paid much attention to her back then, but he sure noticed her now. In those days, she'd simply been too young, but in the present, their two-year age gap was nothing. And in maturity there was a substantial difference between how he was at seventeen and how he was now at thirty.

Gil shook his head. "Don't go reading anything into her staying here. She's accustomed to the Beverly Hills–movie star lifestyle. To Noelle, Twilight must be as boring as watching paint dry."

"Don't be so quick to write her off. From what I've read on the internet, she's not a glitz and glamour girl."

"You've looked her up?"

"You know I Google everyone who stays here."

"This level of investigation sounds like more than a mere internet search."

"They call her the Wedding Whisperer."

"What's that supposed to mean?"

"She has a knack for calming anxious brides and making sure weddings go off without a hitch. She was on *The Klatch*."

Gil frowned. "What's that?"

Gretchen looked at him as if he'd fallen off a turnip truck. "Just the hottest morning talk show on TV."

"Um, even more reason why the likes of Noelle Curry wouldn't be interested in a small-town guy like me."

"Oh, I wouldn't be too sure of that." Gretchen waggled a finger at him. "There's no crush like your first and you were definitely hers."

"But she wasn't mine."

"Who was your first crush?"

"Jeez, Gretch. That was a million years ago. I don't even recall."

"Well, that doesn't matter. What does matter is that for the next six weeks a very attractive woman, who you've got chemistry with, will be living right here at the Merry Cherub."

Gretchen was over-the-top with this, but Gil couldn't deny that Noelle had piqued his interest. Nothing wrong with exploring the attraction.

After all, what was the worst that could happen? Noelle would return to LA and his life would go on the way it was. They'd have a fun, casual flirtation. No harm, no foul. For the first time in a very long time, Gil wondered *what if?*

And another line of lyrics of the song about Noelle bounced into his head.

Nah, nah. So what if she was the first woman to actively pique his interest in years? Nothing could happen. Nothing *would* happen. He was a single dad. His life simply wasn't his own.

While Gil was having sandwiches with Gretchen, Noelle was at Pasta Pappa's with the Buckhorn twins and their mother, Vanessa, her attention totally focused on her clientele. She would do everything in her power to make this the most epic wedding that Twilight, and The Tie for that matter, had ever seen.

Over the course of the past hour and a delicious Greek salad and cheesy garlic bread, Noelle had learned why she would be working with Gil at the Windmill Music Hall.

Sierra's and Sienna's fiancés, Dylan and Cody Maxwell, were former bandmates of Gil's and because of their connection, the grooms-to-be wanted to hold the reception at the Windmill. In light of the excellent acoustics and the historical significance of the old building—it had been a brothel back in the late 1800s—the Buckhorn twins agreed.

It didn't seem fair for Noelle to try to talk the brides and grooms out of their desired wedding reception venue, so she made up her mind to be okay working closely with Gil. This wasn't about her. This was about the couples. Whatever they wanted, she would make happen.

And if her old childhood feelings caused any issues, it was up to her to deal with them in a professional manner. Best course of action? Create strong boundaries between herself and Gil Thomas. Which, granted, might be hard to do considering she'd be living in the apartment above his garage for the next six weeks.

But right now, she needed to concentrate on the job that The Tie was paying her to do. A job that could launch her career into the stratosphere.

"Okay," she said, tapping the information about the reception into her tablet computer. "The venue is set. You've already booked the Windmill for Christmas Eve, Sunday, December 24. Is there any other prep you've done on your own?"

"That's all," Sienna said. She was the older twin, having been born two minutes before Sierra. Since they were identical twins, it was difficult to tell them apart, but Sienna had two piercings in each ear whereas Sierra had only one.

"Well," Sierra said. "We have booked the honeymoon. Two weeks in Bora-Bora."

"But that's all. Nothing else." Sienna nodded.

"Great."

"Do you think six weeks is enough time to get this wedding adequately planned?" Vanessa Buckhorn asked. The twins' mother was in her late forties, with a crisp, tailored style of dress, a lovely auburn pixie haircut, and a thick Texas accent. "It seemed to take The Tie for-*evv*-er to announce the winner and it feels like we're cutting this wedding really close."

"Six weeks is plenty of time," Noelle assured them. "I have strings I can pull if we run into any trouble."

"Like what?" Sierra asked, leaning forward in her seat.

"She's got Hollywood contacts, silly." Sienna nudged her sister with her elbow. To Noelle she said,

"That's why we entered the contest in the first place. Imagine Crescenda Hardwick's daughter planning *our* wedding! It's gonna be epic!"

"We're over the moon to have you." Sierra pressed her palms together.

"By the way," Vanessa said, "would it be crass to ask your mother for an autograph?"

"Crescenda would be thrilled to provide you one," Noelle said. She carried her mother's autographed headshot with her wherever she went for encounters just like this. She took three photos of Crescenda from her portfolio and passed them to the Buckhorns.

Vanessa blushed and placed a palm to her throat. "Oh, my goodness, this is so exciting. I've heard Crescenda's parents used to live right here in Twilight. We've only been in Twilight for twelve years. We're originally from Waco."

"Yes," Noelle said. "But my grandparents moved here after my grandfather retired. Mom never lived in Twilight herself."

"It must have been so wonderful growing up in Hollywood." Sienna sighed.

Not exactly, but Noelle wasn't about to get into that. People enjoyed their fantasies about celebrities. They had no idea about the day-to-day realities of having famous parents—being chased by paparazzi, watching your mother jet off to another country to film a movie while you stayed home with nannies, competing for Crescenda's attention with her fan base. But no one wanted to hear how rough life was for the nepo baby.

Noelle forced a smile. "It was terrific, but you

know, I really enjoyed visiting my grandparents. In Twilight, I got to be just like everyone else."

"I guess the grass is always greener," Vanessa said. "I had dreams of being an actress, but then these two came along and now, well, I wouldn't trade being their mom for all the Oscars in Hollywood." Vanessa beamed at her twins.

Noelle couldn't help feeling a twinge of jealousy. Some people were just natural-born mothers. Crescenda was not. But her mom was lots of fun in other ways. Life was one giant party with Crescenda in charge.

She supposed endless parties seemed glamorous to the average person. She wasn't knocking celebrity. Without it, she wouldn't have her career and despite being unlucky in love herself, Noelle adored planning weddings for others. She and Crescenda were never closer than when Noelle orchestrated one of her mother's weddings.

Sienna rubbed her palms together. "So what's next?"

"Since we're getting a late start today, let's go with what you've already planned. We'll begin with the reception and work backward. How about we head over to the Windmill and get a look at the venue? From there, I can draw up a plan for how the wedding night will flow."

"You'll need to text Gil to make sure the music hall is open," Sierra said. "He's in and out during the day."

"Do you have his number?" Noelle asked, ignoring the blip of her heart at the thought of having Gil's cell number in her phone.

"We sure do." Sienna read Gil's number off her phone screen.

Noelle plugged Gil into her contacts and suddenly she was fifteen again, texting the cool boy across the street.

NOELLE: Hi, it's Noelle Curry.

He answered right away. Hello, Noelle Curry.

The teenager inside her swooned. Can you meet us at the Windmill? I'd like to see where the Buckhorn/Maxwell reception will be held.

Be there in 15. And then he added a laughing emoji. Bookworm.

CHAPTER 4

Bookworm.

Gil's childhood nickname for her.

He'd remembered.

The fifteen-year-old inside her jumped for joy. *Don't let it go to your head.* She had no time for a dalliance.

Outwardly, Noelle gave a slight smile, slipped her cell phone into her purse, paid for their lunch, and left the restaurant with the exuberant Buckhorns.

This was what she loved about wedding planning. Bringing happiness into people's lives.

The twins were chattering at once, filling Noelle's head with their likes and dislikes. She'd never planned a double wedding before and while she found the challenge exciting, it meant she had two brides to please.

Her skills were about to be tested and she welcomed the opportunity, even as she mentally prepped for meltdowns. Glitches were unavoidable. What mattered was the way you handled them.

"Have you given any thoughts to your colors?" Noelle asked as they walked to the Windmill Music Hall on the opposite side of the town square.

"Yellow," Sienna said.

At the same time, her twin said, "Blue."

"No, no, red." Vanessa shook her head. "It's a Christmas wedding."

The Tie would be sending a videographer out to film their nuptials for promotional use and Noelle's contact at the company, Pamela Landry, would be in Twilight for the event as well. It was Noelle's job to make sure the wedding lived up to The Tie's standards since they were footing the bill and that included making sure the colors were elegant, cohesive, and would pop on camera.

"Why don't we have a look at the color wheel when we get to the Windmill, and I'll show you some on-trend suggestions for a winter wedding and see if we can all get on the same page. How does that sound?"

"Good idea." Vanessa put both arms around her daughters' waists and they walked as a cohesive unit, taking up all of the sidewalk.

Seeing a mother and her daughters enjoying each other's company brought a lump to Noelle's throat. The wind gusted off Lake Twilight, and she pulled her blazer tighter around her body. She wished she'd put on the thick, fluffy winter sweater she'd brought.

Shopkeepers had their doors open, an invitation for people to stroll inside. Music oozed from the stores, most of the tunes Christmas themed already. Delicious smells wafted from the restaurants and the Twilight Bakery. A bakery employee stood at the entrance passing out kismet cookie samples.

They stopped for free cookies, and the minute Noelle bit into one, a fresh batch of memories came rushing back as she recalled the legend of the town's beloved Christmas cookie.

"Do you remember when we baked kismet cookies on Christmas Eve and slept with them underneath our pillows?" Sienna giggled.

"How could I forget?" Vanessa said. "I found crumbs in the carpet for weeks afterward."

"The legend didn't work for me though." Sierra stuck out her tongue. "I dreamed of Justin Bieber, and he married someone else."

"Lucky for Dylan." Sienna chuckled. "Or Cody and I would be getting married alone."

"Did you ever make the kismet cookies?" Vanessa asked Noelle.

"I did bake them with my grandmother one year." Noelle smiled at the memory. It was the last Christmas she'd spent with Grammie and Grampie.

"Did you sleep with them under your pillow and dream of your one true love?" Sienna asked.

Noelle shook her head. She wasn't about to tell them, but she *had* dreamed of Gil Thomas that Christmas. Then again, at fifteen, she'd been obsessed with him. Of course she'd dreamed of the boy she'd been crushing on.

The legend claimed if you slept with a kismet cookie underneath your pillow on Christmas Eve, you would dream of your one true love. Pure fantasy of course. Fun, yes, but cookies had no magical matchmaking powers, and she wouldn't indulge such flights of fantasy.

But the cookies were yummy.

"Here we are." Vanessa opened the door to Windmill Music Hall and ushered them inside.

"Hello?" Noelle called, walking through the spacious lobby. "Gil? Are you here?"

"Good afternoon, ladies," said a sexy male voice. She turned.

Gil sauntered down the corridor, a cocky grin on his handsome face.

All the air left her lungs, sliding over her parted lips in a heated rush. Her eyes widened involuntarily in the dim lighting, her pupils drinking him in.

Well-worn Tony Lama cowboy boots, snug-fitting Wranglers hugging his lean hips, blue plaid flannel work shirt underneath the unzipped black hoodie. The sleeves were rolled up, revealing the dark hair of his forearms and the strong muscled wrists of a professional guitar player.

She counted his steps as he got closer. Ten, nine, eight . . .

His hair was cut shorter than he used to wear it, although it was still long enough to sweep the top over to one side in a rakish flop that looked silkily soft.

Seven, six, five . . .

He smelled provocatively of hand soap and sunshine. She inhaled deeply, savoring his scent.

Four, three, two . . .

And then he was directly in front of her. Mere inches away.

"Yeah," he said. "I came in the back door. What would you like to see first? The auditorium or your command center?"

Noelle blinked. "M-my command center?"

"Well, technically it's my office, but I set up a card table, so you'd have a workspace. I know how disconcerting it is on the road while trying to take care of business and not having a central base."

She'd figured she'd just use the Roost as her command center, but a desk at the Windmill in the middle of all the action would be far more convenient.

"That's so thoughtful," she said, touched that he'd make space for her. "I'd love to see it."

"We'll just hang out here," Vanessa said. "Stay out of your way."

"You can come along. I don't mind," Noelle said, a bit panicky at the thought of being left alone with Gil.

"To be honest," Vanessa said, "I wanted to have a tête-à-tête with the twins about getting on the same page regarding wedding colors. With just six weeks to plan, we don't need sibling rivalry gumming up the works."

"Oh, okay."

"This way." Gil led Noelle to the last room on the left, while the Buckhorns stayed in the lobby.

It wasn't a large office, but it was big enough for his desk and a small four-by-four card table. His desk held a twenty-seven-inch desktop Mac that included the computing system in the monitor. The card table was bare except for a lamp and a pencil holder filled with pens and sharpened pencils.

"Have a seat." He held out his arm, indicating she should slip around the side of the card table converted into a desk. "See if the chair is to your liking."

She went to slip past him; just as she did, he shifted his weight, and she ended up accidentally brushing her hip against his.

Gil didn't back up.

"Um . . . er . . . sorry," she mumbled.

"For what?"

"Bumping into you."

"Oh," he said in a sultry tone. "I don't mind."

She didn't know what to say to that, so she made a dash for the chair. It was set a little too high and her feet didn't quite touch the floor. She reached around for the height lever to adjust it, but the controls were loosey-goosey and the chair seat plunged so low her breasts were almost level with the card table.

Noelle readjusted and got the chair at the correct height. She ran her hand along the table. "This was so kind of you. When did you have time to set this up?"

"Just before you got here. I keep the card table in the storage closet. We can get a cloth to cover it, so it doesn't look so plain."

"You're using a beanbag chair," she said, just now noticing the dark green beanbag chair parked behind his desk.

"Normally, I keep it here for my daughter, Josie, for when I have to bring her to work. I gave you my chair and took hers."

"Well, that's not fair to either you or Josie. I'm fine with a simple folding chair if you have one."

"Don't argue with me, Noelle Curry," he said. "You're the guest. You get the good chair. I'll bring a folding chair from home, and I don't want to hear anything else about it."

She stood up, feeling at a disadvantage sitting down. "That bossy alpha stuff doesn't work on me."

"No?" He looked amused.

"No."

"What does?"

"What does what?"

"What works on you?"

"A man who lets me have my way."

The dimple in his cheek deepened. He tossed back his head and chuckled lightly. Noelle studied him, not even trying to hide her appreciation of his gorgeous face.

"You know what this means?"

"What?"

"We're at an impasse. I'm not about to let you sit in an uncomfortable folding chair."

"Ditto."

"You *have* changed," he said. "The Noelle I remember would never have gone toe-to-toe with me."

"I'm all grown up now."

He raked his gaze over her. "Yes, you are."

She sank her top teeth into her lower lip and felt a wave of heat blast up the back of her neck.

The smile disappeared and Gil looked deadly serious, his gaze hooked on her mouth. Her heart skipped a beat and her jaw loosened. He caught her gaze and held it. Her body tensed, suddenly both hot and cold at the same time as a deep, unexpected yearning took hold of her.

It was unsettling.

This hungry craving that had her aching to wrap her arms around his neck, pull his head down, and kiss him until both of their brains spun. She imagined ripping off his clothing, throwing him down on the desk, and having her wicked way with him.

Her cell phone dinged.

She looked down.

The text was from Vanessa. We worked out the color scheme.

"Aah, the great color scheme crisis has been resolved," she said.

"What?"

"Sierra and Sienna couldn't agree on the colors for the wedding. Their mom weighed in too. Want to bet who won?"

"My money's on Vanessa," he said.

Noelle texted back. And the winner is . . . ?

VANESSA: Red.

She raised her head and met Gil's eyes. "How did you know?"

"Sierra and Sienna took guitar lessons from me for a year at their mother's insistence. Vanessa's a woman who knows her own mind." He paused. "Much like Crescenda."

"Thanks for telling me. Forewarned is forearmed. Now I know exactly how to handle her."

"Which means?"

"I need to get the twins alone and find out what they truly want, then go to bat for them with their mother."

"How will you convince her to do what her daughters want?"

"Find a way to make the changes her idea."

"Seems like there's a lot of subterfuge in the wedding planning game."

"Weddings are high drama. It takes a deft hand to keep things running smoothly. That's actually how I became a wedding planner. Keeping Crescenda calm during her numerous nuptials."

"If anyone can handle it, you can."

"The stakes are high." She laughed. "This wedding will stream on The Tie's website and be featured on several entertainment news programs."

"I'm glad you can laugh about it. Feels like a lot of pressure to me."

"Pressure is what makes it exciting." She rubbed her palms together.

"Aah," he said. "You like pressure? Tell me more." He sat down on the end of her card table desk and leaned in.

She had the urge to back up, but there was nowhere to go. The wall was behind her and Gil in front of her. His eyelids were half-lowered, his smile seductive. The man was as explosive as a firecracker.

"There's something you should know," she said. She could not afford to get sidetracked by this man. She had an assignment, and no handsome face was going to sway her from it.

"What's that?"

"I never mix business with pleasure."

Oh-ho, Miss Ego? What if he wasn't interested? What if she'd made an embarrassing assumption? Just because she was hot and bothered by him didn't mean he reciprocated her feelings. She felt the tops of her ears burn. Gosh, she was such a self-conscious goofball.

He didn't say a word, just kept studying her with a steady gaze.

"Okay, that's not true," she said.

"Then you *do* mix business with pleasure?"

"No, I mean . . ." She squirmed. "I just said that to keep you at arm's length."

"I'm listening." He kept staring at her, not moving a muscle.

Just watching, waiting.

"You're hot. Superhot, in fact. I like you. A lot. But here's the deal—I'm here to work, not play."

"And if you were here under different circumstances?"

"I'm not."

"But if you were?"

"Look, you're a forever kind of guy and I don't believe in romantic love. So there's that. And you deserve someone who can love you until the cows come home."

"Until the cows come home? That doesn't sound very LA."

"It's something my Georgia farm boy Grampie used to say."

The amused smile was back. "You've never been in love?"

With you. When I was fifteen.

"I've been in lust," she said. "But I believe what most people think of as 'love' is really just desire."

"What about your grandparents? They seemed in love to me."

"Well, they were an exception."

"My parents love each other."

"Another exception. Those marriages are few and far between. And besides, who's to say that's not simply companionship and compatibility?"

"You know what?" Gil leaned in so close his terrific scent overtook her nose.

Noelle braced herself for a lecture on the joys of love and marriage. Of course, he believed in love. He'd been married. He was a widower.

"What?" she whispered.

"I tend to agree."

Wow, that was not what she thought he was going to stay. Captivated by his stunning blue eyes, a million questions filled her mind. Why wasn't he a true believer? He was from Twilight after all, where romantic myths and legends ran wild. Had there been trouble in his marriage?

She'd come by her prejudice against wedded bliss fair and square. Her mother had been married and divorced five times. Dad was currently looking for wife number four. Most of the people she knew were divorced or locked in rotten marriages. Being a wedding planner and seeing how engaged couples treated each other in the throes of wedding prep only served to cement her theories.

First came lust, then when that wore off, couples either divorced or fell into a mutually beneficial relationship that, if it succeeded, included companionship, compatibility, and shared values. It was the best anyone could hope for. Life was so much simpler if you just stayed single. But if everyone thought that way, she'd be out of a job.

From the doorway came a shocked gasp. "*You* don't believe in love!"

Startled, Noelle jumped, almost whacking Gil in the chin. He unhitched his hip from the corner of the card table and in unison, they turned to see Vanessa and the twins standing in the doorway looking appalled.

Noelle fumbled for something to say that would smooth the whole thing over, but nothing sprang to mind. Oh dear, her worst nightmare. Having people think badly of her. "I—er . . . this isn't—"

"How can you be our wedding planner when you don't believe in love?" Aghast, Sienna's voice came out hysterical.

"This is bad luck." Sierra wrung her hands. "A terrible omen."

"The girls wanted *you* to plan their wedding because your weddings are so magical. We wanted a movie star's daughter. That's why they entered the essay contest in the first place. That's why we waited so long to start planning. I don't get it. How do you create such beautiful weddings when you don't believe in love?" Vanessa wailed.

Sierra clutched her head in her hands. "What are we going to do?"

"I'm calling Pamela Landry at The Tie, is

what I'm going to do." Vanessa whipped out her phone.

"Wait, wait." Panic gripped Noelle by the throat.

Sienna smacked her palm against her forehead. "This is a total *disaster*."

"It's not," Noelle said, self-preservation kicking in. "And here's the reason why . . ."

CHAPTER 5

Gil watched with amusement as Noelle charmed the Buckhorn twins and their mother, reassuring them that her own beliefs about love had nothing to do with the magical moments she would create for them. She was a wedding planner after all, not a matchmaker. Her worldview didn't matter. This was their celebration.

He didn't get to see the whole resolution though, because halfway through Noelle's spiel, he got a text.

Evelyn White, the principal from Josie's elementary school, sent the message. There's an issue with your daughter. Can you come up here now?

Gil startled and his pulse sprinted. What kind of issue?

EVELYN: It's best if you come see for yourself.
GIL: Be right there.

"I gotta go," he said.
Noelle looked concerned. "Is everything all right?"

"No." He pulled the building keys from his pocket and tossed them to her. "Could you lock up when you're done? There's a pressing issue with my kid."

"Surely," Noelle said. "What do I do with the keys after I lock up?"

"Keep 'em. I've got a spare and anyway you'll need access to the office when I'm not here."

He nodded at the Buckhorns and beelined for the back door.

His heart pounded all the way to Jon Grant Elementary as his imagination conjured up one terrifying scenario after another. He parked, checked in with security, and headed straight for the principal's office.

"Evelyn's not in there," the janitor mopping the floor told him as he flew past.

"Where is she?"

"Miss Reed's second grade classroom."

Miss Reed. That was Josie's teacher. Gil pivoted on his heel and took off running in the opposite direction.

"Watch out," the janitor called. "The floor's we—"

He didn't get the word out before Gil's boots slipped and he went down hard. The janitor rushed over, but Gil waved him away and jumped to his feet. His health didn't matter. Josie was in trouble.

"You okay?" The janitor looked worried.

"I'm fine." His butt and his pride were stinging, but he was good. Trying not to limp, he headed toward Miss Reed's classroom.

Evelyn White met him at the door, her cell phone

in her hand, and motioned him into the hallway. Gil backed up.

"The janitor texted me that you fell. Are you all right?"

"I'm great. Where's Josie? What's happened?"

"She's locked herself in the cloak closet."

"There's a lock on the cloak closet?"

"No, she wedged a ruler against the door handle, and we can't pull it open. We could've forced it and broken the ruler, but we were afraid the sharp pieces might fly up and hit her in the face."

"Smart thinking."

"Nor did we want to create more drama for the students than what Josie's already caused."

That comment made him feel defensive, but he recognized his irritation for what it was. His own guilt.

"We tried coaxing her out, but she's adamant. So I told Miss Reed to go on with her class as if nothing's going on, but of course the kids can't concentrate."

"What happened beforehand?" He rubbed his aching hip.

"Are you sure you're all right? We need to fill out an incident report."

"I'm fine." He grunted. "You can fill out your form later. Tell me about Josie."

"They were out on the playground and when Miss Reed rounded up the children to return to the classroom, she couldn't find your daughter."

"You lost my kid?" Gil scowled.

"No, no. We found her hiding behind the shrubbery. She sprang out, ran into the building, hid in the cloakroom, and she's refusing to come out."

"Did she say why?"

The principal shook her head. "She just keeps telling us to go away."

"Take me to her."

Evelyn White ushered him into the classroom. Every head swiveled to gawk at him. He ignored the teacher and the kids who were still wearing their coats from the playground because Josie had inconvenienced them. He followed the principal to the closed door at the back of the room.

"Josie." Evelyn White rapped her knuckles against the door.

"Go away!"

His daughter's high-pitched voice went through Gil like an electric knife. His child was clearly upset. "Kiddo, it's your dad. Please open the door."

"D-daddy?" She hiccupped and that let him know she'd been crying.

"Come on out, sweetheart. I'm taking you home."

"You should be firmer with her," Evelyn White said. "We can't have disruptions like this in the classroom."

"How 'bout you don't tell me how to raise my kid? I'll deal with it." Gil rubbed his hip again and sent her a look.

The principal got the hint. She didn't want a lawsuit. Not that he'd ever suc—the fall had been his fault—but Mrs. White didn't need to know that.

"Fine, but this behavior needs to end."

"It will."

The door opened and Josie stood there looking so forlorn that his heart broke. Her eyes were red-rimmed and her nose runny. She swiped her face with the sleeve of her jacket. Then she saw everyone was staring at her and she ducked her head, her shoulders hunching forward as she curled inward. He hated seeing his normally spunky child looking so defeated.

Something had happened on that playground, and Gil would darn sure get to the bottom of it.

"C'mon," he said. "Let's go home."

He held out his hand and when Josie slipped her little palm into his and squeezed tightly, Gil was prepared to slay any and all dragons for her.

Thank heavens today was Friday and school was out all next week for the Thanksgiving holiday. By the time classes resumed on the following Monday, this whole thing will have blown over. Unfortunately, there were three concerts scheduled this weekend at the Windmill. He wouldn't have as much time with Josie as he would have liked, but he'd find a way.

Gil helped Josie climb into the back seat of his pickup truck and buckled her up. "Wanna tell me what happened?"

Josie shook her head.

"Something really upset you, huh?"

She nodded.

"But you don't want to talk about it?"

"No."

"It's pretty cold standing here with the wind whipping off the lake. Would hot chocolate with marshmallows from Perks make you feel like talking?"

"Uh-huh."

He grinned and ruffled her hair. "That's what I thought."

"You're not mad at me?"

"Why would I be?"

"Because you had to come to school and get me." She stared down at her lap. "B'cause I caused trouble."

He cupped her chin and lifted it so that she had to look him in the eyes. "When you're in trouble, I will *always* come and get you. No matter where you are, and I will never be mad at you. Got it?"

"Uh-huh."

"We'll go to Perks and then you're gonna tell me what happened. Okay?"

"Okay."

Ten minutes later, they were sitting across from each other at the coffee shop on the town square. Josie stirred her hot chocolate with a peppermint candy cane and watched the miniature marshmallows circle the cup.

"What happened on the playground?" he asked as nonchalantly as he could, peering at her over the rim of his mug.

"Some of the kids started making fun of me."

"What about?"

"Because I don't have a mom."

Gil winced. Kids could be so cruel. If you didn't fit in, weren't part of the norm, it was easy to become a target. "What'd they say?"

Josie's lips puckered. "I don't want to repeat it."

"How can I help you if you won't tell me?" His heart turned over. He hated that kids were picking on her.

"What they said was mean." She paused to dunk a marshmallow with the melting candy cane.

Was it wrong of him to press her? If she didn't want to talk about it, should he leave well enough alone?

"Is this the first time these kids have said mean things to you?"

She shook her head.

"How long has this been going on?" Gil fisted his hand against his thigh, doing his best to keep anger from creeping into his voice. He didn't want Josie believing he was upset with her.

She shrugged.

"A week? A month? All school year?"

"Since Silvey Zucker saw us coming out of the graveyard when we went to visit Mommy."

The hairs on Gil's nape lifted. He didn't like the sound of this. He remembered two of Josie's classmates had been cycling by on their bikes when they'd left the cemetery. Josie had waved at them, but the girls hadn't waved back. It had bothered her then, but apparently something more had been brewing underneath the surface for a while.

Silvey Zucker's dad ran the local car dealership and Ted was one of the richest men in Twilight. Gil was by no means poor—Tammy Jo's life insurance had seen to that—but he didn't have money to throw away on frivolous things like the Zuckers did. Ted Zucker was a loud, flashy braggart who'd been something of a bully back in high school. If

Silvey was anything like her father, it sounded like the apple hadn't fallen far from the tree.

"So this has been going on since Saturday?" This was why Josie had been both cranky and clingy over the past week.

"Uh-huh."

"But these girls have been unkind to you for some time?"

"It just got worse after the graveyard."

"What did that girl say to you, Josie?"

Her bottom lip trembled. "She said Mommy died trying to run away from me because I was so ugly that she'd rather die than have me for a daughter."

It couldn't have hurt him more if someone had taken out a sword and run it through his chest. A red-hot burst of rage boiled through his veins, but he couldn't let Josie see that. He had to keep a grip on his temper. He had to choose his next words carefully.

"You know that's not true, right?"

She nodded.

"Mommy loved you very, very much."

"I know, but they said I'm a freak and that's why you can't find me a new mommy. No one wants me for their kid."

Oh hell's bells. Those little gremlins. Gil gritted his teeth. "Honey, I haven't even been trying to find you a new mommy."

"Because no one will like me?"

"No, no. It has nothing to do with you, sweetheart. I need to fall in love first."

"Like you fell in love with Mommy?'

"Like I did with Mommy," he mumbled.

How did you explain to a seven-year-old that love and lust weren't the same thing when even adults got fooled, mistaking explosive sexual chemistry for something more than it was?

He'd hired Tammy Jo as a singer in his band and there had been a red-hot sizzle right from the beginning. He'd been twenty-two when he and Tammy Jo married because she'd gotten pregnant after one wild weekend on a road trip to Galveston. She'd been on the pill, but she'd also been taking antibiotics and didn't know that antibiotics could make the pill less effective. The condom had also broken that night. Under those circumstances, her pregnancy had seemed fated.

Neither one of them considered any other option but marriage. They were both old-fashioned that way. If it hadn't been for Josie, he didn't know if he and Tammy Jo would have ended up together, but along with the hot sex, they had also respected and admired each other and that went a long way.

In the end, they'd had a solid marriage, but he'd always known Tammy Jo was melancholy at the way things turned out, longing for something more than motherhood. Gil had tried his best to please her, putting her unhappiness down to her postpartum depression and doing what he could to cheer her up. Well, until the end when he'd—

Gil shoved aside his guilt. He kept that part of his life buried down deep.

In order to live with his guilt, he'd convinced himself that time would have changed his wife's outlook and maybe it would have. Tammy Jo hadn't lived long enough for them to resolve their issues. He'd been fully committed to their relationship, but he'd also had a secret longing for a deeper connection. He just didn't know if such a thing was possible for him. Maybe love was all a fantasy encouraged by his lore-loving hometown.

"I don't even remember Mommy," Josie whispered. "I look at her picture and I try and try to remember her, but I can't."

"Come here, baby." Gil scooted his chair back and patted his knee.

Josie got up and came over to sit on his lap. He wrapped his arms around her and hugged her tight. She buried her face against his chest, her warm tears dampening his shirt.

"I want you to ignore those girls. What they say isn't true. Don't listen to them."

"Okay."

"You're going to meet mean people in this world who feel like they have to take their hurt out on others, but we're not like that, are we?"

She shook her head.

"Look at me, kiddo."

She raised her chin and he dabbed at her tears with a napkin he pulled from the holder on the table.

"You're better than that. So when they tease you, just pretend it's the sound of the wind blowing. Don't hide. Don't lock yourself in the cloak closet. Hold your head high and go about your business."

"Okay."

"At first, they might get worse, trying to make you cry and run away again, but you're not going to do that, are you?"

"No."

"That's right. If you don't react, eventually, they'll get tired and leave you alone. Can you do that?"

"I'll try."

"That's all anyone can ask." He smoothed her hair and kissed her forehead. "Now let's forget all about this and go home. I've got a concert tonight, so Aunt Gretchen will look after you, but I'll be home in time to tuck you in bed."

After Gil left, Noelle had spent an hour convincing the Buckhorns that their wedding was indeed in competent hands, and then she led the twins and their mother through the color schemes most appropriate for this year's winter wedding palette. What got them fully on board with her advice was showing them her portfolio of the successful celebrity weddings she'd planned.

All was smoothed over.

Crisis averted. *Whew.*

In the end, Noelle had gotten all three women to compromise on a classy burgundy, navy, and gold palette, putting a color wheel spin on Vanessa's desire for red, Sienna's urge for yellow, and Sierra's hankering for blue.

She texted Pamela Landry at The Tie, telling her about the venue for the reception and the color choices and got the green light. While ostensibly Pamela trusted her judgment as the wedding planner, she still had to run her decisions past the woman since The Tie held the purse strings. If she was truly the best of the best, as Pamela had claimed when The Tie invited her to take part in their contest, why did she have to get permission?

It was annoying, but part of her contract.

She locked up the music venue, stuck Gil's keys in her bag, and headed back to the B&B. She wondered how things had gone with Gil and his daughter. She almost texted to ask him, but that seemed too forward, so she resisted the urge. While Noelle might have had a crush on him when she was a kid, she barely knew the guy now.

Never mind that he was ridiculously attractive.

It had been really nice of him, though, to set up a desk for her at the Windmill, but now she worried about having such close proximity to him. Maybe it was a bad idea. She crinkled her nose.

Her heels clacked against the sidewalk. Her toes were aching. She'd been on her feet most of the afternoon and she couldn't wait to get back to her apartment and kick off her shoes.

She passed by Perks coffee shop and casually gazed in through the big picture windows at the cute café with bistro tables and blue gingham tablecloths.

Inside, she saw Gil sitting at a table, a little girl on his lap. The child had her face buried against his chest so Noelle couldn't see her features, but she could see Gil's. He looked worried as he patted his daughter's back.

At that moment, he raised his head, reaching for the cowboy hat sitting on the table in front of him, and he spied her.

Their gazes met.

She stopped in her tracks, her heart beating wildly. What was it about this man that so revved her cardiovascular system?

He lifted a hand in greeting, offered her a soft smile.

She waved back and then quickly went on her way, not wanting to spoil his tender moment with his child. Yep, sharing an office with him was starting to look more and more like a very bad idea. She'd already screwed up once with the Buckhorns. She couldn't forget she was skating on thin ice. Best to forget all about Gil Thomas and keep her thoughts firmly centered on the wedding.

"And they all lived happily ever after," Gil said, reading the final line of the fairy tale. He closed the book and put it on the nightstand.

Normally, he loved this nighttime ritual when he read Josie a bedtime story and tucked her in, but for some strange reason, he'd been distracted tonight, his mind crammed with thoughts of Noelle Curry. More lyrics for the song he'd been writing about her had flitted through his brain when he'd seen her through the window at Perks, and now he couldn't get the lyrics—or her—out of his head.

And that was simply untenable.

"Happily ever after like you and Mommy?" Josie asked.

"Like Mommy and me." Life wasn't that simple, but right now, Josie needed fairy tales. When she was grown, he'd tell her the truth about his relationship with her mother, but she didn't need to know that for years and years.

"But you're not happy anymore, are you, Daddy?"

What? That pulled Gil up short. Did he really

come across as unhappy? He didn't think so, but here was his kid with evidence to the contrary, and today Gretchen had said the same thing.

"I *am* happy," he said. "Aren't we living happily ever after together? You and me and Aunt Gretchen."

"But we don't have a mommy to love us."

He paused, thinking of the best way to address this. "That's why it hurt you so much when those girls said the mean things that they said. You feel like there's some truth to it?"

"I guess."

He ran a hand through his hair, not knowing what to say.

"Maybe if you found us a new mommy, you could be happy again and we could be a real family."

Was she saying this because she believed having a stepmother would stop the Silvey Zuckers of the world from bullying her? Or was she truly aching for a mother's love?

"What would you like Santa to bring you for Christmas?" he asked, changing the subject. He was in over his head here. He needed some feminine perspective. Later, he'd talk to Gretchen and get her take on the situation. Or maybe give his mother a call.

"I wanna skate in the living snow globe."

"Got your back, kiddo. I entered us in the drawing, but remember it's random chance. We might not win a slot. Is there anything else you want for Christmas? But it can't be a pony. We don't have the space for a pony." Not as long as they were living at the Merry Cherub.

Josie nodded. "I know, you already tol' me. Besides, there's something else I want more."

"More than you want a pony?"

"Lots more."

"Well, let's hear it."

She reached for the rag doll at the foot of her bed. It was the doll Tammy Jo had bought Josie for her second birthday. She tucked the well-loved toy underneath the covers with her.

"You're not going to tell me?"

"You haven't figured it out?" Josie searched his face.

"Sorry, your old pop is a little dense sometimes."

"Why, Daddy . . ." Josie met his gaze and held it. "I want a *mommy* for Christmas."

CHAPTER 6

The next day, Saturday, November 18, Noelle, Vanessa, Sierra, and Sienna had planned to attend the Harvest Craft Fair to see if they could find inexpensive, locally sourced crafts to decorate the tables at the reception.

Noelle woke brimming with ideas for the double wedding. Despite her fears about working in Gil's office, she couldn't wait to get to the Windmill and dive into planning before meeting the Buckhorns at the craft fair at ten. Hopefully, she'd beat him there, do what she needed to do, and leave for the craft fair before he ever showed up.

She grabbed coffee to go and a pumpkin spice muffin from the sideboard at the B&B's dining room and walked to the town square, her laptop computer bag slung over her shoulder.

Inhaling the crisp morning air, she listened to the autumn leaves crunch under the heels of her fashionable ankle boots as she traveled the cobblestone walkway leading into Sweetheart Park.

Yesterday, she'd made a big gaffe by telling Gil that she didn't believe in love within hearing distance of a client. She should have kept her mouth shut, but when the look in his eyes had matched the sexy feelings churning through her body, she'd wanted him to know right up front where he stood with her.

She was all for hot sex, but a relationship? Not so much. For twenty-eight years she'd managed to stay out of long-term romantic entanglements. She had no intentions of leading anyone on.

Especially Gil.

He was a good guy with a young daughter to raise. She wasn't about to complicate the man's life.

"Good morning!" strangers called to her as they passed by.

"Good morning!" Noelle returned the friendly greetings echoing throughout the park.

She'd forgotten how nice it was to live in such a friendly town with a solid sense of community. Nostalgia washed over her, and she found herself missing her grandparents. Grammie had passed away from a sudden heart attack at seventy-one. Losing the love of his life after fifty years of marriage, Grampie had lost the will to live, and four months later, he'd died of a stroke. The death of her grandparents had only strengthened her resolve to avoid marriage. She never wanted to go through the kind of pain her Grampie had gone through after losing his beloved wife.

Love, she'd decided at fifteen, simply made you too vulnerable.

While she was enjoying her visit to Twilight, the town's romantic values certainly clashed with her own, as evidenced by the Sweetheart Tree in the middle of the bifurcating path in front of her.

She paused.

Her stomach did a funny little pitch and roll at the sight of the ancient pecan tree with heavy branches gnarled like old knuckles. Over the years, hundreds of couples had carved their names along with lovey-dovey sentiments into the weathered bark.

The original names, which had started the whole tradition, were those of two of the town's founders, Jon Grant and Rebekka Nash. According to lore, the two teenage sweethearts found their love torn asunder by the Civil War, but they never stopped thinking of each other. Fifteen years later, they met again at twilight on the banks of the Brazos River in the same spot where the town now stood.

In recent years, to preserve the old pecan, a white picket fence had been erected around it, along with a sign that warned: Do Not Deface the Sweetheart Tree.

Offered as a substitute to the lovers longing to be part of the tradition, the town had installed a metal frame around the tree trunk and made available for purchase charms for engraving and attaching to the frame. This innovative feature had not been part of the Sweetheart Tree when Noelle was a teenager.

Impulsively, she hurried to the tree and glanced

over her shoulder. No one was in the immediate vicinity. Gingerly, she stepped over the white picket fence. She leaned in, noticing how much the carvings had faded over time.

Dropping to her knees in the dirt, she searched the base of the tree, hunting for one carving in particular. It took her several minutes of searching, squinting, and pushing away fallen leaves from the roots and then, *boom*, she found it.

Noelle Gil.

Her pulse pounded in her throat as she remembered the pocketknife her grandfather had put in her stocking that final Christmas in Twilight. While her grandparents had napped after the holiday feast, she'd walked to the park to look for tree branches to whittle and spied Gil throwing a football with his dad.

They hadn't seen her, and she'd crouched behind the Sweetheart Tree to watch Gil in motion, admiring the way he moved, so athletic and graceful. She'd glanced down at the names carved on the tree and she'd fisted her hand around the new Swiss Army knife in her coat pocket and the next thing she knew she'd made this carving.

Evidence of youthful foolishness.

She hoped Gil had never seen it. Quickly, she covered the carving back up with a pile of leaves.

"Embarrassing old flame?"

Noelle jumped and turned to see an attractive blonde about her own age opening up the charm kiosk.

"Oh, sorry. I didn't mean to startle you, Noelle."

Noelle blinked. "Do we know each other?"

"We had a few sleepovers whenever you came to visit your grandparents." The woman smiled.

"Benji Truesdale!" Noelle said. "Oh my gosh, I haven't seen you in thirteen years. It's been far too long."

"I've been following your career." Benji pointed at Noelle's laptop case branded with her Once Upon a Wedding logo. "I caught you on *The Klatch*."

"Did you?"

"You were fantastic. You looked so professional and polished. I'm so proud of you, but then again, I always knew you'd do remarkable things." Benji held her arms wide. "Can I have a hug?"

"Oh, absolutely!"

They hugged each other. The years slipped away, and they were fifteen again, as comfortable as they'd been when they'd braided each other's hair and mooned over boy bands together.

"How did we lose touch?" Noelle asked, regretting not having kept up with Benji.

Truth was, in the aftermath of her grandparents' deaths, it had simply hurt too much to think about Twilight. The friends she'd made, the town where she'd spent her holidays and summers, were all painful reminders of what she'd lost, so she'd compartmentalized her life, cutting off this part and tucking it at the back of her mind. Now she regretted that defense mechanism, realizing just how much withdrawing had cost her.

"Well, you lived in LA and once your grandparents were gone, there was no reason for you to come back."

"I should have reached out to you," Noelle said.

"There's no excuse not to have kept in touch. At the very least on social media."

"Hey, I didn't reach out either. Sadly, life gets busy and childhood friendships go by the wayside if you don't tend them."

"I've missed you."

"I missed you too."

"We've got a lot to catch up on." Noelle waved at Benji's left hand. "I see you've gotten married."

"Yes, to Spencer Maxwell. We married last spring."

Since Noelle hadn't gone to school in Twilight, she didn't know many people who hadn't lived on her grandparents' block or been in their orbit, but the name rang a bell. "Is your husband related to Dylan and Cody?"

"Yes, he's their older brother. I'll be in the wedding as the candlelighter."

"That's wonderful! I'm thrilled!"

"We need to hang out. I've got to work the kiosk today. It's a fundraising project for the Angel Tree and I'm on the committee this year. It'll get super busy when the craft fair opens, but after that, let's grab a drink, okay?"

"Yes, let's do." They exchanged phone numbers.

"Oh," Benji said. "Before you go, you might want one of these."

She keyed open the kiosk, rummaged through a stack of boxes stored there, and found what she was looking for. Turning, she pressed a silver coin into Noelle's palm.

It wasn't a normal coin, rather some special sort

of currency with the Oliver Wendell Holmes quote "Love prefers twilight to daylight" on one side and a picture of Jon Grant and Rebekka Nash embracing on the other side of the coin.

"What's this?"

"Twilight's selling bona fide wish-granting coins now." Benji giggled. "A dollar apiece. This one's on me."

"What for?"

"Just in case you have the inclination to make a wish." She nodded in the direction of the Sweetheart Fountain several yards away.

Benji was referring to the local myth that if you threw a coin into the Sweetheart Fountain and made a wish to be reunited with your first love, like Jon Grant and Rebekka Nash, your wish would come true. The fanciful fable brought tourists to Twilight. A mystique totally manufactured by the city council, but it worked. Twilight had turned love into a commodity and now they'd added specialized coins into the mix.

"You know." Benji winked. "About Gil Thomas."

Josie seemed to be her old self again, talking up a storm about the upcoming Thanksgiving holiday as they walked to the B&B for breakfast.

Inside, Gretchen and Delphine scuttled about as they replaced food items on the breakfast buffet, kept the area cleaned, and chatted with the guests. Gil glanced around but didn't see Noelle among the diners.

Raising a hand in greeting, he smiled at his sister

and guided Josie to the buffet. Perks of living on the property of the B&B. Free breakfast. Although he did work it off in repairs, and for a house that was well over a hundred years old, that was no small undertaking.

But he wouldn't have it any other way. Moving to the Merry Cherub had been the best decision he could have made in the aftermath of his wife's death, and Gretchen had told him many times she felt the same way.

He and Josie got their plates and parked themselves at a corner table, leaving the choicer spots for the guests. While Josie dug into her waffles topped high with strawberries and whipped cream, Gil downloaded a popular dating app.

Gretchen and his friends had been urging him to try online dating for a while, but he'd been resistant. After what had happened at Josie's school yesterday and what she'd told him last night about wanting a mommy for Christmas, well, it was clear he needed to get serious about finding a wife.

He wouldn't have a mommy for her by Christmas this year, but maybe by next year if he was lucky.

Except when he thought about dating, Noelle was the one who popped into his head. *She's not a candidate. She'll be gone in six weeks.* Besides, she'd made it clear she didn't believe in love.

To be honest, Gil was a little shaky on the happily-ever-after thing himself. He didn't know if he could find what he was looking for on a dating site.

"Never mind," he muttered and deleted the app.

"What did you say, Daddy?"

"Nothing." Gil looked at his daughter, who had whipped cream on her upper lip. He motioned to it with his finger. "Got a moustache."

"Oops." Josie giggled and scrubbed at her face with a napkin, then beamed, showing her missing front teeth. "Did I get it?"

"You did." He smiled at his daughter. He loved spending time with her. Being a single dad was hard, but he wouldn't change a thing about his life. Josie was his heart and soul.

Gretchen zipped by, carrying a big plastic tub filled with the dishes she'd just bussed.

"Hey, sis," he called. "Have you seen Noelle?"

"She grabbed breakfast on the go and left early."

"Oh," he said, feeling a twinge of disappointment as he finished up his breakfast. "Can you keep an eye on Josie while I pop over to the Windmill and get set up for tonight's concert?"

"Sure thing." To Josie, she said, "Want me to put *Frozen* on for you in the parlor?"

"Yay!" Josie applauded.

"Help me stack these dishes in the dishwasher and then I can watch with you," Gretchen said.

"Aww, Auntie, do I hafta?"

"Yes," Gil said firmly. "You do. Family helps each other."

"Okay." Josie got up to follow her aunt into the kitchen as Gil cleaned off their table.

Remembering he needed to bring an extra chair to the Windmill, he took a folding chair from the attic, tucked it under his arm, and left the B&B, cutting through Sweetheart Park on his way to the music hall.

He hurried past the Sweetheart Fountain with the statues of Jon Grant and Rebekka Nash embracing. Twilight's monument to true love. He passed the fountain every day on his way to work and barely paid attention. If a crow hadn't cawed loudly and pulled his attention in that direction, he wouldn't have seen Noelle.

She was standing on the edge of the fountain, her eyes on the water, as if she was contemplating tossing a coin in. She was silhouetted in the morning sunlight, looking like a goddess with her glossy whiskey-brown hair skimming her shoulders and her stylish clothes molding to her curves.

Gil stopped in his tracks.

Today, she wore thick black leggings, a long red tunic sweater, a red-and-black-checkered headband, and cute little ankle boots. He much preferred her in this casual attire to the professional business suit she'd worn the day before, but she rocked both outfits. Right now, she looked like the lead from a heartwarming Christmas movie.

Damn, but she was breathtaking.

She looked so graceful, her body lithe and strong, her balance on the circular rock wall surrounding the fountain was impeccable. She exercised regularly. That much was clear. Yoga? Dance? Pilates? Maybe all three.

She lifted her chin and gazed at the reunited high school sweethearts cast from concrete. The legend of Jon and Rebekka etched into a plaque.

Toss a coin into the fountain, wish to be reunited with your first love, and you will be.

Noelle drew back her arm.

Watching, Gil stopped breathing. What was she wishing for?

Him?

Excitement pulled along his nerve endings, leaving his body buzzing with energy. What was *that* about?

Noelle executed an underhand toss.

The object left her palm and sailed toward the embracing lovers in the middle of the bubbling fountain.

Gil waited for the coin to splash into the water, but she overshot the fountain, and whatever she'd thrown hit without a sound, falling onto the soft ground strewn with autumn leaves.

She'd missed the water.

Did it negate her wish?

That's when he saw she hadn't thrown a coin at all, but rather, she'd tossed a bite of muffin to a squirrel who scampered across the lawn to snag it and stuff it into his plump little cheeks.

Good grief, Thomas, he chided himself. *What the hell are you thinking? Of course she wasn't making a wish for you. Wise up.*

It might be foolhardy, but so was lying to himself. Truthfully, it was dumb to deny his feelings. He'd *wanted* her to want him. But he had zero chance with her for so many reasons he couldn't begin to count them all.

Before she could catch him gaping at her, Gil turned and jogged the long way around the park.

CHAPTER 7

After spending the morning at the craft fair, No-elle and the Buckhorns found a skilled artisan all four of them liked who was able to customize table ornaments for the reception at a price within their budget.

Feeling triumphant, Noelle texted Benji, asking her to come over and hang out at the Roost.

Eager to catch up with her old friend and pick her brain for local vendors who might best meet her needs for the wedding, she stopped off at the market for wine and the ingredients for a charcuterie board. Carrying her groceries, she skirted the corner of the B&B, opened the gate, and entered the backyard.

She headed for the garage apartment, mentally preparing how she would arrange the meats, fruits, and cheeses on the board, and not paying much at-tention to what was going on around her.

"Hey, lady."

She stopped and looked around to see who'd called to her. A young girl sat cross-legged on the back porch swing with a tablet computer in her lap. Gil's daughter. She looked just like him with the same dark wavy hair and impossibly blue eyes.

"Oh, hello."

"Do you make weddings?"

Noelle smiled. "Yes, I'm a wedding planner."

"Cool. Canna ask you a question?"

"Of course." Noelle went up the steps to join the girl on the porch.

"Sit by me," the girl invited, scooting over on the swing and patting the cushion beside her.

"My name's Noelle. What's yours?" Noelle settled her bags on the floor and held out her hand as she sat down. The girl shook it. Noelle was impressed with her poise.

"Josie."

Gil's daughter was slender with pigtail braids, and a gap-toothed grin. She wore trendy jeans, a fluffy orange sweater, and a popular brand of sneakers. Gil did an excellent job of keeping her dressed in the latest styles. Kudos, Dad. Although, her aunt Gretchen probably had a hand in picking out the child's clothing.

"Nice to meet you, Josie. Are you thinking about getting married?"

"No!" Josie scowled so intently that Noelle squelched a laugh. "It's not for *me*. I'm just a kid. It's for my daddy."

A ripple of weirdness washed over Noelle. Gil was engaged? Why hadn't he mentioned it?

"When is your dad getting married?"

"No, not yet." Josie grinned. "He's gotta fall in

love first, but after that he'll wanna get married so I can have a mommy. Is that something you can help me with?"

"Not until your dad proposes to the woman he falls in love with."

"Oh." Josie's face fell. "He doesn't even go out on dates."

"Tell you what. I'll give you my card and whenever that day comes, you give me a call and I'll return to Twilight to plan his wedding."

Not really knowing why she did it, Noelle reached into her purse for her silver business card carrying case. She took it out. Something else came out of her purse with the case and hit the ground with a *clink*. She handed Josie the card.

Josie looked down and traced the embossed Once Upon a Wedding logo of an open storybook with two entwined wedding rings in the center.

Noelle bent to see what had landed on the porch. It was the coin Benji had given her. She straightened with the coin clutched between her fingers.

"What's that?" Josie eyed the coin.

Noelle held out her palm.

"That's pretty."

"Here." Noelle was never going to throw the silly thing into the fountain. She didn't believe in that nonsense. "You can have it."

"Thank you!" Josie took the coin and slid it into her pocket along with Noelle's business card.

The screen door opened, and Gil's older sister stepped out. "Sweet pea, could you come help me set the table?"

Gretchen looked much as she had thirteen years ago when Noelle had last seen her. The woman's brown hair, a shade lighter than Gil's own, was plaited into one long braid and secured by a kitschy turkey barrette.

"Noelle!" Gretchen squealed and swooped out onto the porch. "At last! We've been like two ships passing in the night. Delphine's been keeping me up with your comings and goings." Gretchen wrapped her in a tight embrace. "It's so good to see you."

"It's good to see you too." Noelle returned the hug.

Gretchen stepped back. "I'm thrilled you're here. How fun that the Buckhorn twins won the essay contest and you're the one planning their wedding!"

"It is a blast to be back in Twilight."

"Who knew you'd become a wedding planner?" Gretchen's laughter lit up the porch. "I figured you'd be a writer or a librarian or a college professor. You were always so book smart."

"I sort of fell into the job, helping my mom with her many weddings." Noelle chuckled. "Turns out I have a natural knack for it."

"It's because you've got such great organizational and observational skills," Gretchen said. "Remember that Christmas we had a neighborhood scavenger hunt and you beat out everyone, even the older kids because you were calm and quiet and took the time to fully read the instructions."

"I won a gingerbread house." Noelle smiled, remembering.

"I was so jealous. I wanted that house so bad."

"And now you own your own gingerbread house."

"I do, don't I." Gretchen laughed. "I guess we've both found our places in the world."

"We have."

"I saw you on *The Klatch*. Delphine and I were watching it together at the front desk and when they introduced you, I started jumping up and down hollering, 'I know her, I know her.' You're the most exciting thing that's happened in this town in, like, forever."

"It's not that big of a deal." Noelle blushed.

"Tell that to the ladies at Hot Legs Salon and Day Spa. They can't stop talking about the wedding."

"So no pressure, right?"

"Oh, you'll handle it. Of that I have no doubt. Listen, you wanna join us for our family dinner? Although we eat pretty early on the weekends because Gil has to be at the music hall by five for tonight's performance."

"What a lovely invitation, but my friend Benji is coming over and we're going to have snacks and drinks and reminisce."

"Oh, yeah, of course. You have groceries." Gretchen waved at the sacks Noelle had set on the porch. "But it's an open invitation. You're welcome anytime."

"I thought you couldn't serve guests any meals but breakfast."

Gretchen waved that off. "Pffft. You're not a guest. You're family."

Nothing was going according to plan.

First, when Gil arrived at the Windmill that morning, he realized he'd forgotten the spare key after giving the original to Noelle the night before. He'd trotted back home, skirting the park again just in case Noelle was still there.

Upon his return to the music hall, he discovered a pipe had burst in one of the restrooms. It had been a relatively easy fix and luckily the floor was concrete, but repair and cleanup had stolen two hours from his day. After that, he had to track down a delivery that had gone awry, find a replacement for the ticket taker who called in sick, and field a call from Principal White, who phoned to check on Josie.

He told her about the Silvey Zucker mean-girl thing, and she promised to look into it. By the time he'd sorted out all that, it was two thirty. His entire schedule had been thrown off by Noelle's arrival, and Gil lived and breathed by his routine. As a single dad, if he didn't keep on track, everything would unravel.

One off-kilter day and already things were starting to fray.

No more of that. He had to keep his mind off Noelle and solidly centered on his daughter.

The Turkey Trot was on Wednesday and today was the last day to get the costume altered. Because of his weekend schedule, Gretchen would have dinner on the table by four, so he had just a little over an hour to go home, get the costume, go to the tailor's, have the fitting, return to the B&B, eat, and then get to the music hall by five to greet the musicians and help them set up for the seven P.M. concert.

Unless he just skipped dinner, which he refused to do. Family dinner was an essential part of his routine.

He rushed home.

Josie was sitting on the porch watching a movie on her tablet computer. "Hi, Daddy."

"Hey, kiddo, whatcha watching?"

"*Spy Kids.*"

"Wanna help your old man get dressed in his turkey costume?"

He could wait until he got to the tailor to change into the costume, but the elderly man who did the tailoring lived just down the block. No need to get dressed at the guy's house when he could easily do it here and just walk over. Yes, it meant parading down the block in a turkey costume, but Gil wasn't afraid of looking silly. He didn't give two hoots and a holler what anyone thought of him. Convenience was key.

"Sure." Josie switched off her tablet and followed him to the carriage house.

"How do I look?" he asked a few minutes later once he was in the costume and peering at his daughter through the eyeholes in the papier-mâché turkey head.

"Your legs are baggy." She giggled.

"Which is why I'm heading to the tailor."

"Can I go with you?"

"Sure. But we gotta hurry."

She took his hand, and they went out on the porch. Gil's gaze shot to the apartment, and he wondered if Noelle had returned. He thought about asking Josie if she'd seen her, but he didn't want to look like he cared that much, so he didn't say anything.

They started down the steps. A pitiful mewling

sound came from the sycamore tree next to the carriage house.

Josie dropped his hand and pointed at a high branch. "Daddy, look. There's a kitten and it's stuck."

Gil followed her finger. Sure enough, a tiny white kitten clung precariously to a limb. "It got up there on its own. It'll find its way down. C'mon, we gotta hurry."

Josie balked and folded her arms over her chest. "It's a baby. We can't just leave her up there."

"If she's still there when we get back, I'll get her."

Josie's mouth turned down and she looked as if she might cry. "Daddy, listen to her. She's *scared*."

Indeed. Once the kitten caught sight of them, her mewling intensified.

"Please." Josie pressed her palms together.

How could he turn his back on a tiny kitten and his daughter's big-eyed plea? He sighed. "Fine."

"Thank you."

"Here, hold this." He took off the turkey head and thrust it at Josie. The dang thing was almost too big for her to hold. He fetched a ladder from the shed, dragged it over to the tree, and, somewhat hampered by the baggy legs of his costume and his cowboy boots, climbed the ladder.

Even when he got to the top rung, the kitten was still out of his reach. Not only that, as he grabbed for it, the little cat hissed and flattened her ears against her head.

Dadgummit. He would have to climb into the tree to get her.

"Be careful, Daddy. Don't hurt her," Josie called from the ground.

"It's not the kitten's health I'm worried about," Gil muttered under his breath. He was slightly acrophobic, but his fear was manageable *if* he didn't look down.

Concentrating on the kitten, he grabbed hold of the limb directly above his head, wedged one foot at the juncture where two strong branches diverged, and pushed off the top of the ladder with his other foot.

That's when the ladder fell, leaving Gil dangling eight feet off the ground.

Noelle and Benji were sitting in the living room of the small apartment, catching up on old times and discussing how little Twilight had changed. Benji had also told her about the best places in town to order wedding invitations, flowers, cake, and gifts for the wedding party. To be certain, she'd double-check reviews, but she trusted her old friend's judgment and felt like she had a head start on the planning. As they were talking, a knock sounded at the front door.

Noelle and Benji exchanged glances.

"Are you expecting company?"

"Other than you? No."

Noelle got up and Benji followed her to the door. She opened it to find Josie Thomas standing there, an oversized papier-mâché turkey head clutched in her hands.

"Hi," Noelle said. "What's up?"

"My daddy."

"Excuse me?"

"He needs you."

"Oh?" Noelle looked over Josie's head to see if Gil was behind her. He was not. "In what way?"

Josie bobbed her head. "He's stuck."

"Stuck?"

"The ladder fell down."

"That sounds problematic," Benji said.

"I tried to lift the ladder, but it was too heavy," Josie explained. "He said to go get help. You were closest."

"Let's go," Noelle said, both intrigued and concerned.

She and Benji followed the girl outside.

Noelle whipped her gaze around the yard looking for a fallen ladder or a stranded Gil but didn't immediately see him.

"Where is he?" Noelle asked the girl.

Josie pointed at a sycamore tree, the top visible beyond the roofline of the carriage house, still wearing its yellow-orange autumn cloak. Noelle took off around the corner of the house, Josie and Benji close behind.

Noelle stopped short and they almost plowed into her. For there, dressed as a turkey, and hanging on to a high branch for dear life, was Gil.

"What on earth are you doing up there dressed as a turkey?" Noelle asked.

Not waiting for a reply, she motioned for Benji Maxwell to help her, and the two women grabbed hold of the ladder and righted it underneath him.

Gil glanced down, so relieved to have help that

he didn't mind a little ribbing. He'd expected his daughter to go for Gretchen, but he'd take whatever he could get. "It's a long story."

"One I'm eager to hear." Noelle sounded amused.

"Me too," Benji said.

Noelle scooted the ladder into place, and Gil touched the top rung with the toe of his cowboy boot and breathed a sigh of relief. Noelle settled both her feet on the bottom rung, standing on the ladder to anchor it in place.

"I'm holding it steady," she said. "You're safe. C'mon down, Thomas Turkey."

Even though his arms ached from dangling, Gil managed a laugh. His dismount from the ladder wasn't particularly graceful, and he had a wild urge to kiss terra firma once his feet were on the ground, but mostly, he was grateful as hell he didn't end up with busted bones.

Noelle stepped back as he came down.

He turned to face her. "Thank you."

"Happy to help." Her smile was wry. "Love the costume."

"It's for the Turkey Trot on Wednesday."

"I figured."

"Sorry to have troubled you."

"No trouble at all. You're running in a turkey costume?"

"I'm the official mascot. I cheer on the runners."

"And the reason you were in a tree?" Noelle folded her arms over her chest and her teasing grin widened. "If memory serves, you're afraid of heights?"

How had she remembered that? Cringing, Gil

felt the tops of his ears burn. One time at the local water park when they were kids, she'd come up behind him at the tallest flume in the park. He'd been trying to gather his courage to follow his friends down, gripping the sides for dear life, but determined to master his fear.

"Are you scared?" she'd asked him.

"Terrified," he confessed because she'd given him such a genuine grin.

"Just close your eyes," she said. "And don't look down. That's what I do."

Then she'd stepped around him, wrapped her arms around herself, and plunged down the flume. After that, he'd had to let go of his fear and follow her. No way was he going to let a younger kid show him up.

He met her gaze. She possessed the same warm, accepting smile now as she had back then.

"A fear I've mostly conquered," he said, reaching into the pocket of his jacket and pulling out the tiny white kitten who'd crawled to him while he'd been suspended, and whom he'd managed to grab onto with one hand and not kill himself in the process.

Noelle, Benji, and Josie let out a collective "Aww."

"I wanna hold her!" Josie said. "Canna hold her?"

The tiny kitten dug her claws into Gil's palm at the commotion and he winced. "Shh," he whispered. "You gotta be gentle. She's a baby and she's scared."

"Okay," Josie whispered back, dropping the papier-mâché turkey head and putting her hands together in front of her.

Gently, Gil transferred the kitten into his daughter's upturned palms.

"She's so little." Josie softly stroked the kitten's head, and soon the kitten began to purr.

"She likes you," Noelle said. "You have a way with cats."

"Canna keep her, Daddy?" Josie asked. "Canna, canna, canna?"

"Honey, she's probably someone's pet. Don't get your hopes up."

"But she might be a stray. She could be a stray."

He didn't want her to get her heart broken over a kitten she might not be able to keep. "We'll take her to the vet in the morning and see if she has a chip or if they've heard of anyone who lost a kitten."

"I'm gonna name her Snowball."

"No, it's too soon to start naming her."

"What are you going to do with her for now?" Benji asked.

"I suppose we'll keep her for the night."

"Yay!" Josie said in an enthusiastic whisper as she scratched the kitten's head. "We'll get her a bowl of cream and a soft bed and—"

A car horn honked, and the driver stuck his head out the window to holler, "Those are some hot turkey legs, Thomas."

Noelle and Benji giggled. Gil rolled his eyes and muttered, "Everyone's a comedian."

"They are some pretty hot legs," Noelle said.

Benji whipped out her phone. "This is *sooo* going on Facebook."

"No, no." Gil held up his palms. "No pictures.

No posting. C'mon, kiddo, bring your kitten inside and we'll get her a soft place to sleep." Putting a palm to the back of his daughter's head, he guided Josie inside and away from his most embarrassing moment.

CHAPTER 8

On Sunday morning, Noelle lounged in bed, grateful for a day to sleep in before diving full force into the wedding planning on Monday. She was still dealing with jet lag and, if she dared to admit it, her growing attraction to Gil.

She couldn't stop thinking about what a great dad he was. Climbing a tree to rescue a kitten for his daughter when he was afraid of heights. The image of him in that tree, dressed in a turkey costume, brought a smile to her face every time it popped into her head.

Which was far more often than it should have. Yes, he was hot. Yes, they had chemistry. Yes, he seemed like a truly nice guy.

But so what?

She was only in town for a short while. Nothing could come of it. She was a city girl through and through and he was a small-town guy. Best to keep him as nothing more than a sexy fantasy slotted far into the back of her mind.

Yawning, she rolled over and was about to go

back to sleep when her cell phone buzzed. Lazily opening one eye, she reached for her phone to see who'd texted.

GIL: Do U want 2 come 2 church with us?

Noelle paused. The only times in her life when Noelle had attended church had been with her grandparents and she wasn't particularly religious, but she threw back the covers, sat up, and stared at his text.

Did she?

GIL: We attend the Presbyterian church, same as the Buckhorns. It's just a few blocks away.

Well, that was convenient. Attending would give her an opportunity to scope out the venue where the Buckhorns wanted to hold their wedding.

NOELLE: Sure.
GIL: Meet us outside in ten. We'll walk over.
NOELLE: C U then.

She tossed her phone on the bed, flew to the closet, and scrambled to get dressed. No time for breakfast. She pulled a power bar from her purse, then gobbled it as she applied her makeup. By the time she reached the bottom of the stairs where Gil, Gretchen, and Josie were waiting for her, she was breathless and oddly excited about church. Not because she wanted to hear a sermon, but because Gil had invited her.

"Good morning," Gretchen said. "Did you sleep well?"

"Wonderfully, thank you."

Gil smiled. "Are you bundled up warmly enough?"

"I think so." The air had a slight chill to it, but her jacket was insulated. "I'll heat up as we walk."

Gil guided everyone through the backyard gate and clicked it closed behind them. She caught a whiff of his aftershave and a helpless smile crawled over her face. He smelled so darn good. Like pumpkin spice and pine.

To Josie, Noelle asked, "How's the kitten?"

Josie looked ready to tear up. "Daddy took her to see Sam this morning and he found out she had a chip."

"Sam Cheek is our vet," Gil explained. "I called him first thing and he opened up the clinic for us."

"The kitten belonged to Ms. Isabel." Josie sounded glum.

"Isabel Merchant is an older lady who lives on the next block," Gil explained. "She'd left her front door open while she was unloading groceries and the kitten got out. She was so grateful that we returned her. Her husband died last month, and her daughter got her the kitten for company."

"So I don't getta keep her." Josie sighed.

"Maybe Santa will bring you a kitten of your own for Christmas," Noelle said.

"Really?" Josie perked right up. "You think so? Dad, can Santa bring me a kitten for Christmas?"

"Honey, having a pet is a big responsibility," Gil said. "You can't just get one on a whim. We have to be sure you're really ready for one. Maybe next year."

"But I loved Snowball." A tear trickled down Josie's cheek.

Noelle felt for the child. It hurt to fall in love with an animal and not be able to keep it.

"Remember, Ms. Isabel said you could go over and visit the kitten anytime you want. Let's start with that."

"I guess so." Josie blew out her breath. "But my heart is kinda broken."

"Hey," Noelle said, looking for something to distract the girl. "Have you ever played I Spy?"

"Yes, yes." Josie's mood lightened immediately. "I spy something pretty."

Noelle looked around. "Is it the pot of chrysanthemums on your neighbor's porch?"

"Nope." Josie shook her head.

"Is it the red ribbon in your Aunt Gretchen's hair?"

"No."

Noelle shot a glance over at Gil. He gave her a gentle smile.

"Give up?" Josie asked.

"No, no. I can do this." Noelle tapped her chin. "You're pretty. Is it you?"

Josie laughed. "No, silly, it's *you*." Then Josie threw a look at Gil over her shoulder. "Isn't Noelle pretty, Daddy?"

Gil's eyes found Noelle's and the smile slipped from his face. "Yes," he said in a serious voice. "Noelle is very pretty."

"You didn't guess it. I win." Josie did a little jig.

But Noelle couldn't help feeling that she was the one who'd won.

Inside the church, Gretchen slid into the pew first, followed by Josie, then Gil, leaving Noelle to slide in beside him. Other people arrived, forcing Noelle to scoot nearer to Gil until they were so close their shoulders were almost touching.

She'd never been in this building; her grandparents had attended the First Baptist Church on the other side of town, but the reverential smell reminded her of them, and she felt a pang of sorrow that Grammie and Grampie were no longer part of her life. She'd lost a lot with their passing—structure, security, a soft place to land.

And yet, here in Twilight, she'd found those qualities again.

Noelle inhaled deeply and tried to focus on what the minister was saying, but her thoughts were all over the place and she couldn't seem to corral them. She sneaked a sidelong glance over at Gil.

Through the stained glass window, bright autumn sun filtered in, bathing his profile in an ethereal light. He looked enrapt. Sustained.

Joyous.

The man looked filled with the Holy Spirit.

His pumpkin spice–and-pine scent tickled her nose again. The fragrance creating an odd but intense longing for something she'd never had. She felt a compelling urge to reach for his hand and press her soft palm against his calloused one.

It was insane.

This feeling.

This yearning.

To keep from following her impulses, she squeezed her hands into fists and dropped them into her lap. The moment felt weighted and special, although she had no good reason for why.

She decided to fully embrace it, this hyperawareness of everything.

The tweed pattern of his wool sports jacket. The sharp crease of his starched dark-wash blue jeans, the cowboy boots that were worn down at the heels. The tiny white dollop of shaving cream right below his earlobe. Then she saw the Barbie Band-Aid wrapped around his left knuckle and started grinning.

When she'd picked the Buckhorn twins' entry as a winner and decided to come to Twilight, she had expected a nostalgic trip down memory lane. What she hadn't expected was for the past to welcome her home with wide open arms.

If fifteen-year-old Noelle could see her now— sitting in the church pew beside Gil Thomas—she'd literally lose her mind with rapture.

He's not yours to claim. Calm down, she told the girl she used to be.

Why had she come to church with him? What game was she playing? She had a life in Los Angeles, and he had his life here. She was fooling herself if she thought anything could come of this thrilling attraction.

She had nothing to offer a traditional man like Gil. He needed a woman who could play wife and mother and love the role to pieces. That just wasn't her. Given her background and her views on romantic love in general and marriage in particular, she just didn't have the tools. She had to honor her truth. She wasn't the marrying kind.

Marriage?

Good grief. You've been in town for three days and you're thinking about marriage? What's happening to you?

She nibbled her bottom lip. She was a wedding planner. Was it so surprising that marriage dominated her mind?

Pull the plug on the fantasies. Live in the here and now.

Josie was wriggling in her seat, turning around and peering over her shoulder, waving at someone.

Gil placed a hand on his daughter's knee, and Josie turned back around to face the front. He smiled down at Josie with such an expression of love on his face that Noelle's heart clutched. Her father had never looked at her that way. Crescenda, either, for that matter. She felt a tug of jealousy then, not resentment that Josie's parent loved her so very much, but a green surge of envy that she'd never experienced that kind of unconditional parental love. Her parents had simply been too self-absorbed to give a child the attention she'd needed.

Gil turned to look at her then, the smile still on his face, transferring that divine light from Josie to Noelle. He shifted, oh-so-slightly, and his knee bumped into hers.

Intentional?

Just barely a touch, but she felt it like a lightning

bolt striking straight to the center of her heart. She sucked in her breath through clenched teeth and fixed her attention on the man in the pulpit.

The minister was talking about the sustaining power of unconditional love. "Real love is not about physical attraction, although that is a necessary component in a healthy, well-rounded romantic relationship. Real love is about wanting the best for the other person, regardless of what it means for you. Real love is caring for others without expecting anything in return."

Noelle cast a sidelong glance at Gil just as he turned to look at her.

Their gazes met.

She felt the impact like a punch to the stomach, hard and quick. His blue eyes burned, twin hot flames. She stopped breathing.

His eyes rounded wide, and his lips parted. She caught a glimpse of his straight white teeth and smelled peppermint on his breath.

"Believe in the power of love," the minister said. "Whenever you put your faith in love there's no reason to worry. Believe that love will show you where you need to go. Let love lead your heart, above all else. Love has the power to transform and heal."

Gil's gaze never left her face.

Noelle couldn't look away. Didn't want to look away.

The minister continued, "As Paul says in First Corinthians: 'Love is patient and kind; love does not envy or boast; it is not arrogant or rude. It does not insist on its own way; it is not irritable or resentful; it does not rejoice at wrongdoing but rejoices with the truth.' And love is what we should strive to live by. Not just with family, friends, and your closest intimates, but with everyone."

Noelle finally took a breath.

The minister signaled the piano player. "Now, let's open our hymnals to page twenty-three and raise our voices as we sing 'My Savior's Love.'"

Gil took the hymnal from the back of the pew in front of them and opened it. He held the old hardcover book out in front of him so she could read along just as Gretchen did the same for Josie. Piano music and the accompanying choir started the song as the congregation joined in.

The service was old-fashioned. Quite unlike the modern megachurch she'd attended once with a friend in LA where the hymns were projected on a jumbotron. This service was intimate and sweet, creating that powerful sense of a close-knit community she'd forgotten existed.

The music welled up inside her, stoking her emotions and bringing a tear to her eye. How much she'd missed this town without even knowing it.

She dabbed at her eye with a knuckle.

Gil touched her wrist.

Noelle looked down to see him pressing a clean handkerchief into her hand. His kindness touched her deeply. She smiled at him through a watery film of tears.

He leaned his head down to hers and whispered, "Thinking about your grandparents?"

She nodded, unable to speak.

Then he did the darnedest thing. Gil slipped his arm around her shoulder, drew her closer, and held the hymnal up higher. Singing in perfect harmony, their grateful voices joined those around them and merged into a tender moment of connection.

And she told herself that tomorrow she'd get her mind back where it belonged, on wedding planning.

"Would you like to eat lunch with us?" Gretchen invited Noelle when the service was over.

Oh yes. She wanted that more than anything, but her emotions were raw after that service. She couldn't stop thinking about how Gil's arm had felt around her shoulder as they'd sung together and about how easily he could derail her from her mission.

She needed distance from this little family. Needed to clear her head and put on her logic goggles. She'd gotten swept away by the religious pageantry, welcoming community, and lingering grief over losing her grandparents.

Time for some boundaries.

"Thank you so much for the invitation, but I've got a lot of work to do," she said, which was certainly true.

"On a Sunday?" Gretchen sounded disappointed.

"The day of the week doesn't matter much to me."

"Please," Josie wheedled. "We're going to Froggy's for fried chicken."

"As tempting as that invitation sounds . . ." And it was tempting. Froggy's made the best fried chicken in the world. "I'm going to have to decline but thank you so much for asking."

"Aww man." Josie scowled. "That stinks."

"Don't pressure her," Gil gently chided his daughter. "Noelle's allowed to make the choices that are right for her. Don't make it difficult for her to say no."

Josie rolled her eyes and Noelle wondered if it was a lecture she'd heard often.

"What did I tell you about eye rolling, missy?"

"That it's rude, but Daddy, I want Noelle to come with us."

"And we don't always get what we want, now do we?"

"No." Josie glowered and tucked her hands into her armpits.

"Would you like it if someone tried to make you feel guilty for not doing what they wanted you to do?"

"No." Her tone softened.

"Tell Noelle you're sorry."

"Sorry," Josie mumbled, toeing the church lawn with the tip of her black patent leather shoe.

"Look Noelle in the eyes when you talk to her." Gil put a hand on his daughter's shoulder.

Josie raised her head and met Noelle's gaze. "Sorry for being bratty."

Noelle smiled. "That's perfectly all right. I can be bratty sometimes too."

Josie returned her smile, and all was well. Noelle waved goodbye to the Thomases as they headed toward the lake and Froggy's while Noelle turned back to the B&B.

Part of her ached to go with them, but the part

of her that knew she had to keep her feet planted firmly on the ground was relieved.

It would be so very easy to fall in love with this town, with this community, with Gil Thomas and his daughter. If she had any hopes of keeping her heart safe, she had to stay on her toes.

Good thing she'd be so busy in the weeks leading up to Christmas that she'd have little time for anything else.

And that's exactly how she wanted things to be. Work had seen her through all of life's ups and downs. It would see her through this too.

After their meal at Froggy's, as they returned to the B&B, Gretchen reminded Gil that he'd promised to winterize the pipes. The forecast warned that the first hard freeze of the year was due to arrive on Thanksgiving evening along with potential snow flurries.

He parked Josie in the parlor of the B&B with a movie and Delphine promised to keep an eye on her. He and his sister gathered supplies and went outside to wrap and cap the water spigots.

Gretchen held the supplies like a surgical nurse in the operating room, passing him the tools as he asked for them.

"Plumber's tape." He held out a palm.

She smacked the roll of tape into his hand and watched as he wrapped it around the coupling. "So what was that all about with Noelle at church?"

"Huh?" He peered over at Gretchen, who'd squatted down beside him.

"You putting your arm around her."

"She was sad about her grandparents. I was just trying to make her feel better."

"Uh-huh." Gretchen's voice held a knowing tone.

"What's that supposed to mean?"

"You're pretty talented at hiding your motivations from yourself."

"Humph."

"You like her."

"Yeah, so what?"

"She likes you too."

"Again, so what?" He grunted. The tape had gotten twisted. Frustrated, he yanked it off, wadded it up, and tossed the mangled tape over his shoulder.

"So, I think you two would make a good couple."

"I don't recall asking your opinion." He peeled off another piece of tape and tried again.

"She wanted to come to lunch with us, I could see it on her face, but she's conflicted," Gretchen said.

"I probably shouldn't have touched her without her permission." He shouldn't have, but when he'd settled his arm on her shoulder, just intending to comfort her, she'd leaned into him and hadn't moved away. "She's setting good boundaries. That's healthy."

"Unless it's just avoidance."

"Can we not talk about it?" he asked, finally getting the tape on correctly. He held out his hand. "Wadding."

Gretchen passed him a worn-out tea towel. "She's good for you."

He raised his head to stare at his sister. "How do you figure?"

"She's shaking you out of your rut."

He curled the towel around the spigot. "We're not having this discussion. I thought I made that clear."

"I know you need the rut in order to keep things on track. I know your routine is important, but you've turned stodgy, Gil, and you're just now thirty. It's time to live a little."

"Cap." He would not indulge his sister by feeding this conversation.

She handed him the Styrofoam cap to fit over the towel-wrapped faucet. "Tammy Jo would want you to move on."

"Moving on is one thing," Gil said. "Leaping into the fire without looking is a whole other prospect."

"And yet you put a desk for her in your office."

"I shouldn't have done that," he mumbled, regretting the impulse already, and he hadn't spent a single hour in his office with Noelle in it. To be honest, he didn't know why he'd offered to share his office. In hindsight, it was a dumb idea, but he didn't know how to reverse it now.

"It's okay to be attracted to her."

"Gretchen, if you don't hush up I'm gonna stuff one of those tea towels in your mouth."

"Idle threats."

He picked up a tea towel from the stack she had on the ground in front of her. "You that confident?"

Laughing, Gretchen raised her palms and tried to get to her feet from her crouching position, but lost her balance and ended on her back.

He pantomimed jamming the towel into her mouth, teasing as they had as kids whenever Gretchen picked on him.

"Um . . . Dad." Josie was standing on the porch looking down at them, tablet tucked under one shoulder. "Why are you being mean to Aunt Gretchen?"

Gretchen tilted her head back so she could see Josie on the porch. "Help me, Jo. Your dad's picking on me."

Josie flew down the steps and flung herself over Gretchen's body. "Dad, Dad, don't hurt Auntie!"

"I'm not hurting her." Gil jumped to his feet, hating that Josie thought he was capable of hurting anyone, much less his own sister.

Gretchen laughed so hard, tears came to her eyes. "We were just teasing, sweet pea. Siblings do that sometimes."

"Oh." Josie's eyes glazed. "I wish I had a sibling."

"Maybe someday." Gretchen winked at Gil. "If your dad will ever glance up from his rut and look around."

Gil put down a hand to help first Josie and then Gretchen off the ground. Chuckling, Gretchen dusted grass from her hair.

"What's a rut?" Josie asked.

"Doing the same thing over and over, day in and day out," Gretchen said.

"Like you're one to talk." Gil glowered.

"Oh, I *am* one to talk. I have a date tonight, so you'll have to forage for your own dinner."

"I can handle that."

"See, taking the first step out of your rut isn't

that hard. Just do one thing each day that's different from the day you did before. Tonight, it's eating at your house instead of mine." With that, Gretchen turned and went up the steps.

"Hey, you're not going to help finish wrapping the pipes?"

"Nope," his sister said. "Consider it your penance for not letting me talk about Noelle."

CHAPTER 9

On Monday morning, Noelle decided to stay holed up in the Roost creating a wedding planning bible and making phone calls instead of going to the Windmill and working at the card table desk in Gil's office. After that inspiring church sermon, being near him felt unsustainable.

At least for today.

In flannel pajamas, bathrobe, and her whimsical Bigfoot house shoes, she'd planned on sneaking into the B&B early before most of the other guests were stirring, grabbing breakfast to go from the buffet, and scurrying back to the apartment.

She darted outside in the morning dusk only to run into Gil, who was leaving the B&B carrying a white box of what looked like donuts.

Busted.

Of course he would catch her when she looked her worst—hair mussed, no makeup, baggy pj's and Bigfoot slippers. She should have taken the time to get dressed. She knew better than to go out in public without looking her best. Crescenda had drilled that into her. Image mattered. So much for her covert, buffet-raiding mission.

Gil, on the other hand, looked magnificent. Rugged cowboy to the max in his shearling jacket, white Western shirt with silver snaps, and snug-fitting Wranglers; those sharp blue eyes and daring dimples looked especially appealing in the dawning sunlight.

"Good morning," he said.

"Morning," she mumbled, fixing her gaze on the roofline above his head and the sycamore tree she'd rescued him from. Her feet pointed in the direction of the B&B, but he seemed inclined to talk.

"Going in for breakfast?"

"Yup."

"I was just picking up mine and Josie's. I let Josie sleep in since she doesn't have school this week."

"Donuts?" She eyed the box. Noelle loved donuts.

"Pastries."

Ack! She loved pastries even more. Though she rarely ate them. Too many carbs, too much sugar.

"Gretchen made kolaches. Three flavors. Apple, cherry, and cheese."

"Apple's my favorite."

"I'm afraid I got the last of those. At the rate the guests were swarming, there might not be any pastries left. But if you want, I'll share mine. I picked up two of each flavor." With his elbow, he motioned toward his house. "Come on in, I'll divvy out a couple for you."

"Umm . . ." Going into his house was the very last thing she wanted, but she did love apple kolaches.

"Gretchen uses the apples from our trees." He inclined his head toward the fruit trees at the back of the property. "And I put on a pot of coffee when I left the house. Coffee and apple kolaches, breakfast of champions."

She should say no. Just thank him and just go on into the B&B or run back to the Roost.

Heavy lids hooded his eyes, the thick lashes giving him an insouciant air. He'd sprouted beard stubble since his shave on Sunday morning and she found the slight scruff wildly appealing. Then again, she loved his smooth, freshly shorn look just as much. Shaven. Unshaven. The man was objectively hot.

"You coming?" He stepped toward the cottage.

Damn her, she was.

He opened the door, stood to one side to let her in. They stepped into the open concept kitchen and living area. He set the box on the countertop, took off his coat, and hung it on the coat tree by the door. Noelle was wearing a bathrobe and he didn't offer to hang it up for her. Yay.

"Just let me check on Josie," he said. "Help yourself to the coffee."

He disappeared down the hallway as Noelle moved to the coffee pot, but he was back before she could find a cup.

"Josie's conked out. I don't know how she can sleep so hard." He trailed off and shrugged. "Kids."

Something was gnawing on him, but she could

see it had nothing to do with her. Best to keep her mouth shut and not dig into it, but that didn't stop her from wanting to erase the frown causing a furrow between his eyebrows and that faraway look in his eyes.

Not her problem to solve.

Gosh, it was so easy to fall back into her people-pleasing, childhood habits. Her therapist had once told her that people-pleasing had been her way of trying to control a chaotic environment. Noelle wasn't sure she bought into that, but hey, she'd managed to survive growing up in her famous parents' shadows, so maybe there was something to it.

"Where did you go?" she asked, studying his face.

He gave a short chuckle that was more snort than laugh. "I was going to ask you the same thing. You seemed a million miles away."

"Not miles," she said. "Decades."

"Thinking about your grandparents?"

That was close enough. She nodded.

"The holidays do bring up old memories." His steady gaze locked on her.

"I don't really get into celebrating the holidays. Not since I lost Grammie and Grampie."

He grinned. "Oh, you will this year. You're back in Twilight and just in case you forgot, we go all out."

"I recall."

"You're coming to Thanksgiving dinner with us," he said. A statement, not a question, as if it was a foregone conclusion.

"What if I have plans?"

"Do you?"

"I could have plans."

"With whom?"

"Benji."

"Then bring her along."

"She did invite me to go out to Thanksgiving dinner with her family. They aren't cooking this year because of all the wedding prep, but I haven't said yes yet."

"I could get Gretchen to ask the Buckhorns and Maxwells to our Thanksgiving dinner. Unless that's crossing a boundary."

"Actually, that might be fun. It would give me an opportunity to socialize with the brides and grooms and learn more about them in an informal environment."

"Consider it done."

"Gretchen won't mind?"

"Gretchen is a more-the-merrier kind of hostess, but I'll run it by her to make sure." He came over to where Noelle stood at the coffee station, his shoulder brushing lightly against hers as he reached for a coffee cup from the rack.

Accidental or on purpose?

She tilted her head and slanted him a sidelong glance.

He was looking down at her, a big grin on his face. Oh, definitely intentional. Gil dipped his head and for one freakish, trapped-in-her-teenage-fantasy second, she thought he was about to kiss her.

She startled in a total *hot-dog-let's-do-this* kind

of way, then realized, a bit embarrassed, that he was going in for the creamer nestled in a turkey-shaped ceramic dish.

He stilled. His hand outstretched.

She held her breath.

His blue eyes glimmered in the light spilling in through the kitchen window and the smile faded from his face. He wasn't quite touching her, but almost.

The air between them quivered with energy.

Hello, Dolly, she was quivering.

He wrapped his hand around the plastic pod of creamer, his forearm inches from her breasts. She should move, get out of the way, but her feet seemed welded to the floor.

Holy wedding vows.

Her body heated from deep within her center, spreading out in all directions, burning her skin, her neck, her cheeks. Time, as a concept, collapsed in on itself and no longer existed. She was pinned to this spot, stabbed by his icy blue eyes, blistered by an intense internal heat.

He'd stopped breathing, his gaze latched on to hers.

Frankly, so had she.

Then his gaze traveled from her eyes, down her nose to her lips and beyond, taking in her pajamas and Bigfoot slippers, and his smile returned, more amused than ever, dimples digging deep.

She delighted him. A thrill raced up her spine, lodged at the base of her brain, blasting red-hot tingles to every nerve ending in her body.

"Love the slippers," he said. "Bigfoot fan?"

"Not particularly. I just like the irony."

"You have small feet?"

"I do. Size five and a half. My mother says she doesn't know how I don't tip over in a strong wind."

"No offense, but your mother's sort of an ass."

"Sometimes." Noelle nodded. "But aren't we all?"

"I love that you have small feet," he said. "Then again, I'd love it if your feet were big."

Love.

A fresh ripple of tingling heat went through her. "Why?"

"Because those feet belong to you."

Her heart beat so hard she could hear it in her ears.

"Are you cold?" he asked.

"Wh-what?" she stammered, then realized, horrified, as his gaze dropped to her breasts, that she hadn't bothered to put on a bra and her nipples had beaded and were poking perkily through her pajama top and bathrobe.

She set down her coffee cup on the counter and wrapped her fluffy bathrobe more tightly around her. *Note to self: In future, do not leave the Roost unless fully dressed.*

"I could turn up the heat."

"No!" She cringed that the word came out so loud and adamant. "I mean, I'm fine. You don't need to fiddle with the thermostat on my account."

"You sure?" He pressed his lips together, suppressing a grin.

"Positive. Let me at those kolaches. I'm starving." She picked up her coffee cup and scurried over to the counter where he'd left the box of pastries, and she sank down on a barstool.

He followed her over and parked himself beside her, disturbingly close. She took a big swallow of coffee to avoid looking at him and it was so hot that she hissed as she gulped it down.

"You okay?"

"Fine."

"I forgot to tell you that my pot brews hot."

Of course it did. Everything about the man was hot.

"You sure you're okay?" he asked.

The roof of her mouth was slightly singed, but she'd live. "Mind if I have a kolache?"

"Go for it." He waved at the box.

She flipped open the lid and stared down at the array of pastries. They looked so delicious. She reached for a paper towel from the roll on the counter, peeled off a sheet, and used it as a makeshift plate for the apple kolache.

Gil did the same, adding a cherry kolache to his paper towel.

Noelle took a bite of her pastry. It tasted so good that she let out an involuntary moan of pleasure. "Oh gosh. Gretchen missed her calling. She could have been a pastry chef."

"Kolaches are her specialty. It's the number one comment on our Yelp reviews. Best kolaches this side of West."

"West what?"

"West is a small Czech community outside of

Waco. They're known for their kolaches. My mom's parents were Czech, and Grandma taught Gretchen how to make pastries. Mom wasn't a baker herself. She claims the skill skips a generation."

"I didn't know your maternal grandparents were Czech."

"Why would you?"

She canted her head and studied him. "There's a lot I don't know about you."

He took a sip of his coffee and held her gaze. "Ditto."

"We might have known each other since childhood, but we haven't really had all that many conversations over the years."

"Now is a great time to change that."

"Is it?"

"Huh?"

"Do we *really* want to get to know each other? I'm flying home on Christmas Day, right after the wedding."

"That gives us five weeks to get to know each other."

"For what reason?" she asked, licking crumble topping off her bottom lip.

"Enjoying each other's company."

"That's all you want?"

His gaze hung on her mouth. "That's all."

"You're not looking for anything else? Because if you are, I'm not your gal. Long-distance relationships just don't work."

"I know," he said. "It's why I stopped touring as a musician and opened the Windmill. I was married and I couldn't keep my marriage afloat and stay out on the road."

"You chose your family over your career." She found that quality admirable. Something neither one of her parents had been able to do.

"Yeah, but I had to be honest with myself. While I love music, I'm only a fair to middling musician. I was never going to have a stellar career. I mean, I could have made a good living as a studio musician, but that would have meant leaving Twilight and I love this place too much to ever leave for good. So I run a music venue to showcase talent better than I am, teach guitar lessons, and write songs. It's enough."

"Wow," she said.

"Unimpressive, huh?"

"Quite the opposite. It's admirable that you know yourself so well and have no delusions of grandeur. You're down-to-earth." After growing up the way she did, with parents who put all their faith in drama and dreams, she found Gil's level-headed approach to life compelling.

"I'm basic. It's okay. I know it."

"Basic is good," she said. "So very good. It means you're solid and dependable and . . ."

"Boring."

"Oh, not in the least, Gil Thomas. I don't know many men who would climb into a sycamore tree in a turkey costume to rescue a kitten."

"Who knew that was the way to your heart?" He winked. "If that impressed you, then come run at the Turkey Trot with me on Wednesday as I run alongside the runners to cheer them on. There, you'll get the costume's full effect. Come see me shake my tail feathers."

"While that does sound tempting, I'm more of a Pilates gal than a runner."

"Who cares? It's for fun and charity. We have a blast. That's all that matters."

His invitation was so tempting that she blurted out, "Yes, okay, I'll do it," before she fully thought it through.

Suddenly, the room seemed to shrink, narrowing down to just the two of them sitting at the counter. Gil's beautiful blue eyes drank her in. She was mesmerized, trapped by his dilating pupils and terrified at the wild feelings ping-ponging around inside her. She dropped her gaze and gave the apple kolache her full attention.

"I meant to thank you," he said.

"For what?"

"I saw the pledge you made in my name for the Polar Plunge. That was very generous of you."

"It was nothing." She polished off the kolache.

"Not true. The money means a lot to the kids in the Special Olympics. But I'm curious about one thing."

"What's that?"

"How did you know about the Polar Plunge?"

She came clean. Telling him that she'd watched him take the dive on the morning she'd rolled into town.

"A bit of a voyeur, are you?" His laughter enriched the kitchen.

She measured off an inch with her thumb and

forefinger. "At least when it comes to handsome Santas stripping off their clothes."

"You think I'm handsome?"

"Don't even pretend otherwise, Mr. Thomas."

His smile deepened, showing off that double dimple again. "There's something I've wanted to ask you."

"Yes?"

He reached into his shirt pocket and pulled out her business card. "I found this in Josie's jeans when I went to do the laundry. What's it about?"

Noelle swallowed hard and shook her head. Was he upset with her? "She asked me to help plan your wedding."

"My *what*?" He looked taken aback.

"I gave her my card and told her to call me when you'd proposed to someone. It was in jest, but she must have taken it to heart. She really wants a mom."

"Yeah." He blew out his breath and ran a hand through his hair. "I know. She told me she wanted a mommy for Christmas. Gotta admit, she took me by surprise. I've been so busy trying to be both mother and father, I didn't realize that no matter how hard I try there are some things I just can't give her. I thought living near Gretchen would help fill the gap, but apparently she's still struggling."

"I'm sorry."

He opened up and told her about Josie's problems at school. "I'm worried about her. I feel like I'm screwing everything up."

"She's a great kid and you're doing a bang-up job parenting her. Believe me, I know what screwed-up parenting looks like and you're a million miles from that."

"Thanks."

"All parents have doubts. The difference is that you really *care*. You want the best for her, and you sacrifice to make that happen. Despite what Hallmark greeting cards would have us think, not all parents are like that."

"Still, you turned out pretty darn amazing, Noelle Curry." His smile was gentle, encouraging.

"Because of my grandparents and the people I met in Twilight."

"Twilight is a special place," he said. "You can see why it feels impossible for me to live anywhere else."

Noelle's cell phone buzzed. She pulled it from the pocket of her sweater and glanced down at the text. It was from her mother.

CRESCENDA: Call me!

Groaning, Noelle stuck her phone back into her pocket.

"Problems?"

"Mama drama."

"Aah."

Noelle pushed back her barstool. "I gotta go. Thanks for the kolaches and coffee. I'm fully fortified for a day of wedding planning."

"My total goal."

"Thanks."

He stood up, towering over her. She had a flashback to the day she'd arrived, and he'd stood head and shoulders above the other Santas. Her mind also called up images of what he'd looked like in the water, the sunlight shimmering off his bare chest.

Gil moved toward her, blocking her exit, and lowered his head.

Noelle stared up at him. "What are you doing?"

"I'm thinking about kissing you." His voice was low, sexy, and hot as hell.

"Seriously?"

"Seriously."

"Wh-why?" They'd already talked about why they were not a good match. Discussed why nothing could come of their attraction. What was he playing at?

"Because you look so gorgeous in those Bigfoot slippers."

"The slippers are a turn-on, huh?"

"*You're* the turn-on, Bookworm."

"B-but we just discussed how long-distance relationships don't work."

"Right now, the distance between us is only a couple of inches."

Her stomach churned, but in a spectacular way, like a kid at Christmas. She moistened her lips. His head dipped even lower. She went up on tiptoe.

Their lips were almost touching . . .

A floorboard creaked.

Simultaneously, their heads shot up.

There Josie stood, yawning and rubbing her eyes. "Morning, Daddy. Morning, Noelle."

They sprang apart.

"Morning," Noelle greeted the girl, pulse thumping.

"Whatcha doin' here?" Josie asked, stretching her arms over her head.

"Um, um . . ." Panicking, she couldn't think of a single reason why she should be in Josie's house alone with the girl's father. Her phone buzzed again. Yes! Saved by the bell.

CRESCENDA: I'm waiting.

"I do have to go." She sidled away from Gil and beat a path to his door. "Enjoy your kolaches."

As the door clicked closed behind her, she could have sworn she heard him say, "To be continued."

CHAPTER 10

His door flew open.

Gil startled.

Noelle stood at the threshold. Her hair buffeted wildly from the gusting wind. More lines to the song he was writing about her pinged around his brain like heated popcorn kernels.

"Could I see you outside for a sec?"

"Uh . . ." He cast a glance at Josie, who was busily noshing a kolache. "BRB, kiddo."

Josie waved a blithe hand.

Gil went outside, closing the door behind him. Noelle had her bathrobe wrapped tightly around her, but he could still see her nipples poking through the material. He tried not to stare. "What is it?"

"What did you mean by that crack?"

"What crack?"

"To be continued."

He shrugged, amused by how riled she seemed. "Seems pretty self-explanatory to me."

"Let's get something straight. It's *not* going to be continued."

"No?" He arched an eyebrow.

"No."

Gil shrugged. "Okay."

"That's it? Just okay?"

"What do you want me to say?"

"That you won't try to kiss me again."

"I won't try to kiss you again," he parroted.

"Because kissing me would be a big mistake."

He couldn't help staring at those plump delicious lips he'd almost kissed. Desire rolled through him, hard and fast. He tried to tell himself it was because he hadn't been with a woman in five years, but he knew this feeling went much deeper than that. There was something about Noelle that endlessly intrigued him, and he didn't know why.

"See, now that's where we disagree," he drawled and then let silence spread out between them.

"Well?" She sank her hands onto her hips, deepened her frown, and tapped one Bigfoot slipper.

"I think kissing you would be the best darn thing that happened to either of us in a very long time."

Did saying that to her freak him out? Oh, yeah, you betcha. But he wasn't the kind of guy who ran from tough emotions. Face life head-on. That was his motto. Those words to live by had gotten him and Josie through some pretty tough times.

Noelle's phone buzzed in her pocket.

"You've got a text."

Her phone buzzed again. She winced and then it buzzed a third time.

"Sounds urgent."

"It's not," she said. "It's my mother."

"Your mother never has emergencies?"

"Quite the opposite. My mother *always* has an emergency."

"She sounds like a handful."

Noelle snorted. "That's putting it lightly."

"It's not that easy, is it? Being the child of a celebrity."

"Perks come with it." Her lips pursed—sweet, pink, kissable lips. "I try to remember that whenever I feel a pity party coming on. Everyone has a cross to bear. Plus, I'm well aware of the privilege afforded to me simply because of who my parents are."

"That's admirable."

She raked her gaze over him, empathy darkening her brown eyes to a deep chestnut color. "Some of us have more crosses to carry than others."

"That doesn't mean you don't deserve kindness and understanding."

A soft sigh escaped her. "If Josie hadn't interrupted us would you have gone through with the kiss?"

"Would you have wanted me to?"

"You're being evasive answering my question with a question."

Was he? Maybe.

"Yes," she said before he could reply.

"Yes?"

"I would have let you kiss me."

"That's good to know." He suppressed the grin that ached to light up his face.

"Which is why it's lucky Josie woke up when she did. If she'd have been one minute later she would have caught us in the middle of a lip-lock."

That thought sobered him.

"We can't . . . there's no room in my life . . . I'm . . . you're . . ."

"I get it." He nodded. "Believe me, I get it."

This feeling between them was too much, too soon. It wasn't rational and they were both logical, grounded people. They had their differences for sure. He was laid-back while she was tightly wound. He was small town, and she was big city. He had traditional values, and she was thoroughly progressive. He was big picture, and she was detail oriented. Yes, there were many places where they did not dovetail, but neither one of them had their head in the clouds. They were sensible. They wouldn't allow lust, passion, and desire to sweep them into something they weren't ready for.

Her phone buzzed again.

"You better take that," he said. "You've got a mom to handle, and I've got a kid to tend."

"Thank you for understanding."

"Sure." He shrugged and gave her his best smile. "That's what friends are for."

"Is that what we are?"

"I hope so. I'd like to think so."

A beautiful light flared in her eyes again and then she was gone, fleeing up the steps and into the Roost.

He watched her go, his heart doing a funny little swoop and dive. Behind him, Josie opened the door.

"Dad, better come inside before I gobble up all the kolaches."

"What is it, Crescenda?" Noelle asked as she flopped down on the couch in the upstairs apartment.

She fingered her lips, thinking about the kiss that hadn't happened. Wishing it *had* happened and then hating that she thought such a silly thing. She simply could not get anything going with Gil. Too much was riding on this wedding for her to get diverted from her goal.

The series of texts Crescenda had sent while she and Gil had been sorting out their feelings consisted of demands. Call me! Call me now! Noelle Elizabeth Curry, call your mother!

"I'm here. What do you want? What's so important that I had to drop everything to call you?"

"Darling, the most *wonderful* thing has happened."

Noelle bit her bottom lip and tensed her shoulders, bracing herself. Crescenda paused for dramatic effect.

Ten, nine, eight . . . *wait for it* . . . seven, six, five . . .

Crescenda exhaled in a loud whoosh.

Four, three, two . . .

"Basil proposed!"

Noelle pulled the phone away from her ear to stare at it in her palm. Oh hell, not again.

If you can't say something nice, don't say anything at all. Grammie's motto played in her head and kept Noelle from blurting the thoughts pushing at the back of her lips. She wanted to jump through the phone screen, teleport to London, grab her mother by the shoulders, and shake some sense into her.

"Do you want to know what my answer was?"

No, not really. Sighing, Noelle brought the phone back to her ear. "I can guess from the thrill in your voice."

"Yes! I said yes! My darling, you'll be planning another wedding come spring."

"How long have you known this man? You've been in London, what, three weeks?"

"I met him in LA when he cast me as the lead."

"Okay, four weeks, that's *so* much better. Forgive me. For a minute there, I thought you were jumping the gun."

"Sarcasm doesn't become you."

"You've been married five times, Mother."

"It just means I'm a hopeless romantic and an eternal optimist. Unlike some sourpusses I could name."

"Or it means you have no idea who you are deep down inside, and you turn to men to give you external validation."

"Humph. You sound like my therapist."

"I just don't want to watch you make yet another mistake."

"Making mistakes is how we grow."

"I think you're supposed to learn from the mistakes, not just keep making them ad nauseam." Okay, maybe she was being too harsh, but darn it, she wasn't ready for stepdad number six.

"Basil's different from the others."

"Maybe he is, and maybe he isn't. Ultimately, this isn't about the men. It's your inability to stick it out when the going gets tough. Any of the guys you were married to could have been a lifelong companion if you didn't cut and run when things got tricky."

"Now you sound just like your father." She sniffed delicately, letting Noelle know she was miffed.

"Maybe you should ask yourself what kind of man proposes to a woman after knowing her for just four weeks?"

"A man in love, that's who." Despite her obvious shortcomings, Crescenda could be quite loveable when she turned on the charm.

"Or a man who's fallen for an image."

"You're being mean."

Was she? Noelle nibbled her bottom lip. She felt wretched. This was how things went between them. She'd known Crescenda for twenty-eight years and still hadn't figured out how to forge a stable relationship with her mother while still maintaining her own identity.

"I don't want to rain on your parade. Basil might be a perfectly wonderful man—"

"He is."

"But if he is, why rush things? Get to know him first before taking the plunge. I'm not saying not to marry him, just take your time for once. Have a really long engagement. Years even."

"I know what's going on here."

Noelle suppressed a sigh. "The only thing going

on here is that I'm concerned about you. Every time you go through a divorce—"

"This time it's for real."

"That's what you said about Marty and Nate and Felix and Jack and I'm pretty sure you must have said the same thing about Dad once upon a time."

"You're jealous. That's the truth of it. Admit it. You're jealous that so many men love me."

"Yeah, Mother, that's it. I'm desperately jealous of you."

"You are!" Crescenda's tone escalated. "You've never had even one man propose to you. No man has ever loved you. You're not allowed to judge me. You don't have a clue what love is." If her mother had pulled out a dagger and plunged it directly into Noelle's heart it wouldn't have hurt as badly as those bitter words.

"I'm going to hang up. We can talk again when you've calmed down."

"Calmed down? I'm perfectly calm. You're the one who's out of control. You're the one who's so miserable you can't be happy for me. What did I ever do to deserve such a wretched child as you?"

DARVO.

She recognized the acronym for what it was. Deny. Attack. Reverse victim and offender. It happened every time she tried to hold her mother accountable for her actions. Noelle knew what was happening and yet every single damn time she walked right into it.

And came out feeling battered and ashamed.

Her therapist said she was a glutton for punishment and part of her wondered if it might be true. What Crescenda had said was correct. Not counting her childhood crush on Gil, Noelle had never been in love, and no one had ever been in love with her, at least not to her knowledge.

And despite planning weddings for a living, she had no clue what real love even looked like.

"So, you and Crescenda Hardwick's daughter. What's up with that?" Derrick Driscoll said to Gil on Tuesday as they sat in the CPA's office going over the previous month's receipts.

"Huh?" Gil blinked at the accountant.

Derrick shrugged. "I'm plugged into the town grapevine. I do taxes for half the businesses in Twilight. What can I say?"

"Nothing is up." He shouldn't have responded. He should have just ignored Derrick's question, but he couldn't seem to help himself.

"I go to the barber shop. People talk. Your haircut looks nice, BTW. Getting spiffy for Noelle?"

That dart hit home. He had gotten a trim yesterday after he'd caught a glimpse of himself in the mirror and noticed how shaggy he looked. "The gossip mill is working overtime. Don't feed the beast."

"I also ran into Delphine and Luther in the checkout line at H-E-B."

"Those two enjoy embellishing things."

"So there's something to embellish?" Derrick seemed to be enjoying himself way too much.

"No."

"Come on, don't be embarrassed. Noelle is a pretty woman. She's smart and successful, although I imagine a big part of her success is due to her parents' celebrity, but that's just icing on the cake."

Why couldn't people in his hometown mind their own business?

"I've heard that Noelle had a huge crush on you when she was a teenager and everyone in town knew about it."

Gil plucked a receipt from the file folder he'd brought with him. "Here's my deductions for the overhead lighting I had to replace in the auditorium."

"Delphine said you invited Noelle into your house for kolaches yesterday morning. Is that a euphemism for—"

Good grief! He had no idea that Derrick enjoyed stirring the gossip pot so much.

Gil scowled. "Do you want to keep playing scales for the next month or would you like to work on 'Free Bird'?"

"'Free Bird'!"

"Then hush up about Noelle, okay?"

"Got it." Derrick's smile was smug. "She's special."

"Yeah, so let's keep her name out of the rumors as a favor to me, okay?"

"Maybe you had a little bit of a crush on her too back in high school?"

No, he hadn't. She'd just been the summer kid across the street, but now he wished he had paid more attention to her.

"You *do* know that getting married would give you a huge tax deduction, right?" Derrick asked.

"I can take away 'Free Bird' as easily as I can gift it." Gil grunted.

Derrick straightened and reached for the receipt. "Lighting, you say?"

CHAPTER 11

At the same time Gil was in Derrick Driscoll's office, Noelle and the two sets of engaged twins walked into the Twilight Bakery right around the corner from the accountant.

Cody and Sienna, and Dylan and Sierra strolled arm-in-arm in front of Noelle, and she felt a bit like a fifth wheel.

Delicious smells wafted up to greet them as she followed the brides- and grooms-to-be inside for the cake tasting. She'd made the appointment for noon so that Dylan and Cody could meet them on their lunch hour. The semiprofessional musicians both worked day jobs for Twilight's Parks and Recreation and played in their own band on nights and weekends.

"Hello!" A cheerful woman who looked to be in her mid to late forties greeted them. She wore her hair swept back off her neck and she was dressed in a sage green prairie skirt and white high-necked, long-sleeved blouse covered by a Thanksgiving-themed apron.

"You're Noelle." The woman shook her hand. "I don't know whether you remember me or not, but I'm Christine, the owner. Welcome back to Twilight."

"I remember you and your delicious baked goods." Noelle recognized Christine from when her grandparents occasionally brought her to the bakery for Sunday breakfast before church. It was nice to see that some things never changed. "It's wonderful to see you again."

"I already know these four." Christine beamed at the twins. "Come on back—I've got the cakes waiting for y'all."

Inside the tasting room, Christine had assembled five different cakes on the long oak wood table. They took their seats.

"Keep in mind, the decorations on the tasting cakes are simple. This is just for tasting purposes. You can embellish your cake as much or as little as you want for your reception. I have a portfolio of wedding cake photographs you can leaf through to select your design." Christine picked up a thick notebook filled with plastic sleeves of photographed wedding cakes she'd done in the past and passed it to Noelle, who sat to her right.

Noelle cracked open the book and blinked at the gorgeously decorated cakes. "You're so talented, Christine."

"Oh." Sierra linked her arm through Dylan's and leaned over to stare at the picture of a cake overflowing with buttercream roses. "That's far too elaborate. We like things simple."

"Excuse me?" Sienna said. "We don't want

meh. This wedding will be all over social media. We need to bring it and Christine can deliver the goods. I say we go all out. The bigger the better."

"Less is more," Sierra said.

"Sometimes," Sienna said, "less is just less."

Dylan and Cody exchanged *let-the-gals-sort-it-out* glances. "How about if we taste the cakes first and then decide on the style later?"

"Good idea." Dylan nodded.

Christine cut the first cake, and then put a wafer-thin slice on each of the five plates, and then passed the plates around the table. "Italian cream. It's my second-best seller."

"What's your first?" Sierra asked.

"Vanilla is always a crowd pleaser for weddings." Christine smiled.

"*Bor*-ing." Sienna rolled her eyes.

Noelle held her tongue. She would give the sisters a chance to work this conflict out on their own before offering compromises. No bride was happy if she felt she had to give up her vision to please others.

Noelle took a bite of cake. "Mmm." The moist Italian cream practically melted in her mouth. "Sooo good."

"I vote for this one." Cody polished off his piece of cake.

"You're jumping the gun," Sierra said to her soon-to-be brother-in-law. "We have four more cakes to taste."

"I'm ready." Dylan waved his fork.

Christine cut the vanilla cake next. It was just as good as the Italian cream. Sometimes, simplest was best, especially with something as traditional as a wedding.

"It's delish," Sienna said. "But I still say we should kick it up a notch."

"On to honey lavender." Christine doled out slices of the third cake.

Cody's nose wrinkled. "You put pot porry in a cake?"

"It's potpourri," Sienna whispered to her fiancé. "And lavender is a legit cake flavor."

Noelle tasted the honey-lavender cake. "It's so light and airy."

"Yes," Sierra said. "It's perfect for a spring or summer reception, not so much for a Christmas wedding."

"It's not as bad as I thought it was gonna be." Cody grunted. "But I like the vanilla one best so far."

"What's next?" Dylan asked.

Christine grinned. "My third most popular, red velvet."

Noelle's LA clientele would turn up their noses at what most would consider a plebeian choice, but Texas had deep Southern roots and in the South, red velvet was queen.

"Now we're talking," Dylan and Cody said simultaneously and rubbed their palms together as Christine served up the red velvet cake.

The red velvet was Noelle's personal favorite so far, but she wouldn't influence the couples by saying so. Besides, they had one more cake to taste.

"This one." Cody put up a hand to cover his mouth as he finished chewing the bite of red velvet.

"Yes." Dylan nodded.

Both Sierra and Sienna shook their heads.

"It feels like a birthday cake." Sienna's jingle bell earrings jangled. "Mom always makes red velvet for birthdays."

"I agree," Sierra said. "It's birthday cake."

Well, at least the sisters were finally on the same page, but now they were in opposition to their grooms.

"What's our final choice?" Noelle asked Christine.

"It's brand-new. I just perfected the recipe." Christine's eyes twinkled. "You would be the first ones to have this as your wedding cake from the Twilight Bakery."

Noelle noticed Sierra's and Sienna's faces lit up. The sisters liked the idea of being special.

"Salted caramel." Christine put the slices onto the five plates.

Everyone dug in.

"Holy moly!" Cody groaned.

"This is orgasmic." Sienna closed her eyes.

"I toasted the vanilla beans in browned butter." Christine blushed. "That adds a lot of extra flavor."

The cake was drool-worthy with salted caramel mousse in the center layers and a baked crumble on top, just like a pie. In Noelle's opinion, it was easily the best they'd tasted, and all of the cakes had been phenomenal. Plus, it would be perfect for a winter wedding, and it would merge beautifully with the gold in the color palette.

"I don't like it," Dylan said.

Everyone stared at him.

"Huh?" Sierra blinked. "Why not?"

"It tastes like butterscotch." Dylan's upper lip crinkled. "You know I hate butterscotch."

"It's not butterscotch," Christine said. "It's made with granulated sugar, not brown sugar the way butterscotch is."

Dylan pushed his plate away and folded his arms over his chest. "I'm not eating butterscotch cake. I vote for the red velvet."

Sierra, his bride-to-be, bit down on her bottom lip. "But all the rest of us love the salted caramel."

"So y'all get what you want and I'm out in the cold?" Dylan looked hurt. "That doesn't seem fair."

He made a good point, but the salted caramel cake fit the wedding in every other way.

"What are we going to do?" Sierra asked Noelle.

Noelle met Christine's gaze. "Could you do a half-and-half? One side salted caramel and the other red velvet?"

"I could do it," Christine said. "But the flavors would clash. I don't recommend it."

"We could have a groom's cake," Noelle said. "I'd have to redo the budget and take money from another area. Maybe trim our floral expenses, but it's the perfect solution."

"Yeah," Dylan said. "Do that. Two cakes are always better than one."

"Oh man." Sienna sighed. "The flowers are so important. I'd hate to cut into the floral budget."

Noelle put on a bright smile. "How about we tackle one challenge at a time. We've sailed over the cake hurdle. Let me worry about reshuffling the budget."

"As long as we get what we want," Sierra said, "I'll be happy."

Getting four people on the same page was no walk in the park, but Noelle would find a way. The couples departed, chattering about the yummy cakes, leaving Noelle to finish up the ordering details with Christine.

"I thought for sure they'd end up with vanilla cake as the compromise," Christine said. "I'm thrilled to get a chance to make the salted caramel. It'll be epic."

"Of that, I have no doubt. After it's prominently featured on The Tie's website, you'll get loads of national orders. I hope you're prepared."

"I'm looking forward to that opportunity. I appreciate you buying locally instead of ordering from a Fort Worth bakery."

"Of course. I'm so glad we got this ironed out."

As Noelle signed the contract, Christine thanked her for her business and added in a lowered tone, "I know you're the Wedding Whisperer, but good luck with those four. You're gonna need it. The Buckhorns are notoriously difficult to please."

"Oh," Noelle said, smiling. "Thanks for the heads-up, but I'm quite used to discerning customers."

While she appreciated Christine's support, Noelle really didn't need that gem of an earworm wriggling through her head.

The Buckhorns are notoriously difficult to please.

The sisters and their mother did have strong opinions, but she hadn't yet seen them being any more difficult than the average family planning a wedding. As much as she liked Christine, she decided not to let the older woman's view of the Buckhorns color her own. Being good at her job meant putting her wants, needs, and opinions in the back seat in service to her customers.

She counted her steps from the park to the Merry Cherub, her gaze fixed on the sidewalk. Five hundred and sixteen, five hundred and seventeen . . . Head down, she rounded the corner of the B&B and *bam!*

Ran smack-dab into Gil's chest.

"Whoa there." His arm went around her waist to steady her. "Woolgathering?"

Suddenly breathless, Noelle stepped back, eager to get away from his breath-stealing body.

"S-sorry. My mind was on wedding planning."

"You've been going full throttle since you got into town. Last night when I took the B&B's garbage to the curb at eleven before I hit the sheets, I saw you through the window still poring over your work."

Hit the sheets.

That terminology called up an erotic image of Gil lounging in bed wearing nothing but a cowboy hat.

She shook her head. "I'll have to remember to keep my blinds closed."

"That won't solve the problem."

"What problem is that?"

"Your workaholism." His grin beguiled her.

"I'm not your problem to solve." She pressed her lips together to keep from returning his grin and encouraging him.

"Aah, that's too bad. Are you still coming to the Turkey Trot tomorrow morning?"

"I shouldn't. I really do have a lot of work to do."

"All work and no play . . ." His dimples deepened. "But really, no pressure. I just thought you might get a kick out of seeing me in the turkey suit."

"I got an eyeful the day you were stranded in the tree."

"But you didn't see me in full strut."

She couldn't help smiling. What would it hurt? She had done well with the wedding cakes today. She'd earned a little free time and he was right, she needed to pace herself. A short break from work wouldn't kill her.

"Okay, you win. I'll give the fun run a shot but only because it's for a worthy cause."

"You won't regret it," he said. "I promise."

Workaholic that she was, Gil half expected her not to show up, but Noelle arrived at the starting line a few minutes before the eight A.M. kickoff on Wednesday morning, November 22. She'd been in town for exactly five days and already, he found himself looking forward to seeing her again.

Her hair was pulled up into a high ponytail that bounced jauntily when she walked. She looked good enough to eat in those yoga pants and that form-fitting purple Lycra jacket that enhanced her porcelain complexion.

Gobble, gobble, gobble.

"You ready?" he asked, unable to corral his grin.

"I came to perform. It'll be good to push my body."

"Working even as you play." He clicked his tongue.

She held up the packet she'd picked up from the registration table. "Could you help me put on my runner's number?"

"Absolutely," he said. "Turn around."

In a graceful twirl, she handed him her packet and pivoted on her heels, giving him her back.

He took the Tyvek number and the safety pins from the packet, and then set the packet on the ground beside his ice chest filled with water bottles for the contestants, and leaned in closer.

Gil tried not to notice how good she smelled as he affixed the number to her clothing. Touching her gave him shivers. This felt too intimate, but he wasn't complaining.

"All done."

She turned around. "Thanks."

"You're welcome." Did he sound breathless? Had she noticed?

"Where's your head?" she asked.

"Huh?"

"Your turkey head."

"Oh," he said, embarrassed. His thoughts had gone to naughty places. He pointed to the nearby picnic table. "Over there. It's hot inside that dang thing and I'm waiting for the race to start before I put it on."

All around them, runners were securing their numbers to their clothing, stretching, and lining up under the starting banner.

"Looks like the time has come," she said, giving him the once-over. Her gaze held amusement. For sure she was having fun, but beneath that look, there was something else. What? Attraction?

In this turkey getup? *Ha! Dream on, Thomas, dream on.* Yeah, he'd been dreaming about her both in and out of bed. A lot. Almost constantly, if he was being honest. Ever since she'd rolled into his life again.

She bounced over to the picnic table in her springy high-end sneakers, picked up the turkey head, and brought it back to him.

"Don't make fun." He took the papier-mâché head from her.

"Oh, I'm not promising that." Her laughter filled the air and gave wings to his hopes.

"Fine." He put on the turkey head and stuck out his arms as wide as they would go. "How do you like me now?"

She pressed her lips together, her eyes dancing with suppressed laughter. "This is definitely a turn-on."

"Yeah?"

"Oh, yeah." Her mouth quirked up in that one-sided grin she used when she was truly happy. "*So* hot."

Gil's heart just about swelled to bursting, which was stupid considering he was dressed like tomorrow's dinner entrée.

"Hey, Turkey Tom," one of the event organizers hollered. "Get over here and start the race. You've got work to do."

Chuckling, Noelle took her place at the end of the line. Back home, she worked out six days a week with either HIIT training, Pilates, or yoga. It had been a while since she'd gone for a run, and she could very well embarrass herself on this three-mile circle around Lake Twilight.

Turkey Tom stood off to one side of the starting line with a bullhorn. "Ready!"

"Ready!" the runners cheered back.

"Set!"

The runners leaned forward, preparing to surge.

"Go!"

Boom.

The starting gun went off, and the runners moved en masse. Even when she had been a regular runner, Noelle had never been particularly fast, so she let the eager beavers stream ahead of her.

She waved at Gil as she jogged past. She wasn't lying when she'd told him the turkey costume was a turn-on. Not because the suit was sexy, but because the man willing to make a fool of himself over a charity event was.

Noelle glanced over her shoulder, mesmerized by him. He'd been pretty va-va-voom as a teenager, but this guy? This guy was in a whole other class. Gil had matured and life had carved the softness from him. He was fully grown, seasoned, and hot as hell.

After the final runner crossed the starting line, Gil fell in behind the group, trotting along with them and hollering encouragement.

She thought about how he'd looked when they'd been talking. How he'd lowered his eyes framed by long, thick lashes and he had given her a sultry look that scorched her girly parts. A day's growth of beard stubble had covered his steely jaw, making him look a little dangerous.

Her pulse quickened and she realized her pacing was off. If she kept running at this tempo, she wouldn't be able to finish the race. She slowed, letting runners she'd passed early go on by her.

From behind, she heard exaggerated pounding and hazarded another look over her shoulder. Here came Gil, flapping his arms, gobbling, and galumphing along.

She burst out laughing.

"Hey, lady," he said to her, his voice muffled inside the costume. "*You* try flying when your butt is this big."

That hit her funny bone just right, and she dissolved into peals of laughter. Staggering and holding her side, she tried to keep running, but it was almost impossible.

"C'mon, c'mon." He jogged beside her. "Knees up like this."

She tried to copy him, but she couldn't stop laughing. "You look . . . you look . . ."

"Handsome?"

"That's not the word that leaps to mind."

"Sexy?"

"Not really."

"It's the big butt, isn't it?"

"Stop making me laugh."

"I could go on a diet . . ."

"No! I like big turkey butts and I cannot lie."

Gil started humming "Baby Got Back" and it sounded tinny coming from inside the turkey head.

Noelle was laughing so hard her side hurt. "Oh,

please," she howled and gripped her flank harder. "Please stop."

He was dancing now. Showing off his mad skills.

Other runners were slowing, peering over their shoulders to see what was going on behind them.

"Y . . . you . . ." Noelle wheezed, caught in the spasm of hysterical laughter. "You're . . ."

"Save your breath. You got a race to run." He was trotting backward now, facing her.

"When did you get to be so much fun?" she asked, gasping for air.

"I was always fun. You just forgot."

"No . . . no . . . you . . ." She could finally haul in a deeper breath and that seemed to quell the giggling fit.

"Yes?" He fell in beside her again.

They were at the very end of the race, all the other runners far ahead of them. Noelle didn't care one bit. She might be competitive in business, but not when having an enjoyable time, and boy, was she enjoying herself.

"You're not as self-conscious as you were," she said. "There's a joy about you now that you didn't have back then. You don't take yourself too seriously."

"Not anymore."

"How did you change?"

"That's an easy question to answer. Josie. Having a kid lets you see the world fresh through their young eyes."

They were jogging so slowly they were almost walking, but this conversation felt weighted, important, and deserving of a more deliberate pace.

"You love Josie very much."

"More than life itself. Until I had her, I didn't really know what unconditional love was. She comes first," he said, his tone heartfelt and earnest. "*Always*."

Of course she did. Noelle wouldn't expect anything less and she admired him all the more for his commitment to fatherhood. Not everyone was that dedicated to their children.

"I must go do my turkey duties, and cheer on the contestants. See you at the finish line."

Waving goodbye, Gil took off at a dead sprint, hurrying to catch up with the pack leaders. He looked so comical, tail feathers flapping as he ran, that Noelle started laughing all over again.

Picking up the pace again toward the end, Noelle avoided last place, barely beating out an octogenarian runner. But she didn't care. It was all in wholesome fun. She'd had no illusions about finishing with a respectable time. It took her forty-seven minutes to complete three miles. The winner did it in twenty-two minutes. But she'd finished the course, and that was enough for Noelle.

Gil was at the finish line, cheering her and the great-grandmother on with the bullhorn as they came down the home stretch. Jogging side by side, the elderly woman regaled Noelle with stories of her family. Props to Gramma, she was crushing eighty-two.

"I want to be you when I grow up," Noelle told the woman. "Sorry to smoke you." Then she poured on the heat, crossing the finish line just ahead of the great-grandmother.

"Next year . . ." The woman panted. "I want a rematch. Same time, same place, I'm taking you down, whippersnapper."

Noelle wouldn't be here next year, but she played along. "It's a date."

The woman gave her a thumbs-up and trotted over to her waiting family of twenty-plus people. They encircled her in a huge group hug and spirited her off to their vehicles. Melancholia, that wistful emotion, wrapped around Noelle's heart. She'd never had that many people turn out for her. What a rich life that woman must lead.

"Hey."

She turned to see Gil, sans the turkey head, smiling softly at her. "Hi there."

"Nice run."

"I finished," Noelle said. "Yay, me."

"I was just thinking . . ." His gaze met hers.

"Yes?" She leaned in and caught her breath.

"This afternoon, I'm taking Josie to a Christmas ornament crafting event for kids at Ye Olde Book Nook. Would you like to come along? It's okay if you don't. I know our small-town traditions must seem silly—"

"Yes, yes. I'd love to come. Thank you for the invitation."

Gil looked ridiculously pleased, and that made Noelle feel special. "I'm glad you're coming along. Josie likes you."

"She's a delightful kid."

"Well," Gil chuckled. "She has her moments."

"As do we all."

His smile wrapped a wreath of happiness around

her, warm as a woolen sweater. "Do you want to walk over with us or meet us at the bookstore at one o'clock?"

"I'd love to walk with you."

Excitement brightened Gil's eyes. "I'll head home, change clothes, pick up Josie from the babysitter, and meet you at the bottom of your stairs at twelve forty-five. How's that sound?"

"Perfect, see you then." Noelle practically floated back to the B&B, so glad she'd taken a break, and she didn't count once, not even on the stairs.

CHAPTER 12

Telling herself that taking time for herself would make her a better wedding planner by coming back to her work refreshed, Noelle was excited about the crafting event. As a kid art had been her second-favorite hobby after reading and she missed it.

Besides, it was a holiday of sorts. Thanksgiving Eve.

By the time they got to Ye Olde Book Nook, everything was set up for the energetic six- and seven-year-olds spilling through the doors.

From a flyer in the window, Noelle read that the crafting event was going on all day with different time slots for different age groups. That was nice. The younger kids wouldn't have to compete with older ones.

Several parents Gil knew came over and he introduced Noelle to them. While organizers checked in the children and showed them where to sit, Gil's friends chatted about the wedding and how lucky it was that the Buckhorn sisters had won The Tie's essay contest.

The bookstore had erected the Christmas ornament–building station at the back of the building. Supplies were arranged in color-coded trays, pipe cleaners in the red bins, plastic straws in the blue, cotton swabs in yellow, colored beads in silver, wine corks in gray, white paper plates in green, thin candy-colored ribbon in purple. It was a rainbow of colors and a plethora of textures beckoning kids to jump in and have fun. Lined up at each station were glue sticks, glitter, children's scissors, tape, and rubber bands.

"Wanna bet how long the supplies stay tidy in those neat little bins?" Noelle asked Gil.

"Five minutes tops." Gil laughed.

Leading the event was an elementary school teacher named Flynn Calloway, a pretty woman in her early forties with naturally curly hair that spilled down her shoulders. Noelle remembered Flynn from the times she'd visited her grandparents in Twilight. Flynn used to run her family's popular restaurant, Froggy's, before they'd sold it.

"Noelle!" Flynn exclaimed, coming around the table to greet her. "I heard you were in town planning the Buckhorn/Maxwell wedding for The Tie. How fun!"

"Dad." Josie tugged on her father's sleeve. "Can I sit by Ian?"

"Why don't you ask Ian?"

A curly-haired boy, who looked a lot like Flynn, was seated at the table. He ducked his head shyly and used his foot to push out the chair next to him so Josie could sit down.

Grinning, Josie plunked into the chair. "Hi, Ian."

Ian's face blushed pink and he mumbled, "Hey."

"Ian's my middle child," Flynn said to Noelle. "His older sister, Grace, will be here for the next time slot with the eight- and nine-year-olds."

"Goodness! You've been busy since the last time I was in Twilight." Noelle smiled.

"Oh, we've got a third." Flynn laughed. "Amos is still too young for arts and crafts. He's with my husband, Jesse."

"That must be so fun."

"Hectic as all get-out, but I wouldn't have it any other way." Flynn wriggled her fingers. "We better get this party started before the wee ones begin bouncing around the room."

At that, the families gathered around. Most children had at least one person with them, either a mom or dad, a grandparent, or stepparent. One had an aunt and uncle. Another lucky kid had not only his parents, but both sets of grandparents with him.

But there was one little girl who sat all alone at the end of the table, keeping her distance from the rest of the children. A quiet child with serious eyes. Empathy wrenched Noelle's heart.

She went over to the girl and crouched down so that she was eye level. "Hi, my name's Noelle. What's yours?"

"Ebby."

"Hello, Ebby. Is your mom or dad in the store?"

Solemnly, Ebby shook her head.

"You're on your own?"

"My dad dropped me off. He's gotta deliver a horse to a customer, but he'll be back later."

"Do you know Ian and Josie?" Noelle nodded toward the two other children.

"No. I go to school in Jubilee."

Noelle felt the little girl's loneliness like a visceral punch and her mind jetted back twenty years to a film set in Boulder, Colorado.

Back then, Crescenda would occasionally take her on location so they could spend "quality mother-daughter time" together and would then promptly forget about her, leaving Noelle to watch TV for endless hours alone in their trailer. This one time, bored after three weeks of cloistering, Noelle had left the trailer and wandered off the set, ending up in some alleyway, petting the flea-bitten dog of a homeless man. Crescenda lost her mind when she learned—several hours after the fact—that Noelle had gone missing. She ordered flea baths and called the cops, threw around accusations. It had been a whole thing.

Even now, Noelle cringed at the memory.

After that, whenever Crescenda filmed on location, she sent Noelle to stay with her grandparents, which had turned out a much better solution for everyone involved.

Noelle put a hand to her stomach. She had to be careful not to project her childhood experiences onto Ebby. But goodness, she sure knew what it felt like—alone in a place where you didn't know anyone and had to fend for yourself with strangers.

"Would you like to come sit by Josie and Ian?" Noelle invited.

Ebby's eyes widened, and a fragile smile lit her little face. "Really?"

"Yes, absolutely. Let's move your chair down."

Face aglow, Ebby hopped up and pushed her chair across the aged hardwood floor and Noelle followed her.

"This is Ebby. I told her she could join us," Noelle said to Gil, Josie, and Ian. "I hope that's okay."

"Sure, sure," Gil said. "C'mon, Ebby, get closer. We've got ornaments to make!"

Ebby beamed as if they'd just given her the best Christmas present ever and Noelle felt as if she'd done a good thing.

Noelle amazed him.

Gil studied her. She crouched between Ebby and Josie's chairs, her face animated, as she helped the children pick out one of the four ornament options available. He hadn't noticed Ebby was alone.

But Noelle had.

He liked that about her. Her keen sense of observation brought things onto her radar that wouldn't even show up for most people. He supposed that trait was one of the things that made her such a good wedding planner.

His mind drifted off into a fantasy about what could happen between them, each scenario featuring Twilight as a backdrop.

Maybe . . .

But why would she want him? He was just an ordinary, small-town guy and she was the daughter of Hollywood celebrities with a successful wedding planning business in LA. Besides, she'd made it perfectly clear she didn't believe in love or the traditional values he held dear. The song he'd starting writing about her tingled through his brain.

Spent her time reading books, writing down her thoughts
Never guessed she'd become something greater than she sought

"Daddy," Josie said. "I'm gonna make a paper plate angel tree topper."

"Huh?" He blinked, upset with himself that he'd been ignoring his kid.

"I'm making an angel."

"That's great, honey. We'll put it on our Christmas tree." He knelt on the floor to his daughter's left. Noelle was still crouching to Josie's right. "What's on your craft list?"

Josie held up a laminated card that Flynn had given her.

"How about you, Ian?" Gil asked the boy. "Have you picked out what you're going to make?"

"Jingle bell ornaments," Ian said.

"Of course you are." Flynn leaned over her side of the table to ruffle her son's hair. "Anything musical and this one gravitates straight for it. He got it from my dad's mother, who danced and sang in burlesque when she was in her twenties. She could also strum a wicked banjo riff and play a mean harmonica."

"You don't say."

Flynn had told him the story of her Vegas show-girl grandmother many more times than once. She seemed to admire her ancestor's bawdiness. Maybe because Flynn had always been such a responsible rule-follower herself.

"And you, Ebby?" Noelle asked the girl.

"Snowflakes!" Ebby said.

Flynn gave Noelle the supplies list for the cotton swab snowflakes. Then she looked from Gil to Noelle and back again. "Since y'all are already invested in three of the designs, one or both of you should go for the Popsicle-and–pipe cleaner reindeers."

"Ooh." Noelle sent Gil a sexy look and rubbed her palms together. "Wanna get a side competition going just between you and me, cowboy?"

Whoa, Noelle was flirting with him! Gil's pulse kicked up, spurred faster by her quirky half grin.

"Let's see which one of us can make the best Popsicle stick, pipe cleaner reindeer." Noelle threw down the gauntlet.

"Go for it!" Josie laughed. "Beat her, Daddy. You can do it."

"I thought we were friends," Noelle said to Josie, pretending her feelings were hurt.

"We are, we are." Josie looked alarmed. "I didn't mean nothing by it."

"I was just teasing," Noelle said. "You gotta be loyal to your dad."

Josie blew out her breath and patted Noelle's hand. "We *are* friends."

"You're my friend too." Ebby searched Noelle's face with anxious eyes. "Right?"

"Yes, I'm your friend and Josie's friend and Ian's friend." Noelle smiled at each child.

"And Daddy's too?" Josie asked.

Noelle met Gil's gaze over the top of his daughter's head.

"And Daddy's too," Noelle echoed, then lightly touched the tip of her tongue to her upper lip and winked at him.

Gil would be the first to admit that his mind leaped to things it had no business jumping to. Like how much fun it would be to tug Noelle's hair from that ponytail and let the silky cascade fall against his bare hands.

Uncool, Thomas, uncool.

Everyone gathered their supplies and went back to their seats to begin their projects. Noelle and Gil returned to their places. They took turns helping each child with their project while also working on their own reindeer ornaments.

"Daddy," Josie said. "Noelle's using a neon green marker to decorate. Reindeer aren't neon green."

"She's avant-garde." Gil wriggled his eyebrows at Noelle. "You can't put her in a box. She'll just bust out of it."

"Daddy's reindeer is brown," Josie said to Noelle. "Like reindeer are *supposed* to be."

"Traditionalism *is* a crowd pleaser." Noelle busily colored the Popsicle stick with the neon green marker. "But there's more than one way to skin a cat."

In that moment, Noelle sounded so much like her Southern grandmother and nothing at all like the polished LA woman in front of him, that Gil did a double take.

"Huh?" Josie wrinkled her nose.

"Just wait." Gil nodded. "It'll turn out good. Trust Noelle on this. She has an artistic eye and attention to detail."

Josie looked skeptical.

"I just now remembered Noelle won the summer art contest at the library," Gil said. "That was the year I worked mowing lawns for the town's public buildings, and they posted her art on the bulletin board."

"I can't believe you remembered that. I'd forgotten all about it myself."

"As I recall, it was a painting of a bride in her wedding dress."

"You do remember." Her gaze latched on to his.

"You were thinking about weddings, even back then."

"I did the painting after Crescenda married Felix, her third husband." As she studied Gil, her eyes took on a sweet light. What was that look? Affection?

A delicious chill went straight through his bones, and it was all he could do to suppress his shudder of desire. Unless he was imagining the whole thing because he *wanted* her to want him. His mind went to that moment in his kitchen when he'd almost kissed her.

Right now, he wished he *had* done it and gotten it out of his system. Because he hadn't been able to think of much else since. The anticipation of what her delicious mouth might taste like had kept him awake at night.

Dominated him.

He ached to kiss her.

A lot.

A whole lot.

Her gaze left his eyes and drifted down to fix on his lips. Oh, hell's bells, he wasn't the only one thinking about kisses.

"Daddy, you're not paying attention."

"What? Oh, sorry." He blinked at his daughter. "What is it?"

"What should I make my angel's hair out of?"

"How about glitter?"

"Oh, yeah! Cool idea. Thanks." Josie took the glitter he offered.

Noelle laughed. "You will be cleaning up glitter for months after Christmas."

"Glitter expert, are you?" He lowered his voice, and his eyes went right back to her full pink lips.

"For Mom's fourth wedding, she had people throw glitter as they left the chapel. She'd already done birdseed, confetti, and bubbles and she was running out of ideas. Never again." Noelle shook her head.

"I defer to your wisdom." He snapped his fingers at his daughter. "Forget the glitter, sweet pea. Why don't you glue down yellow beads for her hair?"

Josie narrowed her eyes. "Nope. I'm using glitter."

Gil looked at Noelle. "Help."

"She's your kid." Noelle grinned and shrugged. "She takes after her dad. Stubborn."

Nailed him.

"I gotta pick my battles," he said. "Guess I'll be cleaning up glitter until next Christmas. In for a penny, in for a pound." He motioned at Josie. "Hand me that glitter, kiddo. My reindeer needs some sparkle."

Once everyone had finished their ornaments, glitter, bits of tissue paper, pipe cleaners, cotton swabs, and straws were strewn everywhere. Gloriously messy, just as any worthy craft project should be.

"And now," Flynn announced, "it's time to judge our entries. The prize winners get kismet cookies!"

"Yay!" The kids cheered, clapped, and wriggled.

"Put your ornaments on the table in front of you for the judging."

Everyone complied. Flynn started at the far end of the long table where Gil and the others sat. She had her hands clasped behind her back and slowly examined each project as she walked past.

"Well," Flynn said. "All the projects are so exceptionally good I simply can't pick one winner. That means everyone gets a kismet cookie!"

A chorus of cheers filled the room.

"What about Daddy and Noelle's ornaments?" Josie said. "Who wins best reindeer?"

"They're grown-ups," Ebby said. "They don't getta win."

"Ebby makes a good point," Flynn said. "We'll let Gil and Noelle sort that out themselves, but what say we give them kismet cookies too?"

"Yeah!" Ian said.

"In fact," Flynn said, "cookies for everyone!"

Flynn passed out the homemade cookies, individually sealed in wax paper pouches, while the parents and children gathered up their ornaments and started filtering out of the bookstore.

"Need some help with cleanup?" Noelle asked Flynn.

"Oh gosh, yes, please, thank you," Flynn said.

Gil went for the broom and dustpan in the corner while Noelle got the children involved in putting the supplies back into the proper bins.

Josie paused, studying the reindeer ornaments that he and Noelle had made. "You're right, Daddy. A neon green reindeer shouldn't work, but it looks exactly like Christmas. Bright and happy. Sorry, but Noelle's reindeer wins."

"Thanks, Josie. I appreciate the compliment," Noelle said.

"I like this one better." Ebby pointed at Gil's reindeer. "It's the way things are *supposed* to be. Nice and normal. No weird stuff."

Over the heads of the kids, Gil met Noelle's eyes. The reindeer ornaments and children's critiques encapsulated the difference in his and Noelle's styles. He was rooted, routine, and conventional. Noelle was flexible, vibrant, and one-of-a-kind.

Nothing in common.

Total opposites.

Yeah, but weren't opposites supposed to attract?

After the craft event at the bookstore, Noelle offered to help Gretchen and Delphine with the baking for the next day's Thanksgiving celebration. It would have been rude, after all, to just retreat when there was so much prep work to do.

There in the bustling kitchen, with Christmas music playing from the radio that sat on the windowsill, she'd spent the late afternoon peeling apples from the backyard tree. But although she was having a blast with the two women, the moment triggered a recall of the very first time she'd baked an apple pie with her Grammie.

The memory crept, soft as a kitten padding on quiet feet, across her mind and she was suddenly filled with so much love and laughter as Grammie showed her how to peel the apples all in one piece and then throw the peel over her shoulder to reveal the initial of her one true love.

Noelle's peel had curled into a distinct G, which had sent her heart fluttering. She'd forgotten all about that precious memory with her grandmother. Impressionable teen that she'd been, Noelle had taken it as a sign that Gil was her one true love.

So silly.

Boy, had she been gullible. Hoping against hope there was such a thing as true love but knowing from watching her parents flail in their numerous relationships, it probably was a big fat lie. How could an apple peel foretell your future?

It couldn't and that was the thing. The magical

nonsense of Twilight's myths and legends was starting to wear her down. If she didn't stay strong in her resolve, she was going to get swept away.

And the very last thing she needed was to fall in love with a small-town dad with amazing dimples and soulful blue eyes.

CHAPTER 13

Thanksgiving Day at the Merry Cherub was, hands down, the best Noelle ever had, and that included the year Crescenda hired a private plane to fly them to a Plymouth Rock celebration with two dozen of her celebrity friends.

Gretchen was hosting an open house in Noelle's honor. Townsfolk could come and go as they pleased, and Noelle was stunned at how many people showed up to meet her. The Buckhorns and Maxwell twins came, along with Benji and her husband, Spencer. Noelle told herself it was just because people wanted to rub shoulders with someone who was celebrity adjacent, but she was surprised at how many people wanted to talk to her about her wedding planning business and her appearance on *The Klatch*. Only a few asked about Crescenda or her father.

It was nice, for a change, to be welcomed for herself, and not for who her mother was.

They had met Ebby's father, Tyler, when he picked up his daughter from the bookstore and Gil had invited them to the Thanksgiving meet-and-greet as well. Josie was thrilled to have someone her age to play with, and the girls took off together.

Gretchen invited Tyler into the kitchen for eggnog and conversation. They learned Tyler lived between Twilight and Jubilee and he'd just gotten divorced. Since school was out for the week, and he hadn't had a babysitter the day before, Tyler had dropped Ebby off at the craft event. He thanked Gil and Noelle profusely for looking after his daughter and showing her so much hospitality. Noelle liked the lanky man who smelled of horses and leather. He seemed really nice.

Since Gretchen and Gil's parents were coming to Twilight for Christmas, they wouldn't be attending the Thanksgiving celebration, but they made up for their absence by Facetiming the family from their lanai in Costa Rica.

After the lavish Thanksgiving dinner that lasted for two hours, some gathered in the kitchen pitching in with cleanup, while others went to the backyard to play games, where it was a lovely fifty-eight degrees and filled with sunshine and a soft breeze, but a norther was predicted for later that evening. So they enjoyed the pleasant weather while they had it.

Noelle fluctuated between the kitchen conversations and the outdoor sports. At one point, Gil coaxed her into joining a game of flag football. She knew little about the sport, but she didn't let that stop her. She took in the quick tutorial Gil gave the participants and assumed her position in the formation.

There were eight people on each team. Included

among the players were Sierra and Sienna, Dylan and Cody, and Benji and Spencer. Dylan and Sierra were on the same team as Noelle and Gil.

Watching Gil bend over to hike the ball was a thing of beauty. Holy Christmas! He'd had a great butt in high school, but now, in his tight-fitting jeans, his thirty-year-old tuchus was absolutely mesmerizing with that flashy red bandana sticking half out of his back pocket.

Noelle was so busy staring at him that she wasn't prepared when everyone began moving. Some going left, others right, a couple of participants plowed straight up the field of play.

Oops, oops! Who had the ball?

Noelle wrung her hands, unsure of what to do, but the basic rule was to drive the ball through the opponents to score a goal.

In a flash, Gil zigzagged in front of her, the ball tucked against his body, and suddenly he was pressing it into her hands. "Head down, dart left, don't let go of the ball."

Happy to follow instructions, Noelle did exactly as he asked, hugging the football against her side as if glued there, and she took off running to the left.

Gil charged right, pretending he still had the ball in his possession. The feint worked. The opposing team went after Gil.

Realizing she was temporarily in the clear, Noelle poured on the heat, sprinting as fast as she could, the goal line in sight. Quickly, the other players recognized she had the ball and came thundering after her.

Eek!

She felt her hair tie loosen and a hank of hair fell from her ponytail to swish into her eyes. But she'd be darned if she was going to let a broken hair tie prevent her from making the goal. The team was counting on her.

Plus, she wanted to earn Gil's respect.

Her teammates rushed to protect her, doing their best to block the opponents and clear a path for Noelle down the field.

Her legs churned, kicking up fresh leaves that had fallen since Gil had raked the yard when they'd returned from the craft event yesterday. She'd watched him from the kitchen window of the B&B as she'd peeled apples while Gretchen and Delphine rolled out pie crust dough.

The goal line wasn't far away. Just a few yards left. But she was out of breath and couldn't see with her hair in her eyes. Her legs felt like she was running through syrup.

"Go, Noelle, go!" Gretchen cheered from the sidelines, and that gave her the encouragement she needed to push forward.

Almost there, almost there, she chanted to herself.

Cody Maxwell jumped in front of her, while his bride-to-be, Sienna, grabbed for the flag sticking out of Noelle's back pocket.

The couple was ganging up on her.

Noelle swung her butt away from Sienna's reach, as Sierra came to Noelle's defense and ran interference, slipping adroitly between Noelle and her twin.

"Go, Noelle!" Sierra said. "You can do it!"

Noelle kept running, even though her lungs were crying out for air. She might stand on her feet all day as she helped a waffling bride shop for wedding dresses, but sprinting was a whole other skill.

Someone came up behind her, running faster than she was, angling for the flag in her pocket.

Gracious, but the other team was relentless!

She could hear the person breathing down her neck, panting just as heavily as she was. Noelle didn't look to see who it was. The goal line lay just ahead of her.

Almost there, almost there.

Noelle flew across the ground, her hair streaming out behind her. She was going to make it, oh yes, she was!

Behind her, the pounding feet grew louder.

"Go, Noelle, go!" More people hollered from the sidelines.

So focused was she on the end zone that Noelle never looked down and she didn't see the coiled-up garden hose partially hidden by the leaves until it was too late.

The toe of her sneaker caught the edge of the hose. She was moving so fast that there was no chance for recovery.

She was going down!

Instinct had her putting out her hands to catch herself and the ball popped from where she'd stowed it between her elbow and her ribcage. She did a face-plant as the ball bounced away.

Rats. So close.

Her tumble caused a chain reaction. The person running behind her was also traveling too fast to stop. The next thing she knew, someone was lying on top of her.

"Are you okay?"

That's when she realized the someone was Gil. It hadn't been an opposing teammate coming after her. It had been Gil running to block people from snatching her flag.

Aww.

His chest pressed flat against her spine, his belt buckle pressing into her lower back. It was cold against her bare skin where her sweater had ridden up during the spill.

"Noelle?"

She didn't answer because she couldn't catch her breath. Not with him squashing her lungs.

"Uh." She grunted and closed her eyes, concentrating on getting in air.

Gil scrambled off her and gently flipped her over. "Noelle, are you hurt? Please answer me if you can."

Slowly, she opened her eyes.

He was stretched out beside her on the ground, propped up on one elbow, leaning over, and looking concerned. Lightly, he patted her cheeks. "Noelle?"

Her gaze fixed on his lips.

The game had stopped, and everyone gathered, circling around her, but their faces blurred like an impressionist's painting in the rain, and she could only focus on one face, one pair of eyes, one sexy mouth.

Gil.

More than anything in the world, she wanted

him to kiss her. Ached for it. The heat in his eyes told her he felt the same way.

"Noelle?" His brow knitted.

His blue eyes peered at her from beneath half-lowered lids. His lashes were thick enough to use as paintbrushes. The bit of beard stubble ringing his jaw gave him a rakish look that both excited her and gave her pause. Her feelings were treading dangerously close to something she was afraid to feel. A smart woman wouldn't go there, not even in her mind.

His mouth stretched thin with concern. "Are you all right?"

"I was about to ask you the same thing."

"I'm not the one who face-planted into a pile of leaves." His chuckle was soft and reassuring.

People were staring, but for once in her life, Noelle didn't care what anyone else thought. Every ounce of her attention was fixed on this man who was so very close to her. His rich masculine scent filled her nose and her heart galloped. For one cuckoo moment, she could've sworn he was going to kiss her in front of everyone.

In fact, her body prepared for the impact of his mouth against hers, warming and softening and . . .

"Noelle," he murmured.

"Gil," she whispered back, full of feels.

They stared into each other's eyes for the longest time and then he moved away, and she felt her body go completely limp.

"You never answered my question. Are you hurt?"

Hurt, no? Stunned into silence? Oh, yeah.

"I—I'm . . ." She was about to say that she was all right, but was she? Her world had been knocked off-kilter.

She had feelings for Gil.

Deepening feelings.

Big-time.

And when he scrambled to his feet and held out his hand to help her up, a wide, warm smile on his handsome face, Noelle knew she was in serious trouble. Because if Gil had the slightest inclination of taking her to bed, by gosh, she would let him.

Because she desperately needed to focus on her job, and it seemed the only way to do that was through scratching this sexual itch for Gil that simply wouldn't leave her alone.

At dusk, everyone who'd been playing flag football and hanging around the house headed to the tree lighting ceremony. The big event that officially kicked off Twilight's Christmas holiday season.

Gil was thrilled Noelle wanted to come along.

Delphine and her husband, Luther, stayed behind to hold down the fort at the Merry Cherub so Gretchen could attend as well.

On the town square, the atmosphere was festive with carolers dressed in period costumes strolling the streets and wishing everyone a Merry Christmas in a melodious singsong. Delicious smells filled the air from kiosks roasting chestnuts, frying funnel cakes, and spinning cotton candy. Shopkeepers, who'd opened just for the evening event, passed out free warm apple cider and nonalcoholic eggnog.

Keyed up, Josie and Ebby held hands, and skipped

along in front of their group. Gil was happy that his daughter had made a new friend, and it was all thanks to Noelle's kindness. Ebby's father, Tyler, seemed grateful to be invited along as well. He and Gretchen were discussing cooking. Tyler was trying to learn how to cook instead of just picking up something to go or opening cans for Ebby's dinner and Gretchen seemed to love giving him pointers.

Gil cast a sidelong glance over at Noelle, who walked beside him, her face aglow as she took in the sights. Seeing her bundled up in a cute pink ski parka, her dark hair curling against her shoulders, Gil felt his pulse quicken. Falling on her during their flag football game had knocked all common sense from his head.

She turned to him, her perfectly shaped lips shiny with pink lip gloss. "I'd forgotten just how big Twilight does Christmas."

"We do go all out."

Noelle took a deep breath and closed her eyes, a beatific smile on her face. "I've missed this."

Gil stared down at her. Did her lips taste like honey? He imagined they did.

"Dad! Dad! Hurry before all the good spots are gone!" Josie broke through his reverie, rushing over to grab his arm and drag him toward the thirty-foot pine erected on the courthouse lawn.

"Oh, okay." Grinning, he held out his palm to Noelle. "Please take my hand. I don't know if I can handle this much joy without help."

Laughing, Noelle sank her hand in his as Josie pulled them like a plow horse, Ebby dancing alongside them.

When they reached the tree, people parted, smiling at the exuberant children. A makeshift stage and scaffolding had been erected for the ceremony.

"C'mon Josie, we've got a spot right here for you," said an older man in his seventies. Earl and his wife, Raylene Pringle, were patrons of the Windmill. They rarely missed a show and had VIP seats. Dressed as Santa, Earl waved them over. Raylene stood beside her husband, costumed as Mrs. Claus.

"We get to stand with Santa?" Ebby asked in awe.

"You do." Earl patted his belly and ho-ho-ho'd. "Step right up here, young'un."

Ebby and Josie crowded closer. Gil and Noelle hung back, letting the kids have the best vantage point. The crowd thickened as more people arrived.

"Do you remember that time you were trampled by the Christmas tree crowd and lost Baby Jesus from the manger?" Gil asked.

"I didn't until I came back to Twilight. You saved my life."

"I was so scared you'd gotten hurt."

"Just my tender feelings. You made me feel so much better about losing Jesus." She smiled at him.

"Glad I could help." He smiled back, feeling ten feet tall in the glow of her grin.

Mayor Moe Schebly climbed the stage and sauntered up to the microphone. "Welcome, welcome, Twilightites and visitors alike!"

His voice boomed out across the night that had grown chilly after sundown. People rubbed their palms together and breathed out frosty air. Gil wanted to put his arm around Noelle so badly he couldn't think straight, but that seemed too forward, especially in public for everyone to see.

"This year's tree lighting is extra special," Mayor Schebly went on. "For those of you who don't know, Sienna and Sierra Buckhorn and their fiancés, Cody and Dylan Maxwell, won first place in The Tie's essay contest. Their prize is to have their wedding planned right here in Twilight, by none other than Noelle Curry, the daughter of veteran actor Crescenda Hardwick and documentary filmmaker Clinton Curry. Noelle was part of our community for many summers when she visited her grandparents here when she was a kid. Please, help me give a warm welcome to Noelle! Please come up on stage!"

Thunderous applause echoed throughout the town square.

"Did you know he was going to invite me onstage?" Noelle whispered to Gil.

"I did not, or I would have given you a heads-up that he was going to do so."

"Maybe The Tie put him up to it," she said. "Pamela Landry, my point person in the company, has been pushing me to promote, promote, promote."

Moe waved Noelle and the two sets of twins up onto the stage.

Gil felt Noelle tense beside him. She didn't want to do this. "Do you want me to go up with you?"

"Yes, please." She looked so grateful it tugged at his heartstrings. No matter how self-confident she appeared, deep down inside she was still shy.

The bystanders parted, letting them through as Gil escorted her to the stage. He had his hand on her wrist and could feel the hot pounding of her pulse. She really was uncomfortable in the limelight.

He heard her counting softly under her breath as they went up the steps. *One, two, three, four . . .*

She might be nervous, but other than the counting, she didn't show it.

Appearing poised and assured, Noelle smiled at the crowd. With polished aplomb, she regaled the crowd with the details about the upcoming wedding and The Tie's involvement, then she quickly passed the mike to Sienna, who launched into a spiel about how and why they'd entered the contest. Sierra said a few words, as did Dylan and Cody. When Cody was finished, he gave the mike back to Noelle.

"Anyone have questions?" Noelle asked the audience.

"Will Crescenda Hardwick be here for the wedding?" someone asked.

"No," Noelle said. "My mother's filming a movie in London."

The crowd made a collective noise of disappointment.

"I'm going to turn this back over to Mayor Schebly," Noelle said. "I know you all are eager to decorate the tree. If you want to know more about the wedding, you can ask me or the twins whenever you see us around town."

"Thank you, Noelle." Mayor Schebly took over the mike. "Doesn't she have the perfect name for our town?" Then he reached for the comically oversized switch that would turn on the tree. "Y'all ready to light this big boy up?"

Amidst a chorus of cheers, Noelle reached for Gil's hand so he could help her from the stage. He loved how she trusted him to be there for her.

"Thank you for coming with me," she whispered. "You made that so much easier."

People elbowed closer to the tree and Noelle shifted nearer to Gil, making room. Her hip brushed lightly against his side, and it was all he could do not to put his arm around her shoulder and pull her even closer.

Mayor Schebly lit the Christmas tree as people oohed and aahed.

Tubs filled with ornaments had been set up around the base of the tree. Santa Claus Earl enlisted Gil and Noelle to help pass out decorations to the children so they could adorn the lower tree branches, while adult volunteers climbed the scaffolding to reach the higher boughs.

Josie and Ebby joined the throng of kids racing to find a place to hang their ornaments. Their enthusiasm was a joy to watch.

As soon as Noelle grabbed an ornament to pass along, some excited child snatched it from her hand. "Wow, this is a free-for-all."

"Yep, that's the fun of it. Don't you remember?"

"I do."

Gil passed Noelle a puppet of Rudolph the Reindeer to give to the next kid in line.

"Oops, his red nose fell off," she said.

"Pretend it's one of the other eight reindeers."

"You know how to think on your feet. Just like

you did with me and Baby Jesus." Laughing, Noelle gave the puppet to a little boy. "Here's Dancer."

Reaching out for the next ornament to pass along to another child, her fingers touched Gil's as he handed her a snowman ornament dangling from a red ribbon. Static electricity crackled from her to him, and Gil felt a hot, sharp *snap*.

He felt a little breathless. Lie. He felt a lot breathless and sort of dizzy.

She looked up into his face and in that moment, they shared a sweet connection. Gil stopped breathing altogether and watched as Noelle's pupils dilated. He was feeling something powerful, and from the expression on her face, so was she.

"What if?" she whispered.

Gil stared into her eyes, unable to speak.

"What if what?" Benji Maxwell asked, popping up beside Noelle.

"Eep!" Noelle startled. "Tie a jingle bell around your neck, will ya?"

"Why? Then I couldn't eavesdrop." Benji grinned and waggled a finger at them. "Were you two telling secrets?"

"No!" they said in unison and sprang apart.

Noelle spun to the left, Gil to the right, each looking in the tubs for more ornaments to pass out, but all the tubs were empty. The tree was fully decorated.

"Wow," Noelle said. "That was fast. I thought it would take longer."

"The night is still young," Gil said. "Only seven thirty. I don't have to put Josie to bed for another hour."

"We were talking about going for hot chocolate and Christmas cookies," Benji said. "You guys wanna come?"

"Who's 'we'?" Noelle asked.

"Me, Spence, Gretchen, Josie, Ebby and her dad, Tyler." Benji got a sly look on her face. "Or maybe you guys would like some alone time?"

"No!" Noelle and Gil said.

"Well, come on then, the coffee shop is filling up fast, although the others went on ahead to grab us one of the big tables. Hopefully, the wait won't be too long." Benji started toward the coffee shop.

"You really want to go?" Gil asked Noelle. "Don't feel obligated. You can bow out."

"What? And miss out on a hot chocolate date with the best-looking guy in town?" Noelle teased. "Not on your life."

He held his hand out to her and when Noelle took it, he knew things had changed between them. He didn't know how or when; he only knew that he liked it.

CHAPTER 14

Okay, was Noelle flirting with him?

If he wasn't mistaken, she'd just rubbed the toe of her boot against his ankle as they sat at a table across from each other at Perks, but maybe it was just an accidental brushing, and he was projecting his desires onto her. He didn't want to assume anything, because right now, his heart was jumping to all kinds of hopeful conclusions.

Gil grinned at her over the rim of his hot chocolate mug.

She lowered her lashes and angled a coy glance at him.

Nope, not an accident.

Noelle said something to Benji, who was sitting beside her. Benji laughed hysterically, but Gil missed what she'd said. He was too busy buzzing from where her boot tip had touched his ankle.

Powerful urges overtook him, and he wanted to kiss her more than anything in the world. But his sister and his daughter were sitting at the same table, as were other guests from the Merry Cherub.

They'd ended up pushing three tables together when the Buckhorn twins and their fiancés arrived as well. It was a festive atmosphere, filled with wedding talk and Christmas plans.

In the lively, crowded café, rich with the smell of ground coffee beans and freshly baked cookies, Gil breathed it all in and zeroed his gaze on Noelle's gorgeous face.

Her eyes glowed. She looked absolutely radiant. She cupped her chin in her palm, rested her elbow on the table, and leaned in toward Benji, mesmerized by her old friend's story.

He studied Noelle.

Her makeup was understated. Her lips a glossy pink. Her eyeshadow was only a slightly darker shade than her skin tone. She knew how to present herself in a polished, yet natural way. A pleasing package. Her smile was relaxed and mischievous. She wore a fluffy red sweater sewed with golden threads that sparkled like Christmas itself.

She tucked a strand of hair behind her ear, a casual, graceful gesture that enchanted him. His teeth longed to nibble that sweet ear and taste her salty skin. Her laughter intoxicated him, high and melodious.

There. He felt it. Another gentle bump against his ankle.

Oh, she *was* playing footsie with him. Never mind that she had a plausible denial if he were to bring it up later. A rush of heat spread throughout his body.

She glanced at him, her eyes heavy-lidded, a little bit drowsy. A soft smile crawled across her lips and their gazes fused. In his heart of hearts, if they hadn't been surrounded by chattering people and the hissing of coffee machines he would have leaned across that table, pulled her close to him, and kissed her until they were both senseless.

As a matter of principle, Gil tried not to cuss. He had a seven-year-old daughter in the house after all. But holy shit! He wanted Noelle so badly that he could taste it.

Carolers came through the door singing "Jingle Bells" as they bunched around the counter to submit their orders.

"We should scoot," Noelle said. "Give the new arrivals a place to sit."

"Yes," Gil agreed. "It's bedtime for the little ones."

"Aww man," Josie said. "Why? Tomorrow isn't a school day."

"Because your father says so, Little Miss." Gil gave his daughter an affectionate grin and bopped her nose with his index finger. "Put on your coat."

"You too, Ebby," Tyler said.

"Since there's no school tomorrow, would you two like to have a sleepover?" Gretchen invited. "We could watch *Elf* and pop popcorn on the stove."

"Yay!" Josie clapped.

"Dad, can I?" Ebby asked Tyler.

"Wait, what?" Gil's eyes went wide. "I'm not prepared to host a sleepover."

"You're not invited," Gretchen said, looking from her brother to Noelle and back again. "*I'm* hosting the sleepover, so you have nothing to do. The girls can sleep on the floor of my bedroom in sleeping bags."

Gretchen looked innocent as if the offer were spontaneous and carefree, but something in her grin suggested she was playing matchmaker. Otherwise, why would she extend this spur-of-the-moment invitation, if not to free up her younger brother's evening?

"Can I, Dad?" Ebby begged. "Please."

"You don't have any pj's," Tyler said.

"Josie has lots of extra pj's that Ebby could borrow," said Gretchen, the problem solver.

"All right then." Tyler nodded. "I'll pick her up in the morning, say eight o'clock?"

Josie and Ebby squealed, joined hands, and jumped around the coffee shop.

"You sure you're prepared for this?" Gil asked his sister.

"Easy-peasy."

"I'm picking up the tab for the table," Gil said. "Happy holidays, everyone."

Amidst grateful thank-yous people pushed back chairs, got to their feet, and slipped on their coats. It was so nice of him to treat.

Gretchen looped her purse strap over her shoulder. "C'mon, girls. Let's head back to the B&B."

Putting a palm on each girl's head, Gretchen nudged them toward the door. Noelle didn't miss the exchange when Gretchen turned her head to give her brother a wink as she left the building.

Most definitely the B&B owner was playing matchmaker.

Gil helped Noelle with her coat, a gentlemanly gesture. He was an old-fashioned guy. It was quaint. It was adorable.

And it bothered her.

Not because she disliked his courtly manners, but precisely because she did. She loved them, in fact. And that brought up feelings of vulnerability. She could put on her own coat, thank you very much. She could open her own doors and pull out her own chair. She didn't want or need to be hoisted onto a pedestal.

But when he zipped up her coat and put her knitted beanie on her head, she gulped. Being treasured and cared for scared the pants off her.

He left cash on the table to cover the bill, along with a generous tip, and then offered her his elbow. "Walk through Sweetheart Park to see the lights?"

She shouldn't. It wasn't smart, but she felt helpless to resist. Linking her arm through his, Noelle took a deep breath to steady herself. It was just a walk, nothing more.

Out on the street, the crowd had thinned. The shops and kiosks were closed, but people still strolled through the square and several groups were entering and exiting Sweetheart Park, which was decorated with a lavish Christmas display.

A sense of wonder lit Noelle up. It was so pretty here. Magical.

She shivered, not so much from the temperature that had dropped a few degrees while they'd been inside the coffee shop, but from the specialness of this day. She would remember it forever.

"You're cold." Gil released her arm to slip his hand around her waist and draw her closer to his body heat. "The wind's shifted directions. The norther's coming in."

They walked in lockstep, hip to hip. It felt nice, this gentle connection.

"Look at that." Gil pointed at the inflatable North Pole village. "It's a new feature this year."

Santa Claus swayed in the breeze, almost as if he was waving, beckoning them deeper into the park. "Winter Wonderland" played from the outdoor speakers. It was wondrous indeed.

"Do you think your sister is trying to play matchmaker?" Noelle asked.

"What?" Gil looked startled at the idea. "No . . . Do you think so?"

"She offered to host an impromptu sleepover for two seven-year-olds. That doesn't strike you as suspicious?"

"Huh." Gil pondered that. "Maybe you're right. She has been bugging me about dating again. She's got a new fella even though she hasn't brought him around yet. She says it's too soon for them to meet each other's families, but my sister is happier than I've ever seen her. I guess she wants me to feel the same. Do you suppose this is her unsubtle way of throwing us together?"

"Yes."

"Do you mind?"

Did she? "Do you want to date me, Gil?"

"Better question, do you want to date me?"

More than anything. "I'm only here for another month."

"Then it's back off to Hollywood."

"All I can offer you is sex. Can you deal with that?"

"What are you suggesting?" He stopped walking, turned to face her, and put both hands on her waist.

"It's been fun spending time with you."

"I feel the same."

"You've got a nice life here. A wonderful daughter, and a business that you love. Despite all that you suffered you've come out of it with a great attitude. I'm proud of you and the life you've created for yourself, Gil Thomas."

"Ditto, Noelle Curry."

"It might not have the country music career you once imagined for yourself, but from my eyes, you've got it all."

He met her gaze. "Not everything."

The way he looked at her stole Noelle's breath away. She gulped. That look sent shivers running down her spine. Unable to tolerate the full brunt of his stare, she glanced up at the night sky.

"Oh look! It's snowing." She pointed up at the gentle flakes slowly drifting to earth. The ground wasn't cold enough for snow to stick, but that didn't dampen her joy.

"Beautiful," Gil said, but he wasn't looking at the sky. His gaze was locked on her.

This time, she didn't look away. "We don't get snow in LA."

"We don't get it much here either. More often than not, any precipitation we get is ice."

"I'm glad we're here to see it together."

"Me too."

He reached for her hand, and she took it. They stood like wide-eyed children staring up at the sky, watching the silent snowflakes settle over the park.

"Too bad it won't stick," Noelle said. "We could make snow angels."

"You look like a snow angel." He reached up to brush away the snow collecting on her hair.

His touch heated her, warm as an electric blanket. She closed her eyes, tilted her head back, and stuck out her tongue to catch the snow and giggled as the thickening flakes landed in her mouth. It tasted like chilly air and hope.

So much irrational hope.

"You look happy," he said.

She closed her mouth and straightened, again finding his gaze. There was something about him, something more than the brief history they'd shared. He possessed a quality that was as appealing as it was unexpected. Gil was comfortable in his own skin. He knew who he was and in Noelle's world of actors, producers, filmmakers, and stars, who were always pretending to be something or someone they weren't, that was a rare commodity.

Impulsively, she kissed him, springing forward to lightly press her lips to his and then falling back.

"What was that?" He looked and sounded amused.

She pointed upward at the tree branch they were standing beneath. "Mistletoe."

"Aha," he said. "A handy excuse. I'll take advantage of it."

He dispatched the minuscule distance between them, gathering her into his arms and kissing her.

A long and lingering kiss that stirred yearning deep inside her. *This*. This was what she had been missing. All this time.

Gil.

His lips were firm, but his kiss was gentle. In it, she tasted the past and the promise of a future she didn't dare dream of. Because she liked him. A lot. And she wanted to kiss him endlessly for hours and hours.

He was a good man who made her feel safe, and whenever she was with him she experienced a deep peace that she'd never felt with anyone else beyond her grandparents.

Gil reached up and cupped her face with both palms, deepening the kiss, touching the tip of his tongue to her lips.

Helplessly, she parted her teeth, inviting him to take things further. A kiss suspended in this fairy-tale moment. As if they were captured in a time capsule. Where past and future merged into this magnificent present.

Noelle allowed herself to revel in this sweet twinkling without expectations or demands. She experienced his mouth, the heat and the moisture and the flavor of the peppermint candy cane he'd used to stir his hot chocolate.

The snow came down in quickening flurries, dusting everything around them in white. On and on they kissed, cherishing this special time in their budding relationship.

Finally, Gil broke the connection. "Whew."

"Understatement of the month."

"We're getting soaked. Come on, let's get in out of the weather."

"Goodbye, snow." She waved at the sky as Gil took her hand and pulled her toward the park exit. The lights, obviously on a timer, winked off, bathing them in snowy darkness. They made their way guided only by moonlight.

Laughing, they rushed toward the Merry Cherub, hand in hand. It felt like something from a romantic movie. She wanted to bottle this moment and put it in a snow globe to pull out and shake up for those future moments when she felt nostalgic about this night. Tomorrow, she would wake up and go back to planning the Buckhorn/Maxwell wedding, but for tonight she couldn't get enough of this wintry allure.

When they reached the carriage house at the B&B, Gil hesitated at the steps leading to the upstairs apartment. He looked as if he wanted to invite her in, but she had no real idea what he was thinking.

Sex would only complicate things. They lived in different states. Had different lifestyles. Different values. A romance couldn't go anywhere. They both knew it. But that didn't stop her from wanting him.

What was wrong with a little fling?

Well, for one thing, he was a good dad and he wanted to set an example for his daughter. She liked that about him. That he put his child first.

"I guess this is good night," he said, but longing filled his eyes.

"Yes."

"I had a great time."

"Me too."

"Maybe we could . . ." His eyes never left her face.

She put her hand on the railing, aching to linger, to ask for another kiss, but the snow was coming down furiously now and the steps were only going to get slicker.

Noelle licked her lips.

Gil stared.

"I should go up."

"Yes."

He wrapped his hand around her waist, tugged her closer.

"Oh!"

His eyelids lowered along with his head, and he covered her mouth with his in a kiss that was initially soft and gentle, but within two seconds, became hard, hot, and demanding.

And *she* was the one who took them to that electric place.

CHAPTER 15

At the force of Noelle's return kiss, Gil felt all his resolve leave his body. A soft little moan escaped her lips and he was a goner. She nipped and licked, her tongue teasing an invitation.

Take me.

Finally, panting, he broke the kiss. She was breathing just as fast and shallowly as he was.

"Your place?"

"Yes," she murmured and raced up the steps to the Roost.

Gil spared a glance at the B&B to see if anyone was watching. No one was as far as he could tell—all the blinds were closed tight—and he took off after her.

She waited for him inside the apartment, door thrown open, snowflakes blowing in . . . waiting. Her puffy lips glistened wetly in the entryway light.

He stood in the darkness staring at her. She looked so damn beautiful, so captivating that she took his breath away.

This was the time for him to come to his senses.

Things were moving fast. He wasn't accustomed to traveling at such dizzying speed. But that was part of the appeal, wasn't it?

She crooked her finger.

He took common sense, wadded it into a ball, tossed it over his shoulder, and flew across that threshold.

Noelle welcomed him with open arms, enfolded him into her embrace, and kicked the door closed with her foot. She kissed him long and hard, and then she pulled back and stared straight into his eyes.

"Are we sure we want to do this?"

Gil meant to tell her no. He should have told her no, but he wanted her so much, even if only for one night. He would take any crumbs he could get.

"Noelle . . ." He opened his mouth, uncertain of what he was about to say, but he got no further.

"Shh." She took hold of the front of his shirt and yanked him to her.

He did not resist. He hovered, her hand fisting the flannel in the middle of his chest as she searched his face.

Going up on tiptoe, she planted a hot kiss at the juncture where his neck and jawline met right behind his ear.

Gil shuddered. How had she gone so unerringly to one of his erogenous zones? Her busy little mouth rendered him mute. Gil closed his eyes, clenched his hands, tried to muster up the will to resist . . .

But he didn't want to.

He wanted her.

Had to have her.

She was as necessary to him right now as breathing. She nibbled his earlobe while one naughty hand slipped underneath his shirt, and she planed her palm over his abdomen.

"Heaven help me." He groaned.

"Pay attention."

"Bookworm, that's the problem. I can't think about anything *but* getting you into bed."

"Good. Perfect. We have the same goal. Now, where were we?" She pressed those hot little lips on his throat and Gil stopped thinking altogether.

His body was fully erect in every way possible. It had been a very long time since he'd been this hard, if ever. Cradling the back of her head in his palm, Gil took over, sealing her lips, plumbing the sweet depths of her hot mouth, branding her with his kisses until he was certain she was as breathless and addled as him.

Gil ached for her in a way he'd never ached for another. She represented his past—and dare he hope—his future? Was he wishing for too much? Was he rushing down a merry path that could lead to nowhere but disaster?

"I've waited a long time for you," Noelle whispered around the pressure of his mouth. "I've dreamed of this moment since I was a teenager."

"Wh-what?" He paused, pulled back, and looked down at her.

"I used to have teenage wet dreams about you," she confessed. "I never thought I'd actually get a chance to live out my fantasy."

Slightly alarmed, he cupped her cheek with his palm and peered into her soft brown eyes. "Don't put me on a pedestal, Noelle. I'm bound to fall off."

"I'm not. That was the teenage me. I'm going into this with my eyes wide open, Gil. I just want to enjoy this moment with you, 'kay?"

"Are you sure?"

"Let's don't overanalyze it." She paused. "Please. This is just fun. That's all. We're grown consenting adults. We know how to protect ourselves. We're allowed to enjoy each other's bodies, no strings attached. I know you're a traditionalist and this loosey-goosey approach is probably rubbing you the wrong way, but I want you. Here. Tonight. I hope that's enough."

He *did* want more, but things were complicated. He had no right to ask for them. She'd given him her terms. It was his choice to decide whether he could abide by them or not.

"Deal," he said, because the last thing he wanted was to leave without making love to her.

"I'm serious, Gil. Sleeping together changes nothing between us."

"Got it."

She hitched in a deep breath. "Whew, I'm glad we got that sorted."

He kissed her quickly, a sweet enticing peck, and then peered down at her. He traced a knuckle across her chin and felt the soft thud of her pulse against his skin.

"Gil," she whispered, looking uncertain for the first time since he'd come into her space.

Dipping his head, he captured her mouth again,

a tentative kiss that belied the wild passion storming inside him.

Her teeth parted on a gentle exhale, and she sank against his chest, curling her hands into fists as if to keep herself from ripping off his clothes. He had the same desperate need raging inside of him, but he was determined to take his time. He vowed to savor every minute, in case they never did this again.

Noelle's body heat seeped through his clothing, and he felt sweat pop out on his forehead and upper lip. He was so hard that he could think of nothing but this woman and what he wanted to give her. Not just with his body, but with his heart as well. But she'd made it clear she did not want his heart.

He could compartmentalize and keep his emotions tucked away. If that's what she needed from him, he'd give it to her.

Barely able to control himself, he took her hand in his and led her into the bedroom awash in angels.

Noelle's pulse jumped like a sprinter at the sound of the starting gun.

She was nervous, oh boy, so very nervous, but she wanted this man more than she'd wanted anything in a very long time. From the moment she'd seen him strutting across the road in sexy Santa mode, she'd ached for this.

No, that wasn't true. This night had been thirteen years in the making as her teenage fantasy finally came to life.

He turned to her. "Are you absolutely sure this is what you want?"

One, two, three, four . . .

Counting away her fears, Noelle gazed deeply into his eyes and all at once, she understood that he was just as nervous as she was. Knowing that eased her own anxiety. Even though this was just fun and games and nothing more, they did care about each other. No matter what happened, this was a good thing.

"I'm ready for this," she said. "I'm ready for *you*."

"Hell, yes." His mouth found hers again and he gave her the most wonderful kiss that curled her toes inside her ankle boots. He seemed to know just how much pressure and heat to put into his kisses and she wanted more, more, more.

He slipped the sleeve of her top off her shoulder and lightly bit her skin at her collar bone. He smelled of a manly cologne and pure, sexy Gil.

She threw back her head and let out a low moan.

A smug chuckle escaped him as his lips burned a trail of heated kisses. Her entire body softened, and she felt as if she were made of gelatin, wobbly and sweet.

"Look at me," she whispered.

He raised his head, his lips shiny in the muted glow of the night-light. She reached for his shirt and button by button, *one, two, three, four, five, six . . .* slowly opened his shirt until she fully revealed the delicious muscles hiding underneath his clothing.

She traced her fingertips over his skin, drawing a shudder from him, and then she peeled his shirt from his shoulders, and let it drift to the floor.

Once he was stripped bare to the waist, Gil stepped back. "My turn to remove something."

He reached to unclasp the necklace cradled at her cleavage. Carefully, he settled it on the bedside table, before turning back to plant hot kisses against her throat.

And so they went, slowly undressing each other, marveling at what their exploration uncovered.

He took off her top, his fingers tickling electrical impulses along her back. She shivered again and buried her head against his shoulder, reveling in the sweetness as he softly kissed her temple.

"You are so beautiful."

"I'm not. My mother tells me all the time I'm actually rather plain."

"I know she's your mom, and you love her, but she's also an asshole," he said. "I hope that doesn't offend you. You're damn beautiful to me, Noelle Curry, and I don't want to hear anything to the contrary, ever again. Got it?"

"Okay." She thrilled to the fact that Gil found her attractive.

He wasn't lying. His body gave him away. He was hard as a brick and his eyes were heavy with lust. She would take him at his word.

He wanted her.

And boy, did she want him.

Once they were both fully naked, he took her by the hand and led her to the bed. Gil's body did not disappoint. In the flesh, the man was just as magnificent as in her fantasies, if not more so.

His blue eyes lit up. "God, you are so gorgeous. I feel like the luckiest man on the planet."

In that moment, maybe for the first time in her life, she truly *felt* gorgeous.

And seen.

Fully seen for who she was. Not Crescenda Hardwick's daughter, not Clint Curry's offspring, but simply Noelle. Overwhelmed, she blinked, fighting off the tears of joy. She was that moved, felt that connected to him. She would have to be careful. She was in deep.

"C'mere." He held his arms wide.

She stepped into the welcoming circle of his embrace and felt an inner click, a sense of rightness, that feeling of homecoming again, all the stronger now.

He held her against him for the longest time. He speared his fingers through her hair and his breath was warm against her cheek.

"You smell like heaven."

This time, she kissed him.

With one arm, he reached out and pulled back the covers, while keeping his other arm securely wrapped around her waist. The sheets smelled of fabric softener, floral and fresh.

She slid over to make more room for him.

He turned on his left side and she on her right and they lay in the bed gazing into each other's eyes, belly to belly, hip to hip, heart to heart.

"I could stare at you all night," he said.

"Hmm. I hope you do much more than that."

"I want to take our time. I want this to be good for you. For us both." He trailed a finger over her cheek. "I'm so glad you came back to Twilight."

"Me too."

She felt his erection grow even harder. How was that possible? He was already granite. She felt her own body grow wet and soften, preparing for him.

Noelle ran her palm over his shoulder and down his arm, interlaced her fingers with his, and raised his hand to kiss the back of his knuckles. She wanted him so desperately. Wanted him more than ever.

Pressing her hips forward, she egged him on, inviting him into the timeless dance of physical love.

His calloused palm slid over her hip and curled down around to cup her butt. He spent an inordinately wicked amount of time caressing her bottom and teasing her with his touch.

While he did that, she licked his chest and nibbled at a nipple. He groaned a phrase, but she couldn't quite make out what it was, but thought he said something along the lines of "Oh yeah, *that*."

He explored her with his fingers, seeking out what she liked and what she didn't, trying to find the rhythm that pleased her most. Reading her like a roadmap, his hands worked their magic, coaxing and teasing her arousal, as his mouth took their kisses to a whole new level.

The entire universe dissolved into this room, this man, this sweet memory. Only the two of them existed as they clung to each other, hungry and desperate.

He wrapped his arm around her and rolled her onto her back, levering himself above her, bracing his weight on his forearms as he peered into her eyes. "Noelle, you are the most incredible woman I've ever known."

This man was not given to hyperbole. His compliment touched her deeply. She wanted so much to trust her growing feelings. In the dark of night, it was easy to believe that they could have something monumental together.

But would it last in the light of day? No, she couldn't entertain that thought. She'd set down the rules and she was sticking to them. This was fun and games. Nothing more. It didn't need to be anything more.

"Do you have protect—"

"Yes. In my luggage." She hopped out of bed, went to the closet, dug around for the condoms she kept in a zippered compartment, just in case. She tossed a packet to him and hurried back to bed.

He tore open the foil with his teeth.

Giggling, she helped him put the condom on, making it part of their foreplay, and then teasingly she kissed his sheathed shaft.

He groaned. "I don't know how long I can last. It's been years since I've been with a woman. Not since Tammy Jo."

That pulled her up short.

She wished he hadn't spoken his late wife's name, but she couldn't be squeamish about this. Tammy Jo had existed, and he'd had a daughter with her. Reality was reality. Best to face that head-on.

"Why not?"

"I . . . It's . . ."

"Because you were devoted to her?" Noelle asked. "Is that why you've had no lovers since her?"

"No, it's because I have a daughter. Whatever I do reflects back on Josie. I couldn't bring myself to introduce her to women with whom I knew there was no future. I've had friends who've done that kind of thing after a divorce and when casual flings ended messily it affected their kids in negative ways. I just couldn't do that to my child."

Oh dear. This was some serious pressure. She was the first woman he'd had sex with in five years. She found it both touching and worrisome. Was he putting too much pressure and expectations on this? On her. On them?

"What does that mean about me?" she asked.

"It means I'm so very glad to be here with you. It means we don't have to label this. It means we can just enjoy the night."

"Are you sure?"

"I can keep it light. I can keep things in check. I promise."

Disappointment enveloped her in melancholy arms as she *wanted* this to mean something to him despite her assertions to the contrary. Wanted it desperately. But she was so afraid to ask for what she wanted. So afraid this wouldn't work out. Instead, she pretended she didn't want more.

A smart woman with this much doubt would get out of bed and run away or send him packing, but when it came to Gil, she was not smart.

Her heart led her. She couldn't have pried herself from his embrace if the house had been on fire. She was that attached to him.

She was going to get hurt, she could feel it in her bones, but she would accept all that pain for one night of exquisite pleasure with her fantasy man.

He kneaded her shoulder muscles moving up her neck, his fingers finding tender spots and then soothing them with steady, rhythmic strokes. His fingers were at her scalp, rotating circles through her hair. His touch felt so good, she moaned again and curled against him as his fingers massaged, stroked, and caressed.

Gil kissed the pulse underneath her chin, causing her to throb all over. She nibbled the sensitive skin on the underside of his arm, and he shuddered against her.

They shifted and explored.

He licked the back of her knee, finding more places that caused her to writhe and groan. She ran her tongue over his body, giving as good as she got. They teased each other until they both reached a frantic pitch, perspiring, breathing heavily, aching for release.

His thumbs brushed her nipples and she let out a hungry whimper. Had she ever felt this much excruciating pleasure? She was overpowered, overwhelmed, and overcome.

"Take me, Gil. Please, make love to me now." She needed the abyss of his body to take away her fears and doubts.

"Yes, ma'am."

The way he was looking at her made her feel like the queen of the world. His eyes said he cherished her, admired her, respected her. How she longed to believe that. A pleasurable heat spread across her chest, into her neck, and up her face to burn her cheeks.

She'd waited so long for this moment, most of that time unaware that she'd even been waiting.

Slowly, he entered her body and she clung to him like a life raft, her fingers curling around his upper arms and pulling him more deeply inside her. She sucked in a deep breath and closed her eyes, committing every movement, every whisper, every taste to memory.

She would never forget this encounter, no matter how long she lived, this moment where her dreams finally came true.

He was tender with her, easy and careful. Nothing rushed. Nothing thoughtless. Every thrust considered and measured.

Gil was building something. Their dual pleasure his goal. Each stroke taking them further down this road to oblivion.

Each thrust and retreat created dizzying waves of pleasure that reverberated throughout her body. Crashing her senses. Wrecking her soul. Pushing her higher and faster into the gathering vortex.

"More," she begged. She was panting, barely able to speak.

"Easy, dear heart," he said.

He sounded so wonderfully old-fashioned, a throwback to a gentler time. He was nothing like the men she knew in LA, fast and slick and cosmopolitan. This man was salt of the earth, rooted and stable.

It was a heady concoction for a woman who'd grown up without many roots or much stability.

She threaded her fingers through his hair and pulled his head down to kiss him, her lips plumbing his as he moved within her. She raised her hips to meet his thrusts, urging him on, urging him deeper and deeper.

"Don't hold back," she begged. "Let me have all of you. I want all of you now."

It was as if her words were a match and Gil was gasoline. He was inflamed and he inflamed her, and they went up together.

All control vanished. Ruining his careful efforts. They were wild things. Animals in rut. Writhing, bucking, groaning.

Faster. Harder. He gave her every inch of himself. Sending her flying to the stars, stretching her, burning her, lighting a fuse in her so incandescent she feared she would never be the same again.

"Just let go," Gil said, his voice garbled.

His arms were around her, holding her, steadying her. It felt as if they were sprinting as fast as they could into the great unknown.

"I've got you. You're safe. I'll never let anything bad happen to you."

Waves gathered. Rippled over her. The arcs of sensation intensifying and tightening. *Lost.* She'd thought she was forever lost, but in his strong arms, she was found—treasured, cherished, and cared for.

And nothing else mattered.

She let go then, fully releasing any need to control the outcome. That's when the spasms overtook her. Tore through her body, ruptured her mind into a million beautiful pieces. She fell, shattered, and seconds after, he followed her into his own exalted release.

CHAPTER 16

As Gil slept beside her, Noelle lay on her back staring up at the ceiling. One of his arms was banded across her waist, his head facedown in his pillow. She loved the feel of him anchoring her in place, holding her steady, making her feel safe.

Grinning, she felt tears leak from the corners of her eyes and slide into her ears.

Joy.

So this was what pure joy felt like.

She thought of the other men she'd been with. Losing her virginity far later than her friends, in college at twenty. A fumbling affair that ended quicker than it had taken to get undressed. She'd gone out with the guy a few more times, until Crescenda started flirting with him. Then there was a short-lived fling with one of Crescenda's co-stars. She'd done that mostly to tick her mother off. A sweet summer affair in Greece that ended the second she found out about his wife. And then, a one-night stand when she'd felt too depressed to be alone. That had been more poison than antidote. She'd had no lasting connections with any of those men. No deeper meaning. No lingering bond.

A pretty empty love life when she thought about it.

And now, she was here with Gil. For the first time in her life, someone had truly made love to her. This was so much more than sex.

And that terrified her. No matter how much she claimed this was just for fun, it was not. She wouldn't walk away from this scot-free.

Gil stirred, tightening his arm around her and pulling her closer. "Noelle, are you really here with me?"

"It's true. It's real. I'm here." She pinched her thigh under the covers, hardly able to believe it herself.

He turned his head and shifted, pressing his lips to her temple. "I feared you were a mirage. That this was a dream."

"Me too."

"You look so cute with your hair all wild and free like when you were a teenager."

"Hey, I spend a lot of time and money smoothing out my hair."

"But why?"

Why? Control. Her hair was something she could control. She put up a hand to smooth her mad curls, but Gil touched her wrist.

"Leave it," he said. "Please. I love it when you're easy and relaxed."

Love.

Gil had said the word *love* in conjunction with her, even if he was just talking about her hair. *Ulp.* Hope was a kite, flying off to the sun.

"What's next?" He traced a finger down the length of her nose.

"Huh?" She startled. Before she'd invited him up they'd had a serious talk about sex being nothing more than fun and games. Was he trying to change the rules on her now? And if so, was she happy about it?

Happy? Maybe. But panicky too. She wasn't ready for this.

For him.

"With the wedding prep," he said. "What comes next?"

"Oh. The wedding." *Whew.* Except now disappointment filled up her lungs along with the deep breath she pulled in.

"On Monday, we're heading to Fort Worth to the nearest bridal shop to pick out the dresses."

"Sooo," he said. "That means you're free for the entire weekend?"

"I have planning to do and a progress report to file for Pamela Landry at The Tie."

"Yeah," he said. "And I have two concerts this Friday and Saturday night, but maybe we could hang out on Sunday?"

Did she want to encourage this? Her body said, "Oh boy, yes!" Her mind said, "Keep your distance."

And her heart? Well, it lub-dubbed all the faster.

"No pressure," he said. "Just wanted to throw that out there in case you had free time on your hands. Think about it and let me know."

"Okay."

He nodded, but she could tell he was disappointed, that he'd wanted a different answer. "You need time."

"I do."

"Please understand that I don't want to control you."

For a woman who'd spent her life being controlled by her mother, his statement felt like freedom. Gil was putting his own wants and needs aside.

For her.

"I wish we could stay wrapped in our little cocoon forever." Gil sighed.

"Me too." She snuggled against his chest.

Gil kissed her, his hand moving slowly across her breast. She wriggled into him, excited by the goose bumps his touch stirred.

She ran a palm over his chest, playing with the whorl of dark hair between his nipples. She traced her fingers over his honed muscles. He was in such terrific shape.

"Do you have any idea what you're doing to me, woman?" He groaned.

"What?"

"I think we're going to need another condom. You okay with that?"

"I thought you'd never ask." She flew from the bed, retrieved a second condom, and raced back into his arms.

"Noelle," he whispered as his mouth claimed hers.

They kissed endlessly, slowly discovering each other for the second time that night. Gil cradled her in his arms and stared down into her face. She'd never looked more beautiful—vulnerable and scared but willing to take a chance.

On him.

He felt honored and so very lucky. "You're amazing."

"You're not so bad yourself, cowboy."

He laughed. "I haven't been a cowboy in a very long time."

"Once a rodeo cowboy, always a rodeo cowboy."

Her inquisitive fingers tracked from his chin, down his neck, to his chest, and even lower to the six-inch, faded scar along his left flank that was barely visible in darkness. Goose bumps spread over his skin at her tender touch.

"What happened here?"

"Brazos Buckeroo."

"Who?"

"One ornery Brahman bull."

"Ouch."

"That's when I quit the rodeo."

"Understandably." She shivered. "So glad I wasn't around to see that. How long was your recovery time?"

"Three months. That's when I went all in on music. My guitar skills really improved during my recovery and music saved my sanity."

"I'm glad you found your true path."

"You found yours too. Planning weddings suits you."

"You think so?"

"Oh, yeah. It uses all your best skills—organized, resourceful, detail oriented."

"Speaking of . . ." Her fingers left his scar and

skated lower still. "Let's stay on task. I need more kisses."

"Yes, ma'am."

They kissed. Everywhere. He branded her breasts with his lips, and then moved lower and lower, discovering exactly what caused her to quiver, which places made her quake, and what drew keening noises from her gorgeous pink mouth.

"That's it, Noelle. Let me know what you like."

"I like you," she said, turning the tables on him, flipping him onto his back as she straddled his body and gazed down into his eyes.

He caught his breath, in awe of her.

Then she gave as she good as she'd gotten. Her mouth was as thrill seeking as his, nibbling, tasting, on a seek-and-find mission that left Gil with his eyes rolling back in his head as her daring little tongue explored the hardest part of him.

The minute her lips went around his erection, Gil's world splintered. He didn't expect her to draw him into her mouth, but once he was there, he rejoiced at the feel of her warmth on his skin.

She took him with unrestrained gusto and Gil lost his mind. She drove him to places he'd never traveled, and he quickly came undone. When she'd finished with him, he lay panting and fisting the covers, struggling to find himself again.

"Bookworm . . . that was . . . you were . . . there are *no* words."

She gave a self-satisfied laugh.

"Pretty proud of yourself, huh?"

"Extremely."

"Hahaha. We'll see what happens when I flip the script."

"Wh-what do you mean?"

"Your turn." He gave a roguish laugh and staked her on the bed, using his body to pin her spread-eagle against the mattress. Next, he kissed her long and deep before he roved his way down her body.

She writhed against him and called him all manner of sweet names and a few dirty ones as well. He found her most responsive spot and plied his tongue there. She went wild. He teased and tempted, dragging things out, making her beg.

"More." She gasped. "Please, *more*."

He did things with his tongue, extending her pleasure, coaxing her to wriggle and buck against him.

"You are a wicked, wicked man."

"No more wicked than you."

She tasted so good—rich and sweet. He couldn't get enough of her. She responded with noises and squirms to every lick, touch, kiss, caress. She was incredibly receptive. Her body highly attuned and sensitive.

"I'm gonna take you someplace special, Noelle."

"Ready and waiting, big guy. Prove it."

"Remember, you asked for this." He went down on her with dedication born of love and reverence; all he wanted to do was to please her and make her feel as good as she'd made him feel.

And when she came, shuddering convulsively against his mouth, he felt prouder of himself than he'd ever felt in a very long time as more song lyrics poured into his head and it became a lullaby, rocking him to sleep.

Sated and happy, Noelle lay in Gil's strong arms, awash in the afterglow.

She'd opened herself up to him in a way she'd never opened herself up to anyone before. Not just her body, but her heart as well. Happy, she closed her eyes and fell asleep.

When she awoke again sometime later, she yawned, stretched, and reached across the bed for Gil. Her hand fell on empty sheets. Sitting up, she pushed hair from her eyes and looked around the room.

She cocked her head, listening for him, wondering if he was in the bathroom, but then her nose caught the scent of coffee, bacon, and eggs. She threw back the covers, got up, put on a bathrobe, and wandered into the kitchen.

"Morning," Gil greeted her from his place at the stove.

"Where did you get ingredients for breakfast? I didn't buy anything."

"Slipped over to the Merry Cherub before Gretchen got up and raided her fridge." He grinned like a pirate who'd stolen treasure.

"Just to cook breakfast for me?"

"Yes, ma'am."

"You've outdone yourself, Mr. Thomas."

"After last night, you deserve all the pampering in the world." He served up a plate of scrambled eggs, bacon, toast, and a cup of strong coffee. "Sit."

She plunked down at the small breakfast table. The food looked delicious. "I didn't know you could cook."

"I'm a single dad. I've developed many nurturing skills."

"What time is it?" She yawned and wondered where she'd put her phone.

"Seven forty. I have to leave."

"You're not going to eat with me?"

"Can't. Gotta get Josie and take her for a dental appointment, but relax and enjoy your breakfast."

"I could come with you."

"Nope. I've got this." He leaned over and kissed the top of her head.

"And when you come back? What happens then?" She hated that she asked it. She didn't want him to feel obligated to spend time with her.

"Josie and I are gonna get a Christmas tree. We put ours up the day after Thanksgiving. It's tradition. And you're invited."

It sounded wonderful. Gil looked optimistic and they'd most certainly had an awesome time, but as she watched him go, Noelle couldn't help feeling like the clock was ticking on their romantic fling.

"You sure look happy this morning," Delphine greeted Gil as he walked through the front door of the Merry Cherub to pick up Josie from her sleepover.

It was only then he realized he'd been humming "All I Want for Christmas Is You." He paused, and grinned at the older woman. "You know what? I *am* happy."

"Good on you." Delphine gave him a thumbs-up.

"Where are Gretchen and Josie?" he asked.

"Parlor." Delphine nodded.

What was once the parlor in the old Victorian now served as a TV and game room for guests. He found his sister braiding Christmas ribbons in Josie's hair as they watched cartoons together.

"Ebby's gone home?" he asked.

"Tyler just picked her up." Gretchen drew a comb through Josie's hair, which was the same color as her late mother's.

Gil felt a twinge of sadness that Tammy Jo hadn't gotten to watch their daughter grow up, but regrets wouldn't take the shine off his happiness. His mind kept returning to his private time with Noelle.

"Thanks, sis, for hosting the sleepover. Much appreciated."

Gretchen met his gaze and her eyes lit up. "Did it give you the time you needed?"

"It did. Thanks."

"Maybe you can return the favor and look after the B&B for me on Sunday? I'd like to visit Jubilee."

"And your mysterious new boyfriend?"

Gretchen gave a *Mona Lisa* smile and shrugged.

"Sure. Consider it done." So much for his idea of spending Sunday with Noelle, but maybe she'd help him B&B-sit.

"Did you have fun with your sleepover?" he asked his daughter, coming to sit on the couch beside Gretchen.

"Brilliant!" Josie turned her head to grin at him. "I like Ebby."

"Whoa, kiddo, stop wriggling or you're gonna have crooked braids," Gretchen said.

"I'm glad you've found a new friend." Gil put a hand on Josie's shoulder and gave her an encouraging squeeze. After that nonsense with the mean girls, he was thrilled Josie had found someone nice to play with.

"Me too!"

"All done." Gretchen put the finishing ribbons on Josie's braids.

"Go get your things. You've got a dentist appointment." He tapped the top of her head.

"Yuck." Josie stuck out her tongue.

"Scoot."

She took off after her belongings and Gil turned to Gretchen. "Hey, thanks for last night. I know Josie enjoyed it."

"You're welcome." Gretchen eyed him. "How was your evening with Noelle?"

He grinned. "Fabulous. Exceptional, actually."

Gretchen held up her crossed fingers. "Here's hoping. I do like Noelle."

"Me too." He felt his smile slip. "I'm just . . ."

"Just what?"

"Well . . ." He rubbed the toe of his boot against the geometric pattern of the rug. "I'm afraid I'll end up hankering for someone who can't stick around."

Gretchen sent him a chiding glance. "Enjoy the holiday and don't worry about forever. Right now is good enough."

"That's what's going on with you and the fellow in Jubilee?"

"Time will tell."

"Oh we're a pair, aren't we?" Gil laughed. "The Thomas kids looking for love in all the wrong places."

"Is that what you're doing?"

He met his sister's steady gaze and spoke aloud the fears in his heart. "I want to believe I'm not, but there's a distinct possibility I'm gonna get my heart broken."

CHAPTER 17

After Gil left, Noelle did her best to keep her mind on her work. She had the wedding bible opened on the kitchen table, tabulated and color coded, and was busy making a list of things she needed to double-check.

But her concentration kept slipping as her mind endlessly wandered back to the best night of her dating life. Her teenage fantasy had come true and no matter how much she told herself she wasn't invested in the outcome, she was lying.

In passing, Gil had mentioned something about shopping for a Christmas tree, but he hadn't confirmed it and she didn't want to hang her hat on that. She would act cool, unbothered, and let things play out naturally.

And if he kept his distance and honored her request for a no-strings-attached affair? Well, okay. She'd had fun and that was the point.

Finally, she managed to nail down her concentration and slipped into the stream of her workflow.

Several minutes later, a knock on the door yanked her back to the present and she sprang up from her chair, breathless and hopeful.

She raced to the door but paused to collect herself. *Chill.* It probably wasn't Gil. He had things to do, a kid to look after. He didn't have the time to hang out with her.

Oh ick, was she feeling sorry for herself? Crossing her fingers, Noelle went up on her toes to peek through the peephole.

It was Gil!

He'd come back.

Thrilled, she threw open the door, ready to fling herself into his arms . . . and saw Josie standing behind him.

"Hey." He smiled at her, his blue eyes soft and inviting.

"Hi."

"Can you go Christmas tree shopping with us now?"

"Yes. Let me get my coat."

They drove out to Joe Cheek's Christmas tree farm, which was packed with customers this lovely Friday after Thanksgiving. Gil introduced her to Joe, who was a friend of his; Joe's wife, Gabi; their five-year-old son, J.D.; and Joe's teenage daughter, Casey, from another relationship.

Noelle liked Gabi instantly and when Gabi told Noelle that she was originally from LA, they got into a big city versus small town discussion.

"I left LA for this one and never looked back." Gabi smiled and put an arm around her husband's waist.

"Don't let her fool you." Joe winked. "She had an adjustment period."

"Mainly because the town rolls up the carpet at nine P.M. I was used to 24-7 grocery stores. But no biggie." Gabi shrugged. "I just learned to be better prepared. I wouldn't trade my life here for anything in the world."

"Ditto." Joe leaned down to kiss his wife's head.

Aww. They were such a sweet couple. If Noelle lived in Twilight, she could see herself becoming fast friends with Gabi, who was just a couple of years older than she was.

"We're here for a tree!" Josie said. "We want the bestest one you have."

"Whatcha looking for?" Joe asked. "Virginia pine? Leland cypress? Carolina Sapphire?"

"Dad?" Josie asked, her eyes uncertain as she slipped her little hand into her father's.

"We'll just take a look around," Gil said. "If that's okay."

"Sure, sure. Do you want to chop your own?" Joe asked. "We have gloves and axes you can borrow, or I can come cut it for you."

"Brought my own equipment," Gil said, pulling gloves from his pocket and opening his jacket to reveal a small hatchet dangling from his tool belt. A little thrill went through Noelle. She had a thing for men who were good with tools.

"Great." Joe winked. "Make yourselves at home."

They wandered through the rows of trees, looking for the perfect one. Josie skipped ahead of them, humming under her breath as she ran a hand over the Christmas trees she passed by.

"She's happy." Gil nodded at his daughter. "She's had a tough time of it at school lately. There are a couple of girls who've been picking on her for not having a mother."

"Oh," Noelle said. "The wretched little beasts."

Gil laughed and the jovial sound lit her up inside. "I'm sure the girls have issues of their own, but it hurts to watch your kid bump up against life's thorny thistles."

"I can't imagine how tough that is."

He shrugged. "It's part of her growth. I wish I could Bubble Wrap her and carry her around on a pillow, but I've got to let her learn on her own."

Noelle smiled at him. "You're a good dad."

"I try." He jammed his hands into the pockets of his shearling jacket. "But I'm terrified of screwing this up."

"I'd be worried if you weren't terrified. Raising a kid is a huge responsibility."

"Yeah, but she already has one huge strike against her. Losing your mom when you're a kid does a number on you, no two ways about it."

Noelle wasn't sure why she did it, other than Gil looked like he could use some reassurance, but without even thinking, she slipped her arm around his elbow and leaned in close to him.

He stopped walking. She could see the pulse at his throat throbbing as fast as her own. She paused beside him.

"Noelle . . ."

"Yes?" She turned her body to face him and tilted her head up. Their gazes met.

"Are we doing the wrong thing?"

What did he mean by that? She studied his face, trying to get a read on him, but his expression was noncommittal.

He disentangled his arm from hers and she felt a pang in the center of her chest. She stepped back. Breathing room. They both needed breathing room.

"Dad! What about this one?" Josie disappeared behind a row of trees.

They followed her, Gil's question left hanging in the air. They found Josie staring up at a beautifully shaped tree.

"You have a good eye," Noelle said. "This one is balanced, symmetrical. Excellent job."

Josie blushed and hopped from foot to foot. "Cut it down, Daddy."

"You sure this is the one you want?" Gil asked.

Josie nodded. "I'm certain."

"Okay then, stand back." Gil put on his gloves, took out the hatchet, and bent to chop down the tree Josie had picked. The ping of his axe rang out across the Christmas tree farm.

As they watched him work, Noelle noticed Josie's jacket was thin and she was shivering. Yes, partly from excitement, but the kid was cold and too wound up to say something. Noelle took off her own jacket.

"Here, put this on."

Josie accepted the jacket and slipped her arms through the sleeves. Noelle crouched in front of her to pull up the hood and the zipper. The sleeves were too long, and Josie's little hands disappeared inside them.

"Thank you," Josie said through chattering teeth. "I was cold."

"I noticed."

"But now, *you'll* be frozen."

"No, I have an extra-thick sweater." The wind was breezy, but she'd rather be chilled herself than have Josie suffer. "I'll be just fine."

The beaming grin Josie gave her warmed Noelle inside out.

"Thanks for looking out for her."

Noelle straightened to see Gil had finished chopping down the tree and was staring at her with such admiration in his eyes that her heart skipped a beat.

"I should have gotten her a heavier jacket."

"Glad I could help."

"Here, you take my jacket. I've worked up a sweat and I'm hot."

Yes you are, she thought as he took off his jacket and draped it around her shoulders. She slipped her arms inside the sleeves. He stuck the hatchet into his tool belt and bent to heft the fallen pine onto his shoulder.

Her heart flopped into her throat. Holy smokes, the man was sexy as hell.

"Josie?" Gil glanced around for his daughter.

She'd been right there with them. Where had she gone? Noelle grimaced. She been so busy ogling Josie's hot dad, she hadn't been paying attention to the girl.

"Did you see where she went?" he asked.

Shaking her head, she stepped through to the next row of trees. A couple, a few years older than

Gil, were eyeballing trees, but there was no sign of Josie.

"She's not in that row."

"She knows better than to go off on her own." His forehead wrinkled as he set the tree back down on the ground. He raised his voice. "JoJo, where are you?"

No answer.

"Darn that kid," he muttered. "Stay here in case she comes back. I'll go look for her."

"Try not to panic. She couldn't have gone far." Even as she tried to reassure him, she felt her own anxiety building. Yikes. Parenthood was stressful.

One, two, three, four . . .

Gil disappeared through the rows of trees lined up like regimented soldiers and even though people were walking all around the Christmas tree farm, in this moment, with no one else in her line of vision, she felt a strange sensation she'd experienced quite often as a child. As if she were all alone in the world, belonging nowhere and to no one.

"Psst, Noelle."

She turned to see Josie poking her head out from behind a Christmas tree. Why was she hiding?

"Here she is, Gil," Noelle called out.

"*Shh.*" Josie put a finger to her lips. "I don't want *her* to see me."

"Who?"

"Josie, Josie, Josie."

From the thicket of Christmas trees between the rows, stepped a girl about Josie's age. She spoke with an exaggerated vocal fry and slightly mispronounced Josie's name, calling her Jo-*zee*.

The girl was dressed in the latest designer clothing and sported a stylish asymmetrical haircut. Bad vibes radiated off her self-satisfied smirk.

"Well, well, well, if it isn't the girl that locks herself in the cloak closet."

Josie cringed and leaned against Noelle, who wrapped her arm around Gil's daughter, letting her know she wasn't alone. How many times had Noelle faced a mean little bully by herself? More than she could count.

The girl sank her hands on her hips, raked her gaze up and down Josie. "It's rude not to say hello."

Josie's body language changed immediately. Her shoulders slumped, her gaze dropped, and she toed the ground with her sneaker. Ducking her head, she mumbled, "Hello, Silvey."

Instantly, Noelle knew this was the mean girl who'd been pestering Gil's daughter.

From behind Silvey, another girl emerged. She was dressed as a carbon copy of her aggressive friend and went to stand behind Silvey. Clearly, Silvey was the ringleader, and this girl was her minion.

"Look what I found creeping around the Christmas trees, Tabby," Silvey said to the other girl. "A skink."

Tabby lifted her hand in a half wave at Josie.

Silvey batted the girl's hand down. "Don't wave at her, Tabby."

Tabby clasped both hands behind her back and hung her head. "Sorry," she mumbled.

Noelle stepped closer to Josie and stared down the bratty Silvey. Emotions churned inside of her as old memories she didn't want to face flashed through her memory. She'd been in Josie's shoes, bullied because of who her mother was.

"Did you need something?" Noelle asked.

Silvey tossed her head, raised her chin, but couldn't hold on to Noelle's gaze. "We just came to see what Jo-*zee* was doing here."

"What did you think? Buying a Christmas tree like everyone else, and for the record," Noelle said, putting on a smile as false as the one flitting over Silvey's pretty face, "she pronounces her name *Jo*-see. In the future, please address her that way."

Silvey looked taken aback that Noelle had corrected her. Anger narrowed the girl's eyes. The little Pop-Tart was used to running roughshod over people.

Well, the buck stopped here. Noelle took a step toward Silvey. "You did get my message, right? From now on, you're treating Josie with kindness and respect. No more calling her names. No more taunting her. No more bullying. Got it?"

The girl's pupils widened, but she stood her ground and even curled her upper lip into a sneer. Oh, she was used to running her household. No doubt about it. Her parents had abdicated their responsibility.

"What business is it of yours, lady?" Silvey challenged.

Josie came over and slipped her hand in Noelle's. Noelle squeezed it, letting her know she had her back.

Shooting Noelle a grateful look, Josie lifted her

chin, stared Silvey down, and said, "It's her business 'cause she's gonna be my new mommy."

Gil walked up behind Noelle and his daughter. He arrived just in time to hear the tail end of the conversation.

This was a whole new wrinkle. Last night, they'd convinced each other their fling was casual, no strings attached, and he'd been willing to go along with that because it was what Noelle wanted.

Now his daughter had thrown a wrench in things, and he was faced with reality. He'd told himself Josie wouldn't be affected by the casual arrangement he'd formed with Noelle.

He'd been wrong.

Dead wrong.

He shouldn't have gone to Noelle's apartment last night. Should have hightailed it out of there when she'd thrown her door open and invited him in. But the night had been so special and Noelle's sweet kisses so compelling, he'd allowed himself to get swept away by his bodily urges.

It had been a mistake. That was clear now.

No matter how wonderful they'd made each other feel, this wasn't going to end well and now, not only would he get his heart broken, but so would his daughter.

"You girls go on back to your people." Gil stepped between Noelle and Josie and the other girls. "And you have good weekend."

Silvey looked as if she wanted to say something tacky but thought better of it. She shrugged and tossed her head. "C'mon, Tabby. Let's get out of here."

Rolling her eyes at Gil, Silvey turned and led Tabby through the row of trees and out of their line of sight. He was about to say something to Josie but stopped when he saw his daughter's gaze was locked on Noelle.

"Are you mad at me?" Josie asked Noelle.

"Why would I be mad?"

"Because I lied and said you were gonna be my mom."

"While I don't endorse fibbing," Noelle said, "anything is possible."

"Like you could be my mom in an alternate universe?"

"Yeah." Noelle smiled. "Like that."

"Thank you," Josie said. "It was kinda fun pretending you could be my mother."

Noelle's eyes softened. "It's my pleasure."

"Let's get this tree loaded," Gil said.

Ten minutes later, they were in the truck headed home. Josie in her booster seat in the back, Noelle in the passenger seat, filling the cab with her sophisticated cologne. After her kindness to his daughter, Gil wanted to whisk Noelle back to the Roost, carry her to the bedroom, and show her just how much he appreciated her.

Again and again and again.

But that couldn't happen. For one thing, they had a Christmas tree sticking out of the back of his pickup and an excited seven-year-old who couldn't wait to decorate it. Plus, he needed to have a heart-to-heart with his daughter as soon as possible. He had to dispel whatever fantasy she was cooking up about Noelle potentially becoming her new mother and set the record straight.

He pulled into the driveway at the B&B and killed the engine.

"I've got a couple of calls to make," Noelle said with her hand on the door handle. "I had a really fun time with you guys this morning. Thank you for inviting me."

Had she read his mind?

"You're not gonna help us decorate the tree?" Josie sounded so forlorn that it strengthened Gil's resolve. He had to make sure his daughter wasn't getting too invested in Noelle.

"We can't decorate it right away anyway," Gil said. "I've got Derrick's guitar lesson at noon. He'll be here any minute."

"Aww, man." Josie made a face.

"The decorating will keep until tomorrow. I still have to get all the boxes down from the attic. Now give Noelle her jacket back and say thank you while I unload the tree."

"Thank you," Josie said, unbuckling her seat belt and handing Noelle's jacket back to her over the front seat.

"You're very welcome." Noelle's smile was so tender it tugged at Gil's heart. She took off his jacket and left it draped over the middle console. "I'd love to help decorate the tree whenever you're ready."

"Yay!" Josie clapped her hands.

"Scoot on into the house, kiddo," Gil said. "I'll be in with the tree in a jiff."

"'Kay." Josie seemed to have gotten over her disappointment. She hopped out of the truck and went skipping up the sidewalk to the cottage.

Gil turned to Noelle, who looked so self-contained sitting in the passenger seat beside him. "Thanks for intervening with Silvey."

"I've been bullied a time or two myself," Noelle said. "Kids sometimes have chips on their shoulders when your mom is famous, but I suppose most everyone has to deal with bullies at some point in their lives."

In that regard, Gil had been blessed. He'd been privileged and while a time or two some swaggering cowboy had tried to pick a fight when he was on the rodeo circuit, he'd never been bullied in school. He hated that it was happening to his daughter.

"Silvey shouldn't be mistreating Josie, but I bet if you look closer, Silvey is dealing with something unpleasant in her own life and she doesn't have the skills or emotional maturity to handle it and she's taking it out on Josie."

"Yeah." Gil nodded. "I agree." The cab of the pickup was cooling off fast after he'd cut the engine. "I do think we should talk about what Josie said to those girls."

"No need."

"You're not upset that she said you were going to be her new mother?"

They were turned toward each other in the front seat. Her body was tense, shoulders drawn in, and she'd fisted her hands in her lap.

"We shouldn't make a big deal of it. She said it

as a defense against Silvey's taunts. I don't think she believes it. She did apologize to me for lying."

Gil blew out his breath and stabbed a hand through his hair. "I'll talk to her. Make sure she understands what she said was wrong."

"Go easy on her, okay?"

"Of course."

"What about us?" she asked, her voice low.

"Um . . ." He didn't know what to say.

"I mean, we don't want to encourage Josie to think that you and I might—"

"No, no. You're right."

Noelle cleared her throat and tried to smile but her lips sank back down as soon as she'd tipped them up. She crinkled her nose. "Maybe we shouldn't—"

"Right. No more of what we did last night." He said it as if he agreed, but inside he felt empty and sad.

"I probably shouldn't help you decorate the tree either. We don't want to encourage Josie's fantasies."

"Probably not."

"We'll just go back to being friends."

"Friends," he echoed, even though that was not what he wanted.

"I had fun last night, and I'll remember it for the rest of my life." A bittersweet smile crossed her face. She reached over and put a hand on his wrist. "But your child comes first."

"Yes," he said.

"There's nothing more important to a child than a parent who is always there for them. A parent who has their back no matter what. Josie is a lucky little girl. You put your child's welfare before everything else and for that, I love you to pieces."

Then she hopped from the car and raced up the steps to her garage apartment, leaving Gil feeling as if he'd lost something important.

CHAPTER 18

"We gotta have a talk, kiddo." Gil stood in the doorway of Josie's room, scenting the air with the pine needles still clinging to his clothes after he'd hauled the Christmas tree into the living room.

Josie popped out her earbuds. She was lying on her stomach on her bed, swinging her legs in the air and watching children's TV programming on her tablet computer.

"Can you turn off the show? We need to discuss what happened at the Christmas tree farm."

"Okay." She closed her computer and swung her legs around so that she was sitting up.

Gil came over to ease down on the mattress beside her. "I want you to understand that Noelle is only in our lives for a brief time. She can't be your new mom."

"I know." Josie hung her head. "I shouldn't have lied to Silvey."

"It's more than that, sweetheart." He cupped her chin in his palm and gently brought it up until she was looking at him. "I don't want you to start building some happily-ever-after fantasy in your head about the three of us becoming a family."

Josie squirmed away and dropped her gaze. "Why not?"

"Because I don't want you to get hurt when it doesn't work out between me and Noelle."

"But Dad," she said. "What if it *does* work out?"

"It can't. Noelle lives in Los Angeles. She's only in town to plan the Buckhorn twins' wedding. After that, she'll be gone."

"What if she moved here?"

"She has a business in LA. She has a house there. Friends and family."

"Oh." Josie sounded disappointed. He was almost too late to keep her from getting invested. Then she perked up. "What if *we* moved to LA?"

"Honey, love takes time. You can't make sweeping life changes for someone you just met."

"But Aunt Gretchen said you knew Noelle when you were teenagers. Maybe you can throw a coin into the Sweetheart Fountain, and you'll fall in love again like Jon Grant and Rebekka Nash did."

"For one thing, Noelle and I were never boyfriend and girlfriend. We were just neighbors and that was only when Noelle came to visit her grandparents. For another thing, you do know that story about throwing a coin into the fountain is just a fable, right? It isn't real."

"But Jon and Rebekka really did meet at the river at twilight and fall in love all over again. We learned that in history class."

"That part is true but wishing on a coin is made up."

"Like Santa." Josie pulled a face.

"Like Santa."

Last year, that smarty-pants Silvey had been the one to spoil the innocence of the entire first grade class when she'd announced Santa wasn't real and anyone who believed in him was a stupid baby. Gil cringed, remembering when Josie had come home crying and he'd had to tell her Silvey Zucker was right.

"So there's no chance that Noelle—"

He had to nip this fantasy in the bud. "No chance at all, sweetheart. I'm sorry."

Josie's lower lip trembled. "Now Silvey's gonna call me a liar."

"Well, you did lie to her."

"I know." She hung her head.

"I understand why you did it, but there are consequences for our actions."

Josie pounded her forehead with her palm. "I'm a dumb, stupid liar."

"No, no." He pulled her into his arms and rocked her against his chest. "You are not dumb. You just made a mistake. There's nothing wrong with making mistakes as long as you learn from them and do better the next time. Did you learn something?"

Josie nodded. "Yeah. You shouldn't lie."

"That's right. A lie will get found out eventually and lying keeps you from being close to other people."

She cocked her head. "How's that?"

"Because you're showing them a false self. People can't get to know the real you as long as you're lying to them."

"I'm sorry, Daddy."

"I'm not the one you need to apologize to."

"But I already told Noelle that I was sorry."

"Not just Noelle," he said. "You need to tell Silvey that you lied."

He could see her mental cogs whirling. She was trying to get out of confessing to Silvey and he didn't blame her. The girl was bound to make Josie's life miserable over it. Conflicted, he didn't know what to do.

"Could you just take my iPad away?" Her eyes beseeched him.

If she was willing to negotiate away her most prized possession, Josie really didn't want to face Silvey. All the more reason he had to force the issue. Parenting was damn hard. It would be so much easier to lock up her iPad for a week than make her apologize to her enemy. Honestly, he wished he could do that.

"No," he said. "The punishment must match the crime. Telling the truth is the only antidote to a lie."

"If you married Noelle, it wouldn't be a lie." Her eyes pleaded with him to let her off the hook. "She'd be my mom then."

He kept his tone gentle. "I tell you what, when you go to school on Monday and tell Silvey the truth, I'll go with you. She can't say or do anything mean to you with me standing there."

Josie slanted her head and peeked at him through a heavy lock of hair that had fallen over her face. "But what if she's mean after you leave?"

"Then you'll ignore her, like we discussed before."

Josie whimpered and drew her knees to her chest.

"It will be okay. I promise. I've got your back. Always."

"All right. I'll do it."

"Good girl." He gave her a tight hug. "I'm so proud of you."

"Even though I lied?"

"I'm not proud of the lie, but I'm proud of how you're taking responsibility for your actions. That's what makes you a good person, Josie."

A tear rolled down her cheek. "I'm sorry I did wrong."

"Honey, you're going to make mistakes. That's how you learn. What matters is that you take responsibility for your mistakes and do what you can to make amends. Once you apologize to Silvey for lying to her, it's over, forgotten, and we won't mention it again."

"'Kay."

"I love you."

She squeezed him hard. "I love you too, Daddy."

His big, stupid ego swelled up, pleased with himself. He'd navigated that little bump in the road without too much trouble.

But what was he going to do about his growing feelings for Noelle?

"It's okay," Noelle said to her reflection in the mirror as she brushed her teeth before bed. "You knew when you invited him in last night that it was only temporary. It's fine. Really it is."

She'd stayed busy to keep from thinking about what had happened at the Christmas tree farm and spent the rest of the day working on wedding arrangements, sending in an updated report to Pamela Landry at The Tie, and listening to Gil's guitar student stumble through a thoroughly wretched version of "Free Bird" for an hour.

Then later, she'd listened to Josie's giggles and Gil's baritone as they decorated their Christmas tree. She felt a bit sorry for herself, so she stuck in earbuds and sloughed off work, watching an old romantic comedy on her laptop, which just ended up making her feel even worse.

"Look, it was just sex," she said to herself in the mirror as she brushed her teeth, rinsed, and spat. "No big deal. Let it go."

And yet, she had four more weeks in this town. Four more weeks living upstairs from Gil and working with him on the wedding reception. For more weeks of this intense yearning eating her up inside.

She shouldn't have slept with him. It had been fun. More than fun. It had been thrilling and a pleasure, and she wanted more.

A lot more.

That was the problem. The addiction. The need for him. Was this how Crescenda felt whenever she jumped on the rollercoaster of love?

Ack! Was she turning into her mother? Letting the fulfillment of a lusty teenage dream crack her heart wide open?

Her mind scrambled, trying to find a way out, a solution that would let them be together. Short of her giving up her career and moving to Twilight, she didn't see how that could happen. And besides, she was way jumping the gun. Gil might not be interested in anything more than a fun time. Just because Josie was building daydreams about Noelle being her mother, it didn't mean she should fall prey to the idea.

Even though they had a shared history of sorts, she and Gil barely knew each other as grown adults. She would not be like her mother and jump willy-nilly into relationships.

But wasn't that stubborn resistance to the idea of true and lasting love the thing that had kept her alone all these years?

What if she opened her heart to possibilities? What if she stopped worrying about being like her mother? She wasn't Crescenda. Maybe she *could* fall in love without it ending badly if she just dared to take a chance. Maybe she could have what Grammie and Grampie had had. She shared their DNA just as much as she shared her mother's.

Why was she so terrified of getting hurt? What if it worked out?

Her heart fluttered, full of hope.

But what if it didn't?

He didn't see Noelle for the rest of the weekend. She didn't come into the office space where he'd made room for her at the Windmill, and he felt like a dufus every time he looked at that empty card table.

And yet he couldn't bring himself to take it down.

He'd been too forward by setting it up, assuming too much. His motives had been pure, but he'd overstepped. Now he felt as if he'd been behind the eight ball with her all along with no way to win. Was she just too afraid to love?

Why did he care so much?

That was the vital question.

Why? Because he couldn't stop thinking about her, couldn't stop feeling as if everything was coming unraveled just as it was getting started. He'd punished Noelle for his daughter's lie, breaking things off with her for Josie's sake. He'd been unfair, but he hadn't seen any other way around it.

So he stayed away from her. Resisting the urge to climb those stairs and knock on her door after he'd put Josie to bed. He averted his gaze from her apartment whenever he came and went. She was hiding out and he wouldn't get in her way.

On Monday morning, when he went to wake Josie for school, he found her in bed, doubled over and clutching her stomach.

"My tummy hurts." She moaned.

He had no doubt she was in pain, her fear and anxiety over facing Silvey was giving her a bellyache, but just to make sure something wasn't physically wrong, Gil took her temperature. 98.6.

"Your temperature is normal, kiddo."

"It *hurts*."

"I'm sure it does. Do you feel like eating breakfast?" he asked.

"No." She moaned and pulled her pillow down over her face.

"Are you going to throw up?"

"Maybe."

Nerves could make a kid throw up as easily as

a virus and he didn't want to discount her feelings and emotional upset. "Do you want me to get you a cool cloth?"

"Uh-huh."

Gil went to the bathroom, dampened a washcloth with cold water, wrung it out, and came back to sit on the bed beside Josie. Gently, he wiped her face.

"I know you're not faking. I know your stomach hurts, but once you get past telling Silvey the truth, it'll get better."

"I can't, Daddy."

"You can. I'll be right with you."

"It really, *really* hurts."

"If you don't go to school today, you'll just have to do it tomorrow."

She peered up at him, looking so pale and miserable it kicked him right in the heart. "I know."

"Come on then. Get up and get dressed and let's get this over with." Feeling wretched that he had to teach her this life lesson, Gil peeled back the covers and coaxed her out of bed.

Half an hour later, they sat in the truck outside Jon Grant Elementary. Josie looked less pale, and she'd stopped clutching her stomach, but her little knee was bobbing up and down uncontrollably. Dang it, why did raising kids have to be so complicated?

"Here's how we're going to handle this," Gil said, hoping to reassure his daughter by being calm and in control. "We're going to Principal White's office, tell her what's happened at the Christmas tree farm, and ask her to call Silvey to the office so you can apologize."

They needed neutral ground for this encounter, and he wanted to knock Silvey off-balance.

"When Silvey gets there, I'll explain you got the wrong impression about my relationship with Noelle, and that you'd like to apologize to Silvey for bending the truth."

"Okay." Josie stared down at her lap and fiddled with the zipper on her jacket.

"That's my girl." Pride for his daughter pushed hard against his chest. They'd get through this, and their relationship would be stronger for it.

As they sat in Evelyn White's office, along with her executive assistant, Marjorie, the principal listened to their story without comment, then she got on the PA system and asked Silvey to come to the office.

A few minutes later, Marjorie ushered Silvey through the door. The girl seemed breathless and a little panicky. Gil would have felt bad for her, except the minute she laid eyes on Josie, her upper lip curled into a sneer. Gil put a hand on his daughter's shoulder, letting her know she wasn't alone.

"What's going on?" Silvey asked, sinking her hands on her hips. "Do I need to call my lawyer?"

Good grief, the kid was outrageous.

Principal White, obviously used to hearing things like this from Silvey, ignored the part about the lawyer. "Josie has something she wants to say to you."

Silvey tossed her head. "Well, I don't want to hear it."

Gil nodded at Josie, who got to her feet and stood eye to eye with Silvey. "I made a mistake at the Christmas tree farm."

Silvey folded her arms over her chest. "Oh, yeah?"

"I told you Noelle is gonna be my mommy, but that's not true."

"I knew it!" Silvey pumped her fist and her eyes narrowed with nasty glee. "I knew you were lying."

Did the girl have to sound so hateful?

Josie cringed, but she stood her ground. "I fibbed and I'm sorry for it."

"Such a liar!"

Gil fisted his hands on his knees, and it was all he could do not to rise up from his chair and loom over the girl who'd been tormenting his daughter.

"Silvey," Principal White said sharply. "There will be no name calling. Josie has apologized and now you will accept her apology."

"In a pig's eye." Silvey snorted.

"Silvey Zucker, if you don't want detention, tell Josie you accept her apology," Evelyn White said.

"Fine." Silvey rolled her eyes. "I accept your apology."

"And Josie." Principal White swung her gaze to Gil's daughter. "If you have any problems on the playground, come speak to me instead of hiding or locking yourself in the cloak closet. Got it?"

"Yes, ma'am," Josie mumbled and hung her head.

"Now, I want you both to shake hands."

Josie and Silvey both looked as if they'd rather put their hands in a wood chipper, but Josie was the first to offer her hand.

Begrudgingly, and only after Principal White pointedly cleared her throat, Silvey shook Josie's hand.

"Josie," Evelyn White said. "Tell Silvey you won't lie to her again."

"I won't lie again." Josie pumped the other girl's hand.

"Now, Silvey, tell Josie you won't make fun of her for not having a mother."

At that, Silvey jerked her hand back, gave an odd little cry, and ran from the office. Principal White nodded at Marjorie, who went after the child.

Josie's eyes widened. "What happened to her?"

Principal White sighed and met Gil's eyes. "Normally, I wouldn't talk about other students when they're not in the room, but I think it's important for you to know where Silvey is coming from. Maybe it will give you both more compassion for her. Besides, it's public knowledge. Silvey's mother abandoned the family last month, and her father has filed for divorce and full custody of Silvey. That's why she's been picking on Josie. The school counselor says Silvey can't bear her own pain, so she's been projecting her bad feelings onto other students who don't have mothers. She sees in them her own loss and she's trying to make herself feel better."

CHAPTER 19

Noelle avoided Gil. She waited for him to leave the B&B before she went in for her breakfast, peeking out the window to watch him and Josie go about their business.

"You're being a creeper," she muttered and closed the curtain, but in all honesty, she didn't trust herself not to cave whenever she was around him, so she stayed away.

Ten days after she'd come to Twilight, Noelle left town for the first time since she arrived, riding with the Buckhorns to the nearest bridal shop in Fort Worth. Vanessa drove. Noelle rode shotgun and the twin sisters sat in the back bickering about whether they should dress alike for the wedding or not.

Noelle and Sierra thought matching wedding gowns would look best in pictures, but Vanessa and Sienna lobbied for personal self-expression. Almost every time Noelle had seen the twins together, including now, they'd been dressed in matching outfits, so she didn't quite understand the hesitancy, but it was their wedding. They could pick out whatever dresses they wanted as long as it didn't exceed The Tie's budget.

This was not a hill she was willing to die on.

At the bridal shop, the perky consultant, Becky, met them at the door with mimosas and everything went downhill from there.

Noelle refrained from drinking—she was on the job after all—but Vanessa and her daughters were up for free drinks and after the third round of mimosas, things started getting dicey.

"I understand that you're in love with chiffon," Noelle said as Sierra twirled in a summery frock. The dress was at the top end of their budget, and she still needed to find some wriggle room for the addition of the groom's cake. "But it's sleeveless."

"I have great arms." Sierra flexed her biceps. Indeed, she was buff.

"Keep in mind, this is December. You'll freeze at the reception unless you wear a jacket. The ceilings in the music hall are just too tall to keep the temperature above seventy degrees."

"A jacket would look really clunky," Vanessa said.

"And it's an added expense and this dress maxes out your budget as it is."

"I'm warm natured." Sierra smiled sloppily. "It'll be fine. Besides, we'll be dancing all night long."

"I do love the chiffon. I want it too," Sienna said.

Finally, the twins were on the same page. Noelle breathed a little easier even as Sierra stumbled in her twirl and almost crashed into a rack of dresses. The sharp-eyed consultant rolled the rack out of harm's way.

"Oopsie." Sierra giggled.

"That *is* a gorgeous dress," Sienna said. "I think I do want us to dress alike. Noelle made some salient points about how much more cohesive we'll look in photographs."

"I'm sorry," Becky said. "We only have the one dress in that style."

"The wedding isn't until Christmas Eve. How long will it take for another dress to get here from your supplier?" Noelle asked. Even with the holidays figured into the mix, shipping shouldn't take a month.

"You don't understand. It's a discontinued dress. We can't reorder." Becky looked apologetic.

"Could you check and see if any of the other stores have it in stock?" Noelle asked.

"I can do that." Becky bebopped over to her computer to check inventory at sister stores.

Secretly, Noelle was glad there wasn't another dress to match. Otherwise, she'd have to find a place in the budget for wedding jackets. Despite Sierra's assertions that she'd be fine, Noelle had checked the average Christmas Eve temperature for North Texas, and it was a high of fifty-seven and a low of thirty-seven degrees. If they wore the sleeveless chiffon, they'd have to wear some kind of coverup, no way around it.

"There's a size zero at the South Lake store," Becky said, eyeing the size-six twins. "And there's absolutely nothing else at any of our other locations."

"We're already dieting," Sienna said. "I could try to get to a zero."

"In four weeks?" Vanessa shook her head. "That's just not healthy."

"Besides," Sierra said. "I don't want to be the fat one!"

"Why don't you look at other dresses?" Noelle asked. "Taffeta is great for winter. You'll rustle as you go down the aisle and everyone will hear you coming."

"Eew!" Sierra and Sienna said in unison.

"Scratch taffeta. How do you feel about satin?"

"Too slippery," Sienna said. "I don't want Cody to slide off me."

Noelle didn't bother to ask for edification on that topic.

"How about brocade?" Becky brought over a gorgeous brocade gown.

Sierra stuck out her tongue. "It looks old lady."

"It's our wedding," Sienna said. "We wanna look hot."

"How about crepe?" Noelle said. "It drapes more like chiffon but it's warmer."

"Ooh," Becky said. "We just got in some designer gowns in crepe. Let me go get them."

"Finding the perfect wedding dress is a process," Noelle reassured the brides. "If we can't find something here, we'll drive to Dallas. You will have the dresses of your dreams. I promise."

Becky returned with the crepe dresses and the

twins were at least willing to try them on. Noelle crossed her fingers and held her breath. She and Vanessa sat on the settee and waited for the twins to reappear.

"They're very nervous," Vanessa said, polishing off her third mimosa.

"That's to be expected."

"Not just about the dresses."

Noelle glanced over at the older woman. "What about? Maybe I can help alleviate their concerns."

Vanessa winced. "You can't."

"Give me a chance."

Vanessa hissed through clenched teeth. "See, *you're* the thing they're nervous about."

"What?" Noelle blinked, blindsided. "Me? Why?"

"They can't get past the fact that you don't believe in love." Vanessa bit her bottom lip, leaving crimson lipstick stains on her overly whitened teeth.

For heaven's sakes. She thought they'd put that behind them. What a gaffe she'd made. "Vanessa, I—"

"Mom!" Wearing the crepe wedding dress, Sienna rushed over to where Noelle and Vanessa were sitting.

"Oh honey, the dress is gorgeous. I think you've found the one." Vanessa stood up.

"No, no, listen to me." Sienna wrung her hands. "It's Sierra. She's locked herself in the bathroom and won't come out."

Vanessa jumped up and ran for the bathroom. Noelle followed.

"What's happened?" Noelle asked Sienna.

Sienna stared at her as if Noelle were a fly she found swimming in her soup. "*You*," she said. "You're what's happened."

"Me?" Perplexed, Noelle pressed a hand to her chest. Vanessa stood on the other side of the bathroom door and met Noelle's gaze. "What did I do? If I did something wrong, then I can fix it."

"No you can't!" Sierra said from inside the bathroom.

Simultaneously, Vanessa and Noelle turned to look at Sienna.

"After we tried on the crepe dresses—they're a big 'no,' BTW, that clingy material shows *every* lump and bump—Sierra spied a gown on the sold rack and just had to try it on. Seriously, I tried to talk her out of it, but . . ." Sienna shrugged. "Here we are."

Oh no, what had Sierra done to the dress? Fear catapulted into Noelle's throat. *One, two, three . . .*

The same thought must have occurred to Becky, who quickly shed her people-pleasing demeanor. "If she's messed the dress up, she's paying for it."

"Sierra, no matter what's wrong, we can make this right." Noelle tapped on the door. "Please let me in."

Sobs came from the other side.

Becky narrowed her eyes, folded her arms, and tightened her glare. "That's a ten-thousand-dollar dress."

The boohooing intensified.

Noelle raised her eyebrows at Becky. "That's not helpful."

"Honey, this is Mom," Vanessa said. "Please come out."

"I—I can't." Sierra blubbered on the other side of the door.

"Why not?" Vanessa asked.

"I'm stuck."

Becky pointed at Noelle. "Ten thousand dollars."

"Message received." Noelle held the consultant's stare. "If the dress is damaged The Tie will pay for it."

"That's not coming out of my girls' wedding budget!" Vanessa folded her arms over her chest and shifted her weight onto her right hip. A mirror image of Becky who was leaning to the left.

"No, no." It would be coming out of Noelle's paycheck. She slowed her exhalation, letting the air out in segments, *eight, seven, six . . .* While it wasn't a huge amount of money to her, it would be a lifesaver to her favorite charity for disadvantaged children. But what bothered Noelle more than the loss of money was the damage to her reputation.

"You're jumping to conclusions. The dress could be just fine," Noelle said. "Let's all take a deep breath and calm down. Nothing to get upset about until we know what's going on."

She turned her back to Becky and Vanessa, leaned her head down and knocked softly on the door. "Sierra, let me in."

"Just you." Sierra whimpered.

"Just me."

"Why doesn't she want me?" Vanessa asked Sienna.

"Boundaries, Mom."

Vanessa scowled but held her tongue.

The bathroom door cracked open, and Sierra's red-rimmed blue eyes peeked out. She waved Noelle inside. "Get in here."

Sierra slammed the door closed.

Locked it.

Noelle slipped past the panicky bride. It was pretty crowded in that small bathroom between Sierra, Noelle, and the poufy ten-thousand-dollar wedding gown the bride-to-be had on.

"What's happened to the dress?" Noelle asked, bracing herself for the worst.

"The zipper is stuck." Sierra turned to reveal her back and the zipper hanging halfway up her dress.

"And?" Noelle stepped closer, careful to avoid treading on the train.

Sierra turned back to face Noelle. "Dylan wants to call off the wedding."

"What? Why?"

Sierra plunked down on the closed toilet lid and burst into tears. "Because of you."

They were back to that. What on earth had she done?

Noelle plucked tissues from the box on the sink, crouched in front of Sierra, being extra-careful where she placed her feet.

A knock sounded at the door.

"What's going on in there?" Vanessa asked.

"That's what I'm trying to find out," Noelle said. "Please give me a minute."

"Sierra, honey, it's going to be okay. Mom loves you."

"What will I do?" Sierra said. "Not only has Dylan broken my heart, but Mom and Sienna will flip out."

"Don't worry about them right now." Noelle put

a hand to Sierra's wrist. "How did I cause a rift between you and Dylan?"

"Dylan says you jinxed us because you don't believe in love."

"There's got to be something more behind it," Noelle said. "What does he mean by jinxed?"

"He says ever since you got to town and started planning the wedding, he can't stop thinking about how every day will be just like the day before. Get up, go to work, eat, sleep, sex, rinse, and repeat."

"And his life isn't like that now?"

"Well . . ." Sierra dabbed at her eyes and blew her nose. "It is, but right now he has the option to walk away, to take off on any adventure he wants at a moment's notice."

Noelle rocked back on her heels, her mind scrambling for some way to make this better. If Dylan truly was having second thoughts, Sierra would be better off giving him his freedom, but if he was just feeling generalized ennui and needed to take time away from wedding prep, should she encourage Sierra to just give Dylan some space to work things out?

"And he's tying his unhappiness to my arrival in town."

"Yes. He says he feels so much pressure from the wedding planning process."

"Dylan needs a good swift kick in the ass," Vanessa called from the corridor.

"Mom! Are you eavesdropping?" Sierra looked exasperated. "Get away from the door!"

"Fine." Vanessa heaved an exaggerated sigh.

"I don't hear footsteps walking away," Sierra called.

Stomp, stomp, stomp. Vanessa stormed off, leaving no doubts that her feelings were hurt.

"Oh no," Sierra said. "She's pissed."

Since she'd been in Twilight, Noelle had felt a little jealous of the twins and their close relationship with their mother, but she was beginning to see the appeal of Crescenda's hands-off parenting style.

Independence.

"First things first." Noelle rose to her feet. "Let's get you out of that wedding gown and then we can talk about Dylan."

"Okay." Sierra sniffled, got up, and turned around again so Noelle could work on unsticking the zipper.

Noelle dipped her head to get a better look at the jammed-up dress.

"I'm sorry if I'm being difficult," Sierra said.

"No more so than any other bride a month before their wedding." Noelle worked the zipper, sliding back the piece of material the teeth had gotten caught on.

"Really?"

"Really. This is totally normal."

"So this kind of crisis happens with every wedding?"

"Cold feet is very common."

"What percentage of couples break up at this point?"

"Honestly, less than one percent and when they do call it off, it's always for the best."

"I don't want to call off the wedding . . ." Sierra's voice clotted. She was crying again, her shoulders shaking.

"Shh, shh," Noelle said. "It'll work out."

"You don't know that!"

"I do," Noelle said with authority at the same time she gave a sharp yank, freeing the zipper and pulling it all the way down. The gown was just fine.

Just as she did, Noelle's phone dinged. She pulled it from her pocket. A text from The Tie representative, Pamela Landry.

Call me. Now!

"I'm going to let you get dressed," Noelle said. "Come out when you're ready and we'll talk about Dylan."

"Thank you."

Noelle eased around Sierra, and stepped out into the corridor, steeling herself. The hall was empty, thank heavens. She wouldn't have Vanessa, Becky, and Sienna breathing down her neck when she called Pamela.

Hitting the contact number for Pamela Landry, Noelle brought the phone to her right ear and plugged her left ear to block out the murmur of anxious conversation seeping in from the bridal showroom.

"Hello, Pamela?"

"What in the devil is going on in Texas?" Pamela asked.

"What do you mean?"

"I just got a frantic phone call from the Buckhorn twins' mother. Vanessa says you're a jinx."

Noelle closed her eyes and let the air slowly leak from her lungs. Good grief. "Vanessa is a little reactive. We had an issue, but I'm working to resolve it. I—"

"We've sunk a hundred grand into this wedding, Noelle. It needs to go off without a hitch."

"One of the grooms has cold feet and his bride locked herself in the bathroom. Clichéd, I know, but—"

"No excuses. We can break you as easy as we can make you. We took a chance on an upstart because of who your mother is. If you let us down . . ."

"Is that a threat, Pamela?"

"It's a promise, Curry. You're the Wedding Whisperer, for heaven's sake. Get in there and whisper that bride into wedded bliss or else!"

CHAPTER 20

Gil walked through the back door of the B&B without knocking. He never knocked. The Merry Cherub was his home. He'd gone inside to tell Gretchen what had happened at school with Josie and Silvey and to get a feminine take on things.

What he hadn't expected to find was his sister lip-locked with Ebby's father.

At the sound of the back door snapping shut behind him, Gretchen and Tyler jumped apart.

"Whoa." Gil put up both palms to block his vision and stepped back. "S-sorry."

Gretchen smoothed down her clothes and patted her hair into place. "Um . . . um."

"I'm gonna go." Tyler spun on his heels and headed for the front door, hollering over his shoulder as he went, "I'll call you later."

"What's going on?" Gil asked his sister.

"What do you think?"

"You and Ebby's dad?"

She gave him a coy smile. "Uh-huh."

"What about that cutter in Jubilee you were dating?"

Gretchen's smile deepened. "Tyler *is* the cutter."

Stunned, Gil pulled out a chair from the kitchen table and plunked down. "Why didn't you say something before?"

"Ebby's still reeling over her parents' divorce. Tyler and I are taking things slow. We didn't want to complicate things for her."

It sounded like his own conflict. "Wow."

Gretchen sat down across from him. She bit her bottom lip and looked uncertain. "Be happy for me."

"I am. I'm just caught off guard. Was this a covert way of inviting Tyler and Ebby to Thanksgiving dinner?"

"Do you really think I'm that manipulative?" Gretchen looked hurt. "I just told Tyler about the craft event. I didn't know he was taking Ebby for sure. And I surely didn't know you and Noelle would befriend her and ask Ebby and her dad to dinner."

"So it was just a lucky coincidence."

"You don't know how surprised I was when you walked through the door with them." Gretchen grinned. "And thrilled. I got to spend Thanksgiving with my boo and his girl. Isn't it awesome that Ebby and Josie get along?"

"Pretty cool."

"Please don't say anything to anyone about Tyler and me. Ebby doesn't know about us yet. We thought it was best to wait to tell her until we know for sure we're gonna last."

Gil's mind immediately went to Noelle and how his relationship with her had affected Josie. "Believe me, I get that."

"Are you and Noelle having issues?"

"It's . . . not easy." Knowing his story might help her navigate her relationship with Tyler and his daughter, Gil told her about what had happened between him and Noelle.

"That's tough," Gretchen said. "Thank you for sharing. I won't repeat it."

"I know you won't." He smiled at his sister. "I really am happy for you."

"Thanks. I hope you and Noelle can work things out."

Gil shook his head. "I'm not holding my breath. As you're finding out, things are complicated when you have kids."

"So complicated." Gretchen got a faraway look in her eyes as if she was deep in thought, then blinked and met his gaze. "But love is worth the risk, don't you think?"

Gil spread his hands. "I don't know."

"Don't give up on Noelle because things are difficult," Gretchen said. "You two are good together. It's been a long time since I've seen you so engaged with life. Other people have noticed too."

"Really? Who?"

"Derrick, Delphine, Josie."

"Josie?"

"She told me you smile more since Noelle moved in."

"That kid of mine . . ." He grinned. "She's pretty perceptive."

"Very. She keeps you on your toes."

"Keep that in mind with Ebby. She could be picking up on more than you know."

"Point taken. No more indiscriminate kissing in the kitchen."

"Hey, I just thought of something. If you and Tyler end up getting married, Josie and Ebby will be cousins by marriage."

"Oh, that would be fun."

"They'd both love that."

"Let's not get ahead of ourselves," Gretchen said. "While Tyler is a great guy, he's got a lot of healing to do."

"Don't we all?" Gil asked, thinking of Noelle.

Blackballed.

Her worst fear. Pamela Landry had threatened to blackball her from The Tie—the biggest clearing house for wedding planners—if she didn't fix this. She had to make this right or she'd be stuck planning weddings for Crescenda's friends and acquaintances for the rest of her life and her dreams of independence from her parents' sphere of influence would be over.

Hauling in a deep breath, Noelle powered down her phone, stuck it in her pocket, and went to do what she did best.

People please.

Squaring her shoulders, she walked back to the showroom. Becky was busy steaming wrinkles out of the dress that Sierra had tried on. Vanessa was into her fourth mimosa. Noelle would have to drive them back to Twilight. Sierra was on the settee sobbing, Sienna on her knees in front of her twin, patting her hand and passing her tissues after she discarded another onto the big pile at her feet.

First, to deal with Becky.

Noelle walked over. "Is the dress okay?"

Becky gave her a thumbs-up.

"Thank you for your patience during this stressful time," Noelle said. "You've been invaluable."

Becky looked surprised that she'd been complimented, gave a quick smile and a friendly nod.

The easy part was done. Now to tackle the bull by the horns. Noelle pushed up the sleeves of her faux leather jacket and moved to where Vanessa sat in a chair looking disgruntled.

"Thank you for calling The Tie's attention to my gaffe," she said without a tinge of sarcasm.

Vanessa tensed, got a haughty look on her face, and the vein at her temple pulsed visibly. "You—"

Noelle held up a stop sign palm. She wouldn't allow the woman to go off on her. There was already so much tension in the showroom, a couple of other customers, leafing through the dresses, shied away from them and shot their group worried looks.

"I was blind to my own faults, and I made some mistakes with your daughters. That's totally on me. Thank you for holding me accountable."

Vanessa looked totally taken aback. Her jaw dropped and her narrowed eyes popped round. "I . . . er . . . you're welcome?"

"If you could give me your car keys so I can

drive us back to Twilight and you can enjoy all the mimosas you want."

Without another word, Vanessa surrendered her keys.

"Thank you." Noelle pocketed them. Two down, two to go. The solution here wouldn't be so easy as ingratiating herself.

She took the empty spot on the settee beside Sierra, who was still sobbing so hard her shoulders shook. She waited until the young woman's crying jag slowed and then she said, "I'm sorry this has happened."

"I texted Cody," Sienna said. "And told him our engagement is off too."

"What?" Ah crap. Noelle shifted her gaze to the twin on the floor.

"How can I marry Cody when his brother has treated my twin so shabbily?"

Noelle bit back a sigh. Pamela Landry would not be happy. People had warned her the Buckhorns were not easy to deal with, but she'd had a lifetime of Crescenda and her ilk. She was accustomed to impulsive, passionate people who were prone to overreacting. She could and would find a way to fix this.

The best antidote for drama was a calm demeanor and open curiosity. It didn't matter what she thought or how she would personally handle a situation. Perception was everything and the Buckhorns perceived her as a threat to their happiness. It might not be rational to her mind, but it was in theirs.

Hauling in a deep breath, Noelle counted down her anxiety from *eight, seven, six, five . . .*

The door to the bridal shop flew open with a loud *bang*. Everyone in the showroom jumped.

The Maxwell twins barged in, Cody leading the way. He made a beeline for Sienna. Head down, avoiding Sierra's gaze, his twin brother hung back.

Sienna leaped to her feet. "Cody! What are you doing here? You're supposed to be at work."

"How can I work when my life is falling apart?" He shook his cell phone at her. "What was this text all about?"

"You didn't have to come all the way to Fort Worth. You didn't have to leave work." Sienna pressed a hand to her heart.

"My marriage is at stake. You expect me to sit back and do nothing? I'm here to fight for you," Cody said. "For us."

"We're not married," Sienna said.

"No, but we're gonna be." Cody stepped closer to the settee, his full attention on his bride-to-be. "I don't care what's going on with Dylan and Sierra. This is about you and me. We started going out before they did. I asked you to marry me first. Just because we're twins doesn't mean Dylan and I are joined at the hip. I'm separate from my brother, and you're separate from Sierra."

Yay, Cody. Noelle stayed silent. She'd learned if you gave things time and space they would often work themselves out on their own.

"Do you love me, Sienna?" Cody asked.

"More than anything in the world."

"More than your allegiance to your twin sister?"

Tears shining in her eyes, Sienna nodded.

"C'mere." Cody opened his arms.

Sienna flew into his embrace.

He kissed his bride-to-be passionately, right there in the bridal shop showroom. The other customers and Becky gawked. Someone murmured, "Aww."

Noelle shifted her gaze to Sierra, who'd stopped crying and was peering red-eyed at Dylan. The other Maxwell twin had his hands jammed into his pockets and was intently studying his cowboy boots.

Sierra stood up. "Dylan."

Cody and Sienna separated, but Cody kept his arm around Sienna's waist. As a unit, they turned to stare at Dylan.

In fact, everyone was staring at Dylan.

"Could you please look at me?" Sierra asked.

Slowly, Dylan raised his head and met Sierra's weepy gaze.

"Why did you come here?" she asked.

"Cody made me." He stared down at the floor again.

"Oh." Sierra's bottom lip trembled. "I thought you came for me."

"I told him he needed to man up and tell you in person that he wants out." Cody scowled at his twin. "You don't break an engagement over a text."

Sienna gasped, winced, and brought her fingers to her lips. "I guess I did that to you, didn't I?"

"You did," Cody said. "But I forgive you because I know you didn't mean it. You were just taking up for your sister."

"Did you mean it, Dylan, when you told me you didn't want to marry me?" Sierra asked and moved closer to him. "Are you telling me you don't love me anymore?"

"I love you," Dylan mumbled.

"Then why are you calling off our wedding?"

"Too much pressure." Dylan hunched his shoulders.

"In the text you said it was because you were scared that marriage would get routine and boring. Why would you think that?"

"I dunno." Dylan shrugged.

"Tell her the truth, man," Cody said. "Tell her the real reason why you spooked."

Dylan's head popped up and his dark-eyed gaze drilled straight into Noelle as he pointed a finger. "Because of *her*."

Good grief. Noelle kept her expression as neutral as she could. Why was she such a boogeyman to these people?

"Did you know her mother has been married and divorced five times?" Dylan said. "And it's three times for her dad. It's true. I looked her up on the internet."

"My parents' track record with marriage has nothing to do with me," Noelle said. "And even less to do with you." While that was completely true, Noelle knew she couldn't erase superstition with logic.

"Face it," Dylan said to Sierra. "She's jinxed and she's planning our wedding. What if, because of her, you and me don't last?"

Yeah, blame the wedding planner. How would

she fight this? How could she convince Dylan she was not a jinx? How could she please both Pamela Landry and the couples in front of her and salvage her career? Frantically, Noelle's mind leafed through the viable solutions, but came up empty.

"You told me Noelle doesn't even believe in love. That's at the root of the problem. What kind of person doesn't believe in love and yet becomes a wedding planner? Something's off." Dylan glowered at Noelle. "I don't trust her."

Everyone was staring at her now, waiting to see how Noelle would defend herself.

What? Did the guy think she went around intentionally sabotaging weddings for kicks? His mindset made no sense to her.

Quick, think of something. She had to dig her way out of this, or her career was on the rocks.

"What if we got a new wedding planner?" Sierra asked.

"Marriage is a huge risk." Dylan plowed his fingers through his hair. It was clear to Noelle he was using her as an excuse for his own cold feet and just couldn't admit it to Sierra. "Love is a gamble. Who says we're gonna last?"

"Me," Sierra said. "I do. I say we'll last."

"But how can we last when a jinx is involved?" Dylan glared at Noelle again as if she possessed some magical marriage-busting powers and was gleefully using them against him and Sierra.

"Oh," Noelle said, grasping at straws, searching for any reasonable way to fight back against Dylan's nonsense. "Wait, where did you get the idea that I don't believe in love?"

"That's what you told us at the Windmill the first day you arrived," Sierra said.

"No, that's what I told *Gil*. You just overheard it." Noelle had no idea where she was going with this as her mind scrambled for anything that would get these two back on the same page.

"Are you saying you *do* believe in love?" Looking hopeful, Sierra brought her hands to her heart.

Noelle had snagged their attention. Great. Now what? "Absolutely, I believe in love."

"Then why did you tell Gil that you didn't?" Vanessa asked.

Noelle didn't want to lie. She wasn't a liar. Unless you considered how she'd been lying to herself all these years. Fine. She wouldn't lie. *One, two, three* . . . Noelle gulped and told them the truest thing she knew.

"Because I've been in love with Gil Thomas since I was thirteen years old."

"So you lied to him and said you didn't believe in love because you're in love with him?" Vanessa asked, eyes narrowing. The woman had a suspicious nature. "That doesn't make any sense."

"It was silly. It was foolish. It was irresponsible, and I never should have said it when there was a chance a client could overhear me."

"That's true," Vanessa said. "But *why* did you say it?"

In for a penny, in for a pound. She had to get this double wedding back on track, or her career was a dumpster fire. Blowing this gig with The Tie would forever stain her reputation and limit her future options.

Noelle kept talking, watching their faces. "I wanted Gil to fall in love with me and I was terrified if he knew I loved him my desperation would chase him off. I had no choice but to play it cool and pretend I didn't care. I mean it is weird, right? I've been carrying a torch all this time for a guy who'd barely even noticed me."

"So why didn't you just tell us the truth after Gil went to pick up his daughter that day at the Windmill?" Vanessa asked. "Why not set the record straight right then and there?"

"I didn't know you guys well enough, and I didn't trust the Twilight grapevine. I didn't want the truth getting back to him," Noelle said, making up an explanation on the fly and praying it would work.

"I think it's romantic." Becky, the bridal consultant, sighed.

"Really?" Sienna said. "You're not just saying that to convince us?"

"Really." Noelle nodded.

"You were just playing it cool with Gil, when you actually believed in true love all along?" Sierra asked.

"I was." Noelle grinned. "And it worked too. Gil and I have been seeing each other."

"That's wonderful," Vanessa said. "I'm so happy for you. Gil is a great guy."

"Thanks." She felt like she needed a shower after compromising herself, but she'd done what she had to do to save her job.

"Could there be a wedding in the wedding planner's future?" Becky giggled. "I love it!"

"You hear that, honey?" Sierra beamed at Dylan. "Noelle *does* believe in love. She's not a jinx. Our marriage isn't doomed because she's the one planning our wedding. It's gonna be okay."

Dylan gave Noelle the side-eye. "But how *do* we know she's not just saying that now to keep her job?"

"That's easy enough to find out," Cody said. "We'll just ask Gil the next time we see him."

"I'll text him right now." Dylan pulled out his cell phone.

Ah crap. From the frying pan into the fire.

"Dylan," Noelle said sharply, trying to derail the young man from texting Gil until she'd had a chance to talk to him. "Now that you don't have me to blame, you need to face your own fears. What is it that *you're* so darn scared of?"

Looking cowed, Dylan stuck his phone back in his pocket. "I'm scared it's not going to work out."

"Let's talk this through," Noelle encouraged. "Why do you fear your marriage might fail when you and Sierra are so much in love?"

Dylan swallowed hard, his Adam's apple bobbing. "My uncle Ted is wrecked since his wife ran off with her personal trainer last month and left him to raise Silvey on his own. I've never seen Uncle Ted so out of control. Last night, he was literally sobbing on our mom's shoulder. He's normally so self-confident. I mean if Uncle Ted and Aunt Yvonne can't make it, who can?"

"You're related to Silvey Zucker?" Noelle raised

an eyebrow. Twilight was so darn small. Everyone seemed related to everyone else, by marriage if not by blood.

"Uncle Ted is our mother's younger brother," Dylan said. "I admired him so much. To see him devastated is a punch in the gut. He had everything and now it's all gone."

"I'm scared too, baby," Sierra said, taking Dylan's hand. "Nothing is guaranteed. But I'm not like your aunt Yvonne. I'd never run off and leave you. For one thing, Sienna would kick my ass if the thought even crossed my mind."

"I would do it too." Sienna nodded.

Everyone laughed, but Sierra only had eyes for her groom. "I believe in family. I believe in love. And I believe in *you*, Dilly Bar. There's no reason to be afraid. Sienna and Cody have our backs. Our parents do too. We're as close as you can get to a sure thing. Can you take a chance on us? Because I believe love is worth the risk."

Dylan gazed into Sierra's eyes. His shoulders sagged and he looked relieved. The guy had had a crisis of faith. All he'd been looking for was some reassurance that his life would turn out okay.

"It's okay to have doubts," Noelle said. "Perfectly normal. In fact, good on you for being able to express those doubts rather than tamp them down and hide from your emotions."

"Seriously?" Dylan asked.

"Seriously," said everyone in the room in unison.

Dylan took Sierra's hand. "I'm so sorry, Pookie-Bear. I was a jerk. I got scared. I thought Noelle was the problem, but I can see now I was using her as an excuse. Can you forgive me?"

"Yes!" Sierra flung herself into Dylan's arms and he covered her face in kisses.

"Well," Vanessa said. "I guess we're back to finding the perfect wedding dresses. Becky, bring me another mimosa."

CHAPTER 21

"You gotta help me." Noelle burst into Gil's office at the Windmill looking as if she'd had a near-death experience.

Her normally smooth hair had frizzed in the rain, giving her a mass of bushy curls just as it had when she was fifteen. Her skin was paler than usual, and her eyes were huge. She panted, her chest rapidly rising and falling.

He pushed off from the beanbag chair, having kept it for his seat, hoping against hope she'd come use the office. His comfy office chair was waiting for her if she ever gave it a chance.

"What is it? What's wrong?"

"I'm in big trouble." She pulled up her bottom lip between her teeth, interlaced her fingers, and brought her hands to her heart.

"How can I help?" he asked without a second's hesitation. Noelle needed help. He was there for her. End of story.

"I know it's a whole lot to ask—"

"Say the word. Anything."

"I need you to lie for me."

That pulled him up short. He stepped back, only then realizing he'd drawn so close to her. "Lie?"

"Forget I asked." She wrung her hands. "I shouldn't have asked. You're an honorable guy. You don't lie."

"Lie about what?"

Her gaze landed on his mouth and then slowly tracked up to meet his eyes. "Dating me."

"Wait. What? Whoa." He held up both hands.

She shrank back and he realized his gesture made her feel embarrassed. The last thing he wanted was to shame her.

"I'm sorry." She looked so flustered. Nothing like the confident woman who'd walked into his office that first day with the Buckhorns. "I have no right to ask you to lie for me."

"No," he said, aching for her. More than anything in the world he wanted to pull her into his arms and kiss her until they both forgot their names. "I wouldn't lie for you."

"I understand." She knotted her hand and settled her fist against her stomach. Her shoulders slumped and she turned away.

She looked so sad. So sunk that he blurted, "I won't lie, Noelle, because it's true. I want to date you. Not just for sex, but to see if you and I . . ." He paused. "If there's a real chance for us."

"Wh-what?"

"I like you. A whole lot. And I think you feel the same way about me."

Her soft brown eyes grew even wider. "Y-you do?"

"Yeah," he murmured and covered the space between them until they were mere inches apart.

She stood before him, trembling. Hell, he was trembling too.

"But you said . . . after that mess at the Christmas tree farm with Silvey . . . what about Josie?"

"I'm at war with myself, Noelle. I want to be a good dad, but also I want to be with you too. I don't know the right thing to do. I'm making this up as I go along. I'm floundering."

"Thank you for your honesty."

"But when it comes to Josie . . . I'm not ready to let her know." He paused, thinking about Gretchen and Tyler and how they were keeping their relationship quiet until they were certain they stood a real chance of working out.

"I understand," Noelle said. "You want to keep Josie out of this until you and I can figure out what's going on between us."

"Yeah."

"You're scared of getting hurt."

"Hell, yeah."

"So am I. These feelings—"

"Are pretty overwhelming."

"Yep." She moistened her lips, looking as terrified as he felt.

He reached up, fingers splayed, and cupped the back of her head in his palm. His fingers speared through her cascade of curly hair, holding her in place. Gil lowered his head and kissed her. A sweet, gentle kiss that brought a smile to her face and lit up her eyes.

"What's happening?" she whispered, placing her

palm flat against his chest and gazing up into his face.

"I'm kissing you."

"No, I mean between us." .

"I don't know. Can we just be in the moment?"

"I—" The pulse at her throat fluttered wildly. He couldn't wait to plant a kiss there, feel her heat beneath his mouth. "Say yes."

"I want to, but . . . nothing's changed. I'm leaving town in less than a month and there's Josie to consider. We have to be adults about this. There's a lot of risk here."

"So much for no strings attached, huh?"

"I screwed up. I forced your hand. I should have kept my mouth shut. Now that it's out in the open, we have to deal with our feelings."

"And that's a horrible thing?" Gil's stomach was as jittery as if he'd downed a case of energy drinks in one sitting.

Moaning, she dropped her head into her palms, hid her face from him.

Gently, he wrapped both hands around her shoulders and held her until she finally peered up at him. "Why did you want me to lie for you?"

"I got into trouble with the wedding."

"Tell me." He guided her to sit down in the desk chair parked behind the card table desk. Once she was settled, he moved the beanbag chair closer and plopped down in front of her. "I'm all ears."

Bit by bit, she told him what had happened in the bridal store and why she'd been forced into telling the Buckhorns her business. He hated that she'd been put on the spot, but he was glad she'd had to admit she had feelings for him. Glad he could admit the same for her.

"Yeah," he said. "Dylan and Cody are both pretty superstitious. But Dylan more so than Cody. It's part of the reason our band broke up. Dylan had a nightmare about the biggest gig we'd ever book. He considered it a bad omen and dropped out of the event. That caused a lot of problems and the tension between us built. It was also during the time Tammy Jo was battling postpartum depression and I just couldn't handle that kind of stress both at home and on the job. So I pulled the plug on the band."

"Right when you were on the verge of breaking through."

"Who told you that?"

"Gretchen. She says it's too bad you never got a chance to really see what you could do in the music world."

"Breaking up the band was the right decision." As hard as it had been to end the band, he had no regrets about his decision. It had given him precious time with Tammy Jo and their new baby and that's what had mattered most to him.

"It made a difference for Josie. Your daughter is a wonderful kid and I'd do anything to keep her safe and happy. That's why this is so hard. We have to do what's right for her," Noelle said.

He was so grateful that they were making progress, even if he still wasn't sure where they were headed. Gil rested a hand on her knee clad in sexy black leggings. "Why did you really come back to Twilight?"

She blinked. "What do you mean? I'm here to plan the wedding."

"Benji told me you were the final round judge of the essay contest. You could have picked any of the other entries and yet you chose the Buckhorns. Was their essay that much more compelling than the others? Was it simply the identical twins marrying identical twins thing or did you have ulterior motives in selecting them?"

Her gaze met his. "The twin thing was a factor, but you're right. Their essay, while good, wasn't the best of the best."

"So Twilight did sway your decision."

Noelle shrugged. "Maybe. I was nostalgic for the town. I did have a lot of wonderful memories here and I missed my grandparents."

"Then why did you wait to return? Why not just come back for a visit before now?"

She seemed stumped by his question. "I—I don't know."

"I think you do, deep down inside." He moved his hand from her knee and placed it over her chest. He could feel her heart thundering beneath his palm.

"You think I came back because of you?"

"No." He shook his head. "I think you came back to find *you*. I think you've spent too many years living in your mother's shadow, doing what she wanted you to do, trying your best to please her and never quite accomplishing that goal. I think you lost a piece of yourself when your grandparents died, and I don't think you'll ever be able to fully love anyone, Noelle, until you know who *you* really are."

She looked at him as if he'd shot an arrow straight through the bull's-eye of her heart. "I don't know if I ever will know that. Can you accept me if I don't?"

This wasn't about him. He cared about her either way. This was about Noelle and how she put things in tidy little mental boxes, compartmentalizing her life to keep from facing some unpleasant truths. But he couldn't tell her what she needed to mend herself; she had to figure that out on her own.

Gil couldn't take his eyes off Noelle. The woman stole his breath. More than she ever had before. Looking at her set his desire in concrete. He wanted to get close to her. Be with her.

Love her.

There. He'd acknowledged it.

He wanted Noelle. Not in some distant future way. But now. Today. It wasn't reasonable. He knew that, but he couldn't quell his desire.

Her soft pink lips formed into a tender smile, interrupting the rhythm of his heart. She was so gorgeous, and the moment felt over-the-top romantic. His hopes were leading him down a merry path that he was hungry to follow.

Instead of answering, he got up off the beanbag chair, went to the door, locked it, then came back, pulled her into his arms, and kissed her for all he was worth.

Head whirling, Noelle drank him up, hungry for his kiss, his touch, his distinctly Gil scent.

He grappled for the hem of her sweater and tugged upward. She raised her arms like she was in a stickup, and he peeled the sweater over her head, taking the blouse underneath with it and tossing the whole package of clothing over his shoulder.

Dazzling pulses of pleasure throbbed through her body, burning through any resistance as his pliant lips captured her lips again.

He dispatched her bra, unhooking it with one hand, then kissing the straps off her shoulders, first one and then the other. He paused to kiss her nipples, taking his time. Panting, she sagged against him. Next, he bent and pulled off her boots, followed by her leggings and panties, stripping them down in one smooth move, slipping them over her feet until she was standing buck naked in front of him.

Reaching over, he swept everything off his desk, except for his computer, which he pushed as far against the wall as he could. With a low-throated growl, he turned back, picked her up, and settled her on the sturdy desk.

The wood was cold against her bare butt and instant goose bumps sprang up on her legs and arms. She sucked in air through clenched teeth, her entire body aroused in a way it hadn't ever been before. Being naked while he was still dressed made her feel both vulnerable and oddly powerful.

"You are so damn gorgeous," he said, his voice raspy and thick. His pupils darkened; black dots surrounded by sky blue irises soothing as a still mountain lake. "I could look at you forever."

"I hope you'll do far more than that."

He shook his head, his smile deepening as his gaze roved over her. She felt exposed sitting there in front of him, but the reverential way he was looking at her took Noelle's breath away.

She studied his face, his expression of awe. He was losing his heart to her as she was to him. It was scary and complicated, and she had no idea if it would work out or if they would end up shattered.

All she knew was that she'd never felt this way about anyone else. It was so appealing, the way his fiercely proud gaze took her in. He'd told her he had feelings for her. She'd been in love with him since she was thirteen. She'd told herself it was a crush, lust, hormones, chemistry—and of course, that was all part of this, sure, but her feelings ran far deeper for this mature, grown-up Gil.

He made her feel special, feminine, desirable . . . *Loved*.

Was it really true? Was Gil Thomas falling in love with her? The shy little bookworm across the street?

Her heartbeat sped up. She grasped the front of his Western shirt and pulled him to her, then she yanked on the shirt, popping open all the snaps. Well, she was shy no more.

He shrugged off the shirt.

With shaky fingers, she traced the honed muscles of his fine body, the way she'd ached to do that first day when he stripped off his Santa suit for the Polar Plunge.

She reached for the snap on his jeans. He took two condoms from the back pocket of his Wranglers and tossed them on the desk beside her.

"You're prepared," she said. "Cocky."

"No, hopeful." He smiled down at her and pressed his forehead against hers. "I wished we might do this again."

"You told me we shouldn't."

"Yeah, well, I say a lot of stupid things."

"Duly noted." She giggled and pulled his zipper all the way down.

He took over, shucking his pants in one quick movement that removed his boxer briefs along with his jeans.

And then she got a gander at his fully naked body and for a second, her heart stopped beating. She thought she'd never have the joy of seeing him without clothes again and this was her first time seeing in him nude in the full light of day. His striking handsomeness stole all the air from her lungs.

He hooked a finger underneath her chin and tilted her face up, so she had to stop looking at his most impressive parts and stare into those endless eyes.

"How are you doin'?" he asked.

"I'll be doing much better when you stop yacking and start getting busy."

"Yes, ma'am," he said and picked her up without warning.

She let out a whoop, both of joy and surprise. He sat down on the desk where she'd just been, scooted back a bit, and settled her in his lap. Her knees were on either side of his waist, his impressive penis jutting right in front of her.

He leaned back, propping himself up on his elbows, watching her. It felt scandalous being naked in his office during the middle of the day.

Scandalous and hot as hell.

She leaned over his muscular body, found his lips, and kissed him while his erection jumped and pulsed between them. While she kissed him, he reached up to cup one of her breasts in his palm, lightly strumming his thumb over her nipple.

Her body heated, softened, getting ready for him.

He broke their kiss to trail his mouth over her neck, burning hot kisses down her throat to the pulse pounding at the hollow, sucking and nibbling and teasing and driving her right out of her mind.

While his hand, oh his wicked, wicked hand, went exploring right between her quivering thighs.

His index finger gently touched her most sensitive spot, easy and cajoling. Rubbing in just the right way, with just the right amount of pressure with his calloused fingertip. The hands of a musician. He knew just how to play her.

She couldn't wait anymore. She grabbed for a condom on the desk, ripped the package open with her teeth, and then rocked back against his raised thighs, and leaned down to kiss the head of his shaft before rolling on the condom.

"You're a devil." He gasped.

"And don't you forget it." She laughed, delighted over being in control.

His eyes crinkled at the corners and his lips

curved into a smile that hit her hard as a punch. It was such a happy smile. Filled with joy and glee.

She lowered her head, pressed a million open-mouthed kisses over his chest, his nipples, his belly and beyond, inching closer, ever closer to the place where she most wanted to go.

"Noelle," he murmured.

She stared down at him beneath her, breathing hard, hearing the hammering of her heartbeat in her ears. He thrilled her in ways that no one ever had. She made love to him with her mouth, her teeth, her tongue. Her breath stalled in her throat. This moment felt weighted somehow, special.

His shaft was rock hard, growing harder beneath her mouth.

"C'mere," he said, holding his arms out to her. "I want to kiss you again."

Their mouths met, crashed, crushed, caught fire. Stoked and burned. Flaming high and hot. A blister. A blaze.

"Babe, I can't stand it anymore. I gotta have you. Please, ride me," he begged.

How could she turn down such a heartfelt request? She craved his body like water. Slowly, she slid down over his shaft and they sighed in unison as she settled in, taking him to the hilt.

And when she started to move, he called out her name, arching his hips to push more deeply into her.

Just as frantic as he was, she closed her eyes so she could concentrate, rotating her hips, flying up and down, swaying side to side. Unplanned, this wild rhythm. She was simply following where her body, and his cries of pleasure, led.

She was close. So very close. But she wanted to pace herself, to come when he did. She bit the inside of her cheek, trying her best to hang on to control. Her chest felt tight, her body tense and ready for the explosion she knew was coming.

He angled his hips, responding to her change in pace. Giving her so much damn pleasure, meeting her needs as she met his.

And just when she thought she would shatter, Gil stopped moving.

"Noelle."

Opening her eyes, she peered down at him, trying her best to focus. "Wh-what?"

"Nothing," he said. "I just needed to say your name."

"Oh you!" she cried, frustrated that he'd derailed her drive to the finish, and she started back up again.

Out of control, wanting all of him, right there, right now, she ground her hips against his, taking him with her.

He called her name again, this time deep and guttural, raw and needy.

Then she was there, hollering, "Gil, Gil, Gil," as they went over the edge together, tumbling headlong into their dual release.

She collapsed against him, and he folded his arms around her. They lay on the desk, panting and breathless, shivering and shuddering against the power of their joining. This wasn't a casual thing. It was serious and they'd passed the point of no return.

Panic took over her then and she wanted to squirm away, but he held her tight, pressed his mouth against her ear, and whispered, "What happens next?"

CHAPTER 22

How easy it would be to declare herself madly in love with Gil Thomas and shout it to the world.

Unfortunately, life didn't work that way. Not if you were a sensible adult. You couldn't just live for yourself, responsibilities be damned. That had been her parents' way and Noelle's childhood had been a mess because of it.

Actions had consequences.

Gil had a child. Life wasn't so simple that they could just dive headfirst into their feelings. Josie had already suffered enough, losing her mother and grandparents to a tragedy.

Plus, Noelle had a wedding to pull off. Until the job was finished, she didn't have the luxury of telling Gil she was in love with him, even if she had just done her best to show him.

"We need to be careful," Noelle said. "This is new. We don't know where it's going. I think we should keep it quiet for now."

Gil pulled on his jeans. "What about the Buckhorns and the Maxwells? They need to know we're dating."

Noelle made a face. If the two sets of twins hadn't forced her hand, she wouldn't be here in the first place. Wouldn't have learned Gil had feelings for her too. "Well, obviously, they have to know about us."

"If they know, the whole town is gonna know."

That was true.

"Josie is my main concern. If things don't work out between us, she'll be so confused." Noelle wriggled into her leggings.

"You're right." He nodded. "We are in a fix. I just made her apologize to Silvey this morning for telling her you were going to be her new mother."

At the idea of being Josie's mom, wistful longing shot through Noelle, but it was much too soon to be thinking along those lines.

"What are we going to do?" Noelle put on her bra and scooped her blouse and sweater off the floor.

"Play it by ear?" Gil snapped his shirt closed.

"Be cool around Josie."

"But here at the office?"

"As long as we lock the door." Noelle buttoned her blouse and grinned. "All bets are off."

"And when the wedding is over and it's time for you to go back to LA?" Gil worked his feet into his boots.

"Let's take it one day at a time, okay?" She tugged on her sweater and smoothed down her hair.

Now that she was sated and had saved her job,

her old fears of commitment crept back in. They'd gone out on a limb. This was scary stuff.

With each husband, Crescenda had sworn it was true love, that *this* husband was The One she'd been searching for. That they would live happily ever after forever and ever. Then a year or two later, her mother would become dissatisfied or disillusioned with the man, divorce him, and start the process all over again. For her entire life, Noelle had resisted that willy-nilly feeling of falling headlong into love, and now it was upon her. She felt like a damsel tied to the train tracks as a speeding locomotive headed straight toward her.

"Can we do that?" she asked, hearing anxiety lace her voice.

"Yeah, sure. That'll work." Gil didn't seem happy about it.

"What is it?"

Gil shrugged. "I dunno. Feels like you're backpedaling."

"Not backpedaling," she denied. "Just being cautious."

"Stewing," he said.

"What?"

"You're letting your fears get the better of you."

"And you're not afraid?"

"Hell, yes," he said. "But you're worth the risk, Bookworm."

The way he was looking at her, eyes shining with admiration and respect, sent chills shivering up her arms. Was true and lasting love within her reach?

Gil pulled her to his chest and kissed her, long and sweet and passionate. "What we just did together was special. With you, I feel whole again."

"Oh, Gil."

"I know you're scared. I'm scared too, but love *is* worth the risk, and I want to risk everything with you."

Three joyous weeks passed. Twenty-one spectacular days spent at the Windmill with Gil as they worked side by side in his cozy little office, and twenty-one sizzling nights when he would creep upstairs to Noelle's apartment while Josie slept below. They'd make wild, passionate love and then he'd slip back downstairs, his daughter none the wiser that he'd been gone.

Noelle had asked the Buckhorns and Maxwells to keep quiet about her romance with Gil and once they'd confirmed with him that they were indeed an item—the superstitious buggers—they seemed to have lived up to their word. Neither Noelle nor Gil had been approached by anyone asking about their relationship status.

It turned out, sneaking around was *hot*.

The only downside was that she was left with an empty bed, but even though she didn't want to admit it, she liked a little distance. That sweet, solitary time to herself quelled her fears of being overwhelmed by her feelings.

After the meltdown at the bridal store, everything with the wedding got back on track and things had been glitch-free ever since. Pamela Landry had praised Noelle for calming the Buckhorns and Maxwells and apologized for being so harsh with her over the phone. All was well.

On December 18, one week before Christmas and six days before the Christmas Eve wedding, as Noelle lay in Gil's arms after a rousing round of enthusiastic sex, he gathered her close, kissed her temple, and held her for a long time. Neither one of them spoke about what would happen after the wedding. They'd figure it out when the time came. For now, they were simply enjoying each other's company.

"Your work is really gearing up with the wedding so close."

"Mmm-hm," she murmured, tracing her fingers in the whorl of dark hair at his chest.

"Not much spare time."

"Sadly, no."

"Too busy to carve out a couple of hours on Friday night?"

"I'm sorry, but that's the night of the bachelorette and bachelor parties. It's also the day Pamela Landry and the videographer arrive. I need to be on hand in case something goes awry."

"Oh." He sounded disappointed.

She found his hand in the darkness and interlaced their fingers. "The parties don't start until nine. Is this something we can do earlier in the evening? Maybe I could spare an hour."

"Yes, that's perfect timing. Our time slot is from six to seven."

"Time slot for what?"

"I won the lottery," Gil said.

"Pardon?"

"Oh, not the Powerball or anything." He laughed. "I won the living snow globe lottery. It was Josie's main Christmas wish . . . well, besides a mommy for Christmas and she knows *that's* not happening."

"Um . . . okay."

"I should explain."

"Good idea. Dare I ask what's a living snow globe?"

"It's a portable ice rink. They install it on the courthouse lawn every year four days before Christmas. Over the rink they mount a transparent plastic dome."

"To help keep the ice from melting?" They didn't have an ice rink when she visited her grandparents, but that was thirteen years ago.

"That's how it started, but it looked so much like a snow globe that the creatives in this town drew inspiration and now they've turned it into a whole snow globe winter wonderland."

"Trust Twilight to come up with something no one else has thought of." Noelle chuckled. She loved her adopted hometown.

"They install blowers that shoot out fake snow and swirl it around, so it looks like you're skating inside a snow globe. Everyone really gets into it."

Of that, she had no doubt.

"There's always a theme. This year, it's Teddy Bears on Ice. Professional skaters dress up as teddy bear mascots and there's a snow globe cam, so people from around the world can watch it live online."

"That sounds impressive," she said. "And expensive."

"It's worth it. Next to the Dickens Festival, the

living snow globe is the town's biggest money-maker of the season."

"That sounds adorable. I can't wait to see it. What's the lottery part?"

"Folks are able to join the professional skaters on the ice if they dress thematically, but because of limited space, you have to enter the lottery and hope you get picked and can make it during the time slot you're given. It's supercompetitive."

"Wow and you won tickets! That's wonderful. Josie's going to love it so much."

"I've got three tickets for Friday evening. I entered it for me, Josie, and Gretchen, but Gretchen has her annual cookie club party that night and she can't make it. I was hoping you could go instead."

"Josie didn't want to ask Ebby?"

"No, she specifically asked me to invite you."

"Really?"

"Really."

"Do you think it's okay for us to go out in public together?"

"It's at Josie's request."

Her heart tripped. "I would love to come."

He rewarded her with a kiss. "That's great. You're gonna love it."

Now all she had to do was work out how to slip away from the wedding prep for an hour on Friday evening before the bachelor and bachelorette parties. It would be touch and go, but she'd do what she could to pull it off.

On Thursday night, when Gil slipped up to her apartment after he put Josie to bed, the baby monitor he used to keep tabs on his daughter while he was upstairs with Noelle tucked into his back pocket, he was carrying a shopping bag.

"I got you something."

"Oh?" Noelle asked, greeting him at the door in a terry cloth robe with nothing on underneath. "What is it?"

Gil handed her the bag. "For tomorrow night when we go skating."

Noelle opened it to find a green sweater with a red teddy bear quilted on the front, along with embroidered red lettering that said, I ♥ YOU BEARY MUCH. Her heart caught. Was Gil professing his love? Or was it just a shirt?

She looked up at him.

He grinned. "Do you like it?"

"Aww! Gil, I love it! Thank you. How fitting." She'd been wondering how she was going to dress for the teddy bear–themed skating event.

"Not too corny?" He looked anxious.

"It fits the theme, and it goes perfectly with the outfit I have planned."

"That's why I got it. They were selling them at a kiosk outside the ice rink."

"I need to thank you properly for your gift," she said, opened her robe, and let it drop to the floor.

In ten seconds flat, Gil scooped her into his arms, carried her to the bedroom, and they spent the next hour having a jolly good time.

They made plans to meet at the snow globe at six on Friday evening. The late afternoon arrival of Pamela Landry and the videographer delayed Noelle.

She gave them the rundown on the upcoming wedding activities, got them ensconced in their rooms at the Merry Cherub, recommended a few places where they could go for dinner, and then hurried to the Roost to get ready for her skate date.

After she was dressed, barely able to contain her excitement, she rushed from the Merry Cherub to the courthouse lawn. Shoppers, tourists, and locals headed home from work packed the town square. By the time she reached the snow globe ice rink the courthouse clock was striking six.

Tonight, by going out in public, she and Gil were practically announcing to the world at large that they were a couple.

She spied Gil's smiling face standing out among the throng. He wore a baseball cap with Yogi Bear on it and a Yogi Bear sweatshirt. He spotted her, raising his hand to wave at her. Giddy, she rushed over, skipping around people as if she were Josie's age.

"Hi!" she greeted them.

"Noelle!" Josie wrapped her arms around Noelle's waist and hugged her tight. "You came!"

"Of course I did." Noelle hugged her right back. She smiled so hard her cheeks hurt and when Gil put his hand to her lower back to guide her into the ice rink, she breathed in his woodsy scent. She'd never forget the way he smelled tonight.

A refreshing blast of frigid air greeted guests as fake snowflakes whirled around them inside the ice rink. Noelle thought about the night real snowflakes had fallen in Twilight. The night Gil had first kissed her.

The professional skaters in teddy bear costumes

weaved in and out among the other skaters who, for the most part, like Noelle, wore teddy bear sweaters, or teddy bear print shirts or teddy bear baseball caps. All manner of bears were represented, from polar bears to grizzlies to koalas.

It was bear-a-palooza.

"Yay!" While watching the skaters on the ice, Josie twirled, the flared pink skating skirt she wore over white leggings whirling around her. She looked adorable in a fluffy pink teddy bear–themed sweater and a headband with bear ears on it. "Isn't this fun, Daddy?

"So glad you're happy, baby girl."

"I'm not a baby!"

"You're right. You're not. Let's go rent our skates." Gil smiled after his daughter as she skipped ahead of them and he slipped his hand around Noelle's waist.

"Size five and a half, right?" Gil said as he ordered their skates.

"You remembered."

"I remember everything about you, Bookworm."

Once Josie had her skates on, she took off without them, hollering, "See ya, wouldn't wanna be ya."

"That kid." Gil chuckled.

"She's spunky. You've got your hands full with that one."

"Tell me about it."

"Ma'am?" A girl about Josie's age hovered nearby with her parents. She was clutching a notebook and pencil in her hand.

"Yes?" Noelle said brightly.

"Can I have your autograph?" the little girl asked.

"Why would you want my autograph?"

"'Cause you're making that beautiful wedding."

"Where did you hear that?"

The girl grinned. "Josie and I are in the same class and you're all she can talk about."

"Certainly." Noelle smiled at the girl. It was the first time anyone had asked for her autograph. People had asked if she could get her parents' autograph for them hundreds of times, but no one had ever wanted hers.

She wasn't going to lie. It was a satisfying feeling.

After the little girl broke the ice, others started coming over. Some for autographs, others to ask about the wedding and her parents.

Gil tolerated it for a few minutes, but then he stepped in. "Folks, Noelle came to skate—I'm sure you can appreciate that. You can approach her later."

The crowd that had started forming around her dispersed.

"Thanks," she told Gil. "I didn't know how I was going to get out of that."

"You need a bodyguard."

Oh heavens, that sounded horrible.

The two of them went out onto the ice together but didn't hold hands because of Josie, even though Noelle wanted to hold Gil's hand more than anything. She had self-control. She could keep her hands to herself. They were taking things slow.

She and Gil skated underneath the live-streaming camera installed by the town, and just as she zoomed past the lens, the blowers blasted a fresh round of foam snowflakes into the air.

The crowd let out a collective sigh as the snow-flakes danced and swirled along with the skaters. From the speakers came "Waltz of the Snowflakes." Noelle had to admit the effect was impressive. She wondered what it looked like to the folks watching on the live feed.

Josie skated up to them, her little face aglow. "Noelle, isn't this awesome?"

"Is this your first time skating inside the snow globe?" Noelle asked her.

"Yes," Josie said, "and I love it."

"Me too."

"It *is* special," Gil said, his eyes drilling into hers.

Noelle giggled as the faux snowflakes settled over her. She ran a hand through her hair to dislodge a clump of them.

"You look like a fairy snow princess," Josie said.

"So do you."

Grinning, Josie twirled.

"You're really good," Noelle said. "Where did you learn how to ice-skate?"

"Grandmaw taught me." Josie curtsied.

"Mom takes her to the rink in Fort Worth every Christmas when she and Dad come to visit," Gil said. "She started her off young."

"Grandmaw and Peepaw are coming to see me tomorrow," Josie said. "I can't wait."

"That's nice."

"Mom taught me and Gretchen to skate too." Gil turned and skated backward.

"Oh, now you're just showing off," Noelle said.

"I wanna do that." Josie tried to turn, wobbled,

and almost took a spill, but Noelle reached out to steady her before she tumbled.

"You need a few more lessons first, kiddo." Gil executed a backward figure eight.

"Will you teach me?" Josie asked.

"I want to learn too," Noelle said.

The song changed to "Dance of the Sugar Plum Fairy."

"Skaters, please leave the rink," Moe Schebly requested.

"Aww, man," Josie said. "How come?"

"The professional skaters are putting on a show for us," Gil said, sending Noelle a sultry look.

"A show?" Josie twisted her head around. "What kind of show?"

"Shh." Gil held out his hands, one to Josie, the other to Noelle, and together, the three of them skated to the exit that led to the changing area where the other skaters had assembled to watch what was happening on the ice.

"Daddy." Josie tugged on Gil's hand. "I can't see."

Gil bent and scooped his daughter up, putting her on his shoulders and then stepped to one side, making sure he wasn't blocking anyone else's view of what was happening on the ice. Noelle loved how considerate he was.

He held on to Josie's ankles. Her skates rested against his chest. The blades had to be poking into him, but he seemed unfazed.

Noelle scooted closer to father and daughter, making room as more of the skaters came in off the ice. Once everyone had left the rink, the Teddy Bears skated around the rink, falling into formation to create the shape of a heart.

"Daddy, let me down," Josie said, her tone of voice sharpening.

"What is it?" he asked.

"Silvey Zucker's here." Josie spat out the name as if she had something distasteful in her mouth. "I'm ready to go now."

CHAPTER 23

"Is Silvey still giving you trouble at school?" Gil asked, concerned about his daughter. He wished he knew what was going on in that little brain of hers.

Josie shook her head. "She leaves me alone now."

"Then there's no problem?"

Scowling, Josie folded her arms over her chest. "I didn't know she was gonna be here."

"We're not going to let that stop us from having fun, are we?"

Josie looked from him to Noelle and back again. Her cheeks pinked and Gil wondered if his daughter was thinking about that day at the Christmas tree farm when she'd embarrassed herself.

"No," Josie mumbled.

"C'mon." He took her hand. "Let's go skate. I'll teach you both how to do a figure eight backward."

Josie didn't move.

"What is it?" Gil asked.

"Can Noelle wait here?" Josie asked.

Clearly, the poor kid was self-conscious about

having told Silvey that Noelle was going to be her
new mommy. He wished he could tell Josie that her
dream of a new mother was a possibility, but this
thing with Noelle was still too new and neither one
of them were impulsive people. That kind of commitment would take time and the long distance between them could be a deal breaker. He just didn't
know enough yet to tell his daughter about his feelings for Noelle. Heck, he hadn't even told Noelle yet
that he was falling head over heels in love with her.

Gil shot Noelle a half smile. "Do you mind?"

"Not at all. Go have fun."

Gil winked at her, and she rewarded him with
a soft smile. He took Josie's hand and guided her
out on the ice, just as Silvey and her father entered
the rink.

Noelle enjoyed watching father and daughter together. Gil was such a good dad and so patient
with Josie.

More people came up to her and asked for an
autograph and several minutes passed before she
looked up again.

On the ice, Silvey and her father skated up to Gil
and Josie. Gil had a short exchange with Silvey's
dad. She noticed the two girls barely looked at each
other. Josie glanced over her shoulder in Noelle's
direction.

Noelle smiled and waved.

Quickly jerking her gaze away, Josie did not
wave back.

She wasn't offended. She understood the girl's
embarrassment.

Gil and Josie came off the rink. Josie plunked down some distance away from Noelle and started unlacing her skates while Gil came to sit beside her.

"What's up with her?" Noelle asked.

"She says her feet hurt, but I think it's just an excuse because Silvey is here."

"Ouch!" Noelle crinkled her nose. "She's still pretty sensitive about what happened at the Christmas tree farm."

"She is."

"What did Silvey's dad say to you out on the rink?"

"He asked me if you were seeing anyone."

"What?" Noelle hadn't even met Ted Zucker. Why was the man asking about her?

"He's ready to date. He doesn't like being single and he's eager to find Silvey a new mom. He's heard about you from his nephews and thinks you're hot."

"He moves fast. His wife just left him."

"Some people aren't good alone." Gil studied her face.

"What did you tell him?"

"That you were headed back to LA on Christmas Day."

"And that's it?" Disappointment carved a hole in her stomach. He didn't tell Ted that she and Gil were an item?

"What else was I supposed to say?"

That you're with me. That you're dating me. That I'm your girlfriend.

They stared at each other. People were streaming around them, going on and off the ice, chattering about how much fun they were having. They were just a few feet apart, but to Noelle it suddenly felt like a thousand miles.

Ted Zucker skated up and came off the ice. He wasn't a bad-looking guy in an overgrown frat boy kind of way, but he couldn't hold a candle to Gil.

"Hi," Ted said, thrusting out a hand and ogling her openly. "I'm Silvey's dad."

The guy was bold. She'd give him that. He wouldn't be single for long. She held her breath, waiting for Gil to intervene, to give Ted the bum's rush and tell the man she was with him.

But Gil said nothing.

Not knowing what else to do, Noelle shook Ted's outstretched hand. "Nice to meet you, Ted."

"I run the GMC dealership here in town. My nephews are Cody and Dylan Maxwell. You're Crescenda Hardwick's daughter. Love your mother's movies."

"Thanks."

"You might have heard, I'm newly divorced. Well, technically not divorced yet, but I'm working on it."

"Good for you . . . I guess." Noelle shot a look over at Gil to see if he was going to say anything to Ted about the two of them dating, but Gil wasn't looking at her. He was frowning and scanning the ice rink.

"Is something wrong?" she asked Gil.

"Do you see Josie? I lost her in the crowd and those confounded snowflakes are making it impossible to see her."

"She was right here," Noelle said. "Taking off her skates."

Gil searched the area, but Josie was nowhere in sight. He swung his gaze to the concession stand. Maybe she'd gotten a hot chocolate, although as far as he knew, his daughter didn't have any money for refreshments.

Panic flared icy cold across his skin. He started across the spongy mat flooring, forgetting he still wore his skates, and almost lost his balance. He flailed, grabbing onto the railing that separated the rink from the changing area.

Noelle wrapped her hand around his wrist. "We'll find her."

"Maybe she's with Silvey," Ted said.

Gil already wanted to smash the guy's face in for coming on to Noelle. He didn't want this jackass getting involved in his business. Besides, the last person Josie would hang around with was Silvey.

"Josie," he called, fear slamming hard into his chest and bubbling up from his throat. "Josie!"

What kind of father let his seven-year-old wander off because he'd been too busy fretting over a woman? His ears burned and his heart was a whippet, racing in circles around his chest.

"We'll find her," Noelle repeated, tightening her grip on his arm. She said it with absolute certainty. "She's probably just gone to the bathroom."

"You think she's in the bathroom?" Gil asked. Yes, yes. That made sense.

"Most likely." Noelle smiled gently. "I'll go check."

"I'm going with you."

"To the ladies' room?"

"I'll stand outside."

"Where are the bathrooms?" Noelle glanced around the crowded snow globe. The blowers were kicking up so much faux snow and the crowd was so thick it was hard to see across the rink.

"The portable toilets are outside," Ted said.

"That means she left the rink." The self-assurance in Noelle's voice slipped.

"Let's go." Gil grabbed Noelle's hand.

"Our skates. We've got to change our shoes."

Gil cursed loud enough that heads swiveled. Normally, he would apologize for losing his cool in public, but manners be damned, his daughter was missing.

"Skaters from the six-to-seven-P.M. slot, it's time to leave the ice so the next group can enjoy the snow globe," came the announcement over the PA system.

People had come in and were sitting on the bench where they'd left their boots and Ted Zucker was in their way too.

"Scoot," Gil commanded.

Wide-eyed, both Ted and the other people moved over, letting him and Noelle sit down. Gil clawed at the laces, desperate to get the skates off his feet.

"Slow down," she whispered. "Stay calm."

"Easy for you to say. It's not your kid who's missing."

Noelle drew back.

He was lashing out at her when she only wanted to help, but he couldn't seem to rein in his fear. "I—I'm sorry."

"It's okay. I get it."

Silvey came into the changing area and went over to Ted. "Can we go get pizza?"

"Have you seen Josie?" Gil asked her.

"No." Silvey shook her head.

"Did you say something mean to her?" Gil asked.

"I didn't even talk to her." Silvey jutted up her chin. "You can't blame this on me."

"No one's blaming you, honey," her father said.

Gil felt as if he was about to implode. Normally, he was an easygoing guy, but when it came to his daughter, all bets were off.

"Odds are that Josie is absolutely fine." Noelle tried to smile, but it didn't reach her eyes.

She was right. His daughter was well-known around town. Friends and neighbors would look out for her. He'd taught her what to do in case she got lost. She had her tablet—

Yes! Her computer. He could track her. Why hadn't he already thought of that? He tugged his cell phone from his pocket, checked the app that told him her location. She was right outside, near the portable toilets.

"She's okay. I've got her on my app." He felt all the air leave his lungs and he slumped against the wall.

Noelle picked up the skates he tossed aside and took them to the rental counter along with her own skates. He owed her a better apology after they located Josie.

She came back from the counter with their coats, which she'd retrieved from the coat check. She handed him his shearling jacket along with

Josie's jacket as she pulled on her own coat. Gil clutched Josie's coat. His baby girl was out there in the cold with no coat on.

"This way," Noelle said, guiding him past the people streaming into the changing area to take off their skates. Several people greeted her.

Gil stared at the phone screen, willing Josie to stay put, but the tracker showed she was walking away from the ice rink. "She's on the move!"

"Coming back toward us?"

"No, she's headed away."

"Don't panic. We'll get her. It'll be all right." She sounded so sure of herself, but to Gil, it felt like empty promises.

They exited through the turnstile as a fresh batch of ticketed skaters came in through the entrance. Gil's nerves stretched like overly tuned guitar strings. His gaze was glued to the cell phone screen and the blip that was his daughter as Noelle tugged him across the courthouse lawn. His ankles felt strange from where the skates had been strapped and he had a hollow fear carved deep into his belly.

"Josie!" he hollered.

Shoppers turned to stare at them. Gil was running now. Noelle hurrying to catch up with him. They blasted past the Windmill. There weren't any concerts this weekend because of the wedding reception on Sunday night, but a walking tour group from the Friday night ghost tour were passing by as the bubbly tour guide, Brandy, told the tourists about Twilight's spooky past.

"Brandy," he called. "Did Josie come by here?"

"Yes," Brandy said. "She was running like Jesse

James's ghost was on her heels and she was headed toward Sweetheart Park. She might have been crying. I called to her, but she ignored me."

"Thank you," Gil hollered over his shoulder and kicked up the pace.

Noelle matched his tempo, staying right with him, step for step.

They raced through the park, past strolling couples holding hands, past the Christmas displays and the Sweetheart Tree, Gil's gaze trained on the phone screen.

"She's stopped," he said.

"There she is." Noelle pointed through the darkness aglow with Christmas lights.

Josie stood on the edge of the Sweetheart Fountain, her eyes closed, and her palms pressed to her chest as if she was praying. Then, as Gil and Noelle headed toward her, she reached in her pocket, took out a coin, and tossed it into the water.

"Young lady!" Gil barked. "What did you think you were doing, running off on your own? You know better than that!"

Noelle didn't blame Gil for being upset. His child had gone missing. Any parent might get emotionally dysregulated over something like that, but she'd never seen him looking so freaked out.

Josie turned toward them and jumped off the fountain.

Gil grabbed hold of his daughter's hand. "Why did you leave the ice rink without us?"

"Daddy," Josie said, staring up at her tall father. "I *had* to go."

"But why?"

Josie shifted her gaze to Noelle. "Because Silvey's dad was talking to Noelle and Silvey said Noelle was gonna be *her* mommy, not mine, and I had to do something to stop it."

"So you threw that coin I gave you into the fountain," Noelle said. "And made a wish for your father and me to be together."

Josie nodded. "Aunt Gretchen said you were in love with my daddy when you were young, the same way Rebekka Nash loved Jon Grant. I thought if maybe I threw a coin in the fountain my daddy would love you back and you could really, truly be my mommy."

"Oh sweetheart," Noelle said. "Things just don't work like that."

"Daddy, why can't you love Noelle? Why can't she be my mommy?"

Gil pulled a palm down his face and let out a long sigh. He looked haggard and when he raised his eyes, his face was blank. She had no idea what he was thinking. Did he blame her for Josie's behavior? She was certainly blaming herself. She shouldn't have given the girl that coin. Had no idea why she'd done that other than Josie had admired it.

"Come on, Josie," he said. "Let's go home. It's time to get ready for bed."

"Daddy, are you mad at me?"

"We'll talk about it later."

"Did I do something wrong?"

"Yes, ma'am. You went off without telling me where you were going."

"I'm sorry."

"There will be consequences. We'll discuss your punishment later."

"Yes, sir." She ducked her head, her little voice so forlorn.

Gil put his hand on Josie's shoulder and guided her toward the park exit. Noelle wasn't sure what to do. She wanted to follow them, but she needed to go check on the preparations for the bachelor and bachelorette parties.

"Gil."

He turned back toward her. "Yes."

"Should I come with you?"

He gave a curt shake of his head. "No. This is my problem. You've got work to do and I need to take care of my kid."

She stared at him. She'd never felt so uncertain in her life. What was he thinking? Was he upset with her? Bombarded by self-doubt and unwanted feelings, she stood there, looking at him with pleading eyes. This felt like a monumental rift. Like something they couldn't overcome and yet, she had no idea what it was that she'd done to put that murky expression into his cool blue eyes.

"Noelle!"

She turned to see Pamela Landry and the videographer coming toward her. The videographer was filming the beautifully decorated park.

"Go. Do your thing," Gil said and propelled his daughter toward the B&B.

Before Noelle could say anything more, Pamela rushed over. "This town is so freaking cute! I can't tell you how happy I am you picked the Buckhorn essay as the winning entry. This place will look magnificent on camera. Despite that little hiccup with the Buckhorns at the bridal shop, I think this will be our best wedding contest yet!"

"That's nice," Noelle said, her gaze still fixed on Gil's back as he and Josie walked away. His shoulders were slumped, and he looked defeated. She couldn't help feeling like she'd blown everything up.

The truth was, no matter how hard she tried to tell herself she was immune to the romantic mythology of Twilight's lore, she absolutely was not. She'd fallen for Gil Thomas all over again. Loving him just as hard now as she had at fifteen. She'd tried to convince herself she could play it cool and keep her heart safe, but it simply wasn't true.

She'd gotten hurt and she'd hurt Gil and Josie in the process. Best bet? Bow out. Leave them alone and do what she'd come to town to do.

CHAPTER 24

"Are you absolutely bonkers?" Gretchen stared at Gil as he sat at the kitchen table toying with the napkin holder and looking glum. "You're ending it with the best thing that's happened to you in ages?"

Using the sideboard as a folding table, he pleated the linen napkins in neat triangles. After putting Josie to bed, he'd come inside with the excuse of helping Gretchen prepare for the next morning, but she'd seen straight through his ruse and asked what was bothering him.

"Dude, you light up whenever Noelle walks into the room."

"I do?"

"Please don't tell me you're that dense. She can't take her eyes off you either."

Gil rubbed his forehead with two fingers.

"Talk to me. What is going on inside your head that you want to break up with her?"

"Technically, I can't break up with her because we were never really together."

"Please. You didn't tell people you were together.

It's not the same thing. I've seen you sneaking up those stairs every night for the last three weeks."

"Much like you and Tyler?"

"Leave Tyler out of this."

"You're not telling people about him. How is that any different?"

"Because we *have* decided to let people know about us. He and Ebby are coming over for dinner tomorrow so they can meet Mom and Dad."

"Hey, I'm happy for you."

"Invite Noelle to come to dinner too."

"I can't."

"Why not?"

"I have to end things with her. It's already gone too far."

"Because she lives in LA?"

"That's one reason, yes. Long-distance relationships don't work."

Gretchen rolled her eyes. "You could figure that out if you really wanted to. There's something more going on."

"Well, yeah, there's Josie. She's too attached to this idea of Noelle being her mother. If things don't work out, she'll get her heart broken."

"Like she hasn't already? If you married Noelle, then she would be Josie's mom. Not really seeing the problem. Seems like a win-win to me."

Gil shook his head. "It's not that easy."

"Dumbass," Gretchen muttered, putting the ingredients for overnight oatmeal into the crockpot and closing the lid.

"Things are just getting too complicated. Ted Zucker was trying to ask her out and people were swarming around her asking for her autograph. It's too much."

"You mean you got scared." Gretchen grabbed a sponge and started scrubbing the counter that was already clean.

"Why do you care?"

"Because these last few weeks you've been the happiest that I've seen you since Josie was born and it's all because of Noelle."

"Look, Gretch. There's no way this could work out. Best to stop things now before Josie and I get even more invested."

"So what are you teaching Josie? If things are challenging, don't bother trying?"

That pulled him up short. His sister made a good point. "Noelle and I come from different worlds."

"That's only an obstacle if you let it be one."

"My life isn't my own. How could I ask Noelle to give up what's important to her in order to be with me?"

"Shouldn't Noelle be the one to decide that?"

"You don't get it. You don't have a kid."

"Nope, you're right, I don't." Gretchen tossed the sponge in the sink and raised her arms. "It's none of my business. I'm just the built-in babysitter."

"Hey, that's not fair. I do plenty around here to help."

"I'm not complaining about your work ethic, and I love getting to help raise my niece, but I'm concerned about her welfare too. She needs a mother, Gil."

Gil thought about what Josie told him she wanted for Christmas and cringed. He finished folding the last napkin, got up, settled his arms over his chest, and leaned against the sideboard. "I appreciate everything you do for me and Josie, Gretchen. I don't tell you that enough."

"I'm not looking for validation. I want you to be happy. Noelle makes you happy. Why not get over your resistance? What's at the core of it?"

"That's really none of your business, is it?"

"Ouch. I suppose I deserved that."

"I do value your opinion, Gretchen, and I'll give your advice some thought, but I'm hoping you can respect my decision. If I decide it's best if Josie and I keep our distance from Noelle, please accept it."

"You're a hard nut to crack, little brother." Gretchen untied her apron and hung it on a hook beside the door. "But I'll stay out of your love life."

"Thank you," he said.

He left the Merry Cherub and went across the backyard to his cottage. Pausing at the door, he looked up at the overhead apartment. Noelle would be gone soon, and their short-lived affair would be over.

It was for the best, really. Noelle simply didn't belong in Twilight.

Two more days.

Noelle had two more days to get through and she could go back to her life, having done what she came to Twilight to do. Successfully put on a double wedding for The Tie and forge a new path for her future. And yet, now that she was on the cusp of achieving her goal, it felt like dust in her hands.

She couldn't stop thinking about Gil, the incident

with Josie, and the desperate feeling that they'd lost something important tonight.

Sighing, she watched the grooms-to-be and their friends whooping it up at their bachelor party in the Silver Dollar Saloon on the west side of the town square while the bachelorettes celebrated at Fruit of the Vine to the north, where they were having a bottling party to bottle and label their own wine for the wedding reception.

Finally, she worked up the courage to text Gil. Can we talk later? It's important.

She waited. No answer. Most likely he was tucking Josie in, reading her a bedtime story. Trying not to feel slighted, she stuck her phone back into her pocket. Time to head to Fruit of the Vine and check on the bachelorette party.

Her phone buzzed and her heart leaped. She yanked it from her pocket and her hopes were dashed. Not Gil.

Pamela texted: Get over here. We got a problem.

What now? Noelle hustled over to Fruit of the Vine and found Sienna in tears. Her sister, Benji, Vanessa, and bridesmaids surrounded her. Pamela stood off to one side while the videographer filmed everything.

"What are you doing?" Noelle asked Pamela. "Why are you filming this?"

"Hey, drama sells, and I know you'll fix this." Pamela shrugged. "I have faith in you."

Noelle suppressed an eye roll and went over to where Sienna sat next to a table where empty wine bottles and labels were lined up next to the bottling machine. "What's happened?"

Sienna dropped her head in her hands. "She's gone!"

"Who?"

"Heidi." Sienna wailed. Heidi was Sienna's maid of honor.

"She's dead?" Noelle's hand flew to her throat.

"No, she's not *dead*," Sierra said. "She eloped to Hawaii with some guy she met on the internet two months ago."

Oh whew! Thank God, Heidi was okay.

"What are we going to do?" Sienna wrung her hands. "Where can we find a maid of honor on such short notice?"

"Give me a minute." Noelle's mind whirled, as she leafed through workable solutions.

"Could we just have one maid of honor?" Pamela asked.

Noelle had already thought of that and quickly discarded the idea. "It would mess up the symmetry. The whole thematic concept was twin everything."

"Yeah, yeah." Pamela chuffed. "What if we cut one of Sierra's bridesmaids and use her counterpart as Sienna's maid of honor?"

"That's not fair!" Sierra protested. "Why should one of my friends get sidelined because Sienna's maid of honor eloped?"

"Does anyone know someone who could stand in for Heidi?" Noelle asked.

Vanessa hissed in her breath through clenched teeth. "It's so last-minute."

"What about cousin DeeDee?" Sierra suggested.

"She's three inches taller and fifty pounds heavier

than Heidi. There's no way she could fit into Heidi's dress, not even with alterations," Sienna said.

"Anyone else?" Noelle asked.

"Everyone we want in the wedding is already in it." Sierra drummed her fingernails on the table.

Pamela eyed Noelle. "What about you?"

"Me?" Noelle pressed her palm to her chest.

"You're about the same size as Heidi."

"That's a really good idea." Sienna perked up.

Noelle suppressed a groan. "You guys, I'd be happy to do it, but I'll be so busy behind the scenes—"

"I can do all that," Pamela said. "There's not much difference between being a wedding planner and managing The Tie. The job is the same. Make things run smoothly. Besides, being maid of honor will only take a couple of hours from your other duties."

Everyone was staring at Noelle.

Great.

"Noelle, you're Sienna's maid of honor. Problem solved." Pamela clapped loudly. "Now, chop, chop, that wine won't bottle itself."

It was almost midnight by the time the parties were finally over, and Noelle had finished cleaning up, but Gil had never texted her back.

Pamela and the videographer had already gone back to the B&B. She could have walked over with them, but her heart was still heavy over what had happened with Josie, and she made an excuse to linger.

The streets were silent as the owner of Fruit of the Vine locked the door behind them. "Do you need a ride?" she asked Noelle.

"The walk's not that far."

"You sure? It's cold out."

"I'll be fine."

"Suit yourself." The woman headed for her vehicle.

Once she drove away, there was not another soul around. Even the incessant Christmas music had stopped playing although the string lights on the courthouse were still on. Noelle started walking.

Gil still hadn't texted her back.

Her mind came up with a dozen good excuses. He'd silenced his phone. He'd forgotten to charge it. He'd left it in another room. He'd fallen asleep . . .

But her doubts and fears weren't buying it. They poked at her, mean and relentless. *He doesn't want to hear from you. He's ignoring you. Wise up. It's over.*

She'd intended to go back to the B&B, but that's not where her feet took her. Huddled against the wind, she pulled up the hood on her coat and walked for twenty minutes. As she wound her way through the familiar neighborhood, a mist rolled in off the lake, covering her in the deepest dark, the blackest of nights, the streetlamps obscured by the thickening fog.

It was the lowest she'd felt since coming to Twilight. She felt utterly hopeless. There was no way she could have a happily-ever-after with Gil. A forever love just wasn't in her DNA. She might as well face facts.

The darkness had become so intense, so overwhelming, she wondered if perhaps she'd died and just didn't know it, and yet, she kept walking, placing one foot after the other, moving forward in the soup of her own despair.

Why had she thought coming back to Twilight was a good idea? Why had she thought it would save her? She wished now she'd picked someone else's essay as the winner of The Tie's contest instead of the Buckhorn twins. She'd paid a high price for her nostalgia.

At last, she arrived at her destination. In the darkness, the house was nothing more than lumpy shadows. The little bungalow that had once been her salvation.

Grammie and Grampie's home.

She wished her mother hadn't sold it. Wished she could move here and live in this little town that had once been more home to her than any place she'd ever lived with Crescenda.

She stood there, tears streaming down her cheeks, feeling so much grief she could hardly bear it.

"Oh, Grammie, Grampie, I miss you so much," she whispered into the night. "How did you do it? How did you make love last a lifetime?"

Her grandparents never talked badly about her mother, but after Crescenda's fourth marriage broke up and she'd sent Noelle to stay with them for a few weeks until she could sort herself out, Noelle remembered hearing Grammie mutter to Grampie when she thought their granddaughter wasn't listening, "If Crescenda could just open her heart to the idea that true and lasting love is so much more than fast-beating pulses, breathless whispers, roses, and sonnets, if she could just stay in one place long enough to get the lesson, then she could have what she's desperately searching for."

Noelle had forgotten all about that until now. Could she draw inspiration from her grandmother's advice for her mother? Was she just as closed off as Crescenda, but in a totally different way?

It was a startling thought. Had she used disbelief in romantic love as a way to keep her safe from her mother's chaotic infatuations? Gone in the opposite direction. Rejecting love because her mother embraced it so haplessly?

Gobsmacked, she sank down on the frigid ground.

A car came down the road, headlights cutting through the foggy darkness and that's when she saw it.

The "for sale" sign in the front yard.

CHAPTER 25

After his talk with Gretchen, Gil stewed, second- and third-guessing himself. He stayed up until midnight, waiting for Noelle to come home. He hadn't texted her back because he wasn't sure what to say. Even though it was late, he planned to sit down with her and lay it all out. His feelings, his fears, his hopes, his dreams. It was time to stop holding back.

He'd made that mistake with Tammy Jo, trying to be the big strong tough guy, and keeping his emotions bottled up when he should have been open and honest with her. If he had, maybe she would have been happier.

Gil had made that mistake in his marriage, but he'd learned his lesson. Communication was key and he'd been holding back with Noelle, afraid of scaring her off.

Well, the time had come. She would be leaving on Monday. It was now or never.

They were on the precipice of something important. He was falling in love with her—oh, who was he kidding, he was already in love with her—and he had to know where he stood. If she was serious about this relationship, he needed to know and he needed to know it now, before his daughter got any more invested than she already was.

Heartache might lie ahead of him, but so might the greatest happiness of his life. He was ready to take the risk. Ready to lay everything on the line for her.

He hated seeing his kid hurt, and if Noelle didn't feel the same way about him that he felt about her he had to end this thing tonight. He'd waited too long for a half-hearted romance. He had to know that she was all in. Because he sure as hell was.

So, he checked on Josie, found her sleeping soundly, then went to the garage to finish the song he'd been writing for Noelle, and he waited.

And waited.

And waited.

Knowing her responsibilities to the wedding might have kept her out extra late, he finally gave up and went to bed. His parents were coming in tomorrow and he was picking them up at DFW Airport at nine. His talk with Noelle would have to wait. Both of them had so much going on with this wedding, he didn't know when they'd find the time for a private talk.

As unsatisfactory as it felt, he'd just have to bide his time.

It was two A.M. by the time Noelle got back to the Roost. She'd been walking around Twilight, thinking about her parents and grandparents, her life in

LA, her career, and what a different kind of future might look like.

The day would be utterly hectic as she put the finishing touches on the wedding prep and prepared for her last-minute duties as Sienna's maid of honor. The rehearsal dinner was that night, and she wouldn't have a moment to spare.

Noelle dropped into bed exhausted and immediately fell into a troubled dream where she was being chased by a nameless terror. She woke up bathed in sweat and reached for her phone, flopped back on the pillow, and held it to her chest. *Please.* She turned it on.

Gil hadn't texted.

She felt tears leak from her eyes and run down into her ears. Oh, she was making herself miserable.

Unable to go back to sleep, she got up, made coffee, pulled out the wedding bible, and started going over her to-do list.

At dawn, she heard the door downstairs open. She jumped up from the table, raced to the door, threw it open, and flung herself down the stairs.

Gil was halfway to his truck parked in the side driveway.

"Gil!"

He stopped.

She was breathless, heart slamming against her chest.

He turned.

She came closer.

They stood staring at each other.

"Hi," she whispered, hoping so many things.

The wind was whipping through her pajamas, but she barely noticed.

"I waited up for you, but I guess you had a late night."

"Oh." She blinked. "You did?"

"You texted that you wanted to talk."

She gulped. "You didn't answer me back."

"I figured you were busy."

"I was."

"I just sent Josie into the B&B for breakfast. I'm headed to the airport to pick up my parents or I'd stay and talk now." He didn't smile.

She couldn't get a read on him. "Go, go. It's okay. We don't have to do this."

"Do what?"

"Drag things out. We had a wonderful time. I've loved every minute I've gotten to spend with you and your family. Thank you for a wonderful time."

Gil winced.

A reaction! Hallelujah.

"That sounds like goodbye."

"No," she said. "Not yet. We still have today and tomorrow."

"One of those days is a wedding and Christmas Eve and the day after that, you'll be on a plane back to LA."

"I will."

He looked as if he might say something, but at just that moment a black SUV pulled into the driveway behind his truck and two older people got out. It had been over a decade since she'd seen them, but Noelle recognized the couple right away.

It was Gil's parents, Jim and Marcie Thomas.

"Mom! Dad! I was just on my way to pick you up." He turned toward them, his arms outstretched.

Leaving Noelle behind.

"Surprise!" Jim and Marcie said in unison and embraced their son in a family hug. "We couldn't wait to see you, so we changed our travel plans, caught an early flight, and grabbed an Uber. Where's Josie?"

"Grandmaw! Peepaw!" Josie came flying down the steps of the B&B to get her share of hugs and kisses.

Noelle stood off to one side, watching the loving reunion, and trying not to feel left out. This wasn't her family. She should go.

"Noelle?" Marcie Thomas, wearing a comically ugly Christmas sweater, raised her head and startled as if seeing her for the first time. "Little Noelle Curry? Is that really you?"

"Hi, Mrs. Thomas." Feeling awkward and out of place, Noelle lifted a hand. "Hi, Mr. Thomas. Merry Christmas."

"Oh, my goodness, it's been too long." Without hesitation, Gil's mother covered the distance between them and scooped Noelle into her arms as if she was one of her kids.

Once Marcie was done hugging her, Jim came over to pump her hand. "Well, look at you, Noelle Curry, all grown up."

"Good to see you again, sir."

"Don't sir me. I'm Jim to my friends."

Gretchen trotted out of the house, wiping her

hands on her apron and the embraces and kissing started all over again.

Noelle watched Jim open the back door and usher his wife, daughter, and grandchild inside while Gil went to pick up their luggage from the Uber driver.

"Noelle?" Jim held the door open. "Are you coming? Fair warning, Marcie's making her breakfast tacos and they're the best you'll ever put in your mouth."

"I can't. I've got work to do."

"Noelle's planning the Buckhorn twins' wedding," Gretchen said. "They're getting married tomorrow."

"On Christmas Eve?" Marcie said. "Oh, that will be fun."

"Aah, come on," Jim coaxed. "You gotta fuel your body. Can't send you off on an empty stomach."

"Dad," Gil said. "Let her go."

Let her go.

Noelle mumbled a quick goodbye and raced back to the Roost feeling worse than she had when she'd come bursting out of the apartment. Which was pretty darn crappy indeed.

For the rest of the day, Noelle managed to block Gil out of her mind. Mostly because she had so much work to do, she had no time to think about anything else, which was exactly how she wanted it.

At one point during the rehearsal dinner, a bedraggled Pamela Landry looked at her and said, "You're like what? The spawn of the Energizer Bunny and Mary Poppins? I didn't know one woman could smile so much and with such earnestness."

Noelle just gave her a dazzling grin as she steered a drunken Buckhorn relative to the restroom just before they heaved.

"Truly," Pam said. "You are the Wedding Whisperer. Your instincts are uncanny."

"Nah," Noelle said. "I just had parents who partied."

"Well, appreciate the skills you learned. They've served you well."

"Nice to know something good came from it."

"Don't sell yourself short. You're extraordinary."

"Thank you for the compliment," Noelle said. It was nice to know she would have a career once this was all over, even if her love life was falling apart. But she wasn't getting cocky. She had a wedding to get through.

Anything could go wrong and ruin it all.

Gil, on the other hand, couldn't stop thinking about Noelle. He went along with his parents and Gretchen as they took Josie to several Christmas events, including story hour at Ye Olde Book Nook, where local children's author Sarah Walker did a reading of her newest book, *Santa and the Magic Christmas Cookie*. They went on a scavenger hunt and took Josie to see Santa and ended the day with a shopping trip.

There were no other guests booked at the B&B for the Christmas weekend, besides Pamela Landry, the videographer, and Noelle, and they would be out all evening. So, Mom played the piano while they all gathered around and sang Christmas carols. Later, they all piled into the parlor, and had popcorn and soda while they watched *Elf* and *A Christmas Story*, a Thomas family holiday tradition.

They did all the stuff he normally loved. It was sweet, it was touching, it was heartfelt, and Gil was utterly miserable. He kept wishing Noelle was there to enjoy the festivities with him. But she was not and when it was time to go to bed, she still hadn't come home.

The weather on Sunday, December 24, was crisp and cool with clear skies. A perfect day for a winter Christmas Eve wedding.

Showtime. Noelle was in her element. She'd spent six weeks preparing for this. The wedding was scheduled for four in the afternoon, and Noelle was up at dawn, packing the bridal emergency kit bags and gathering the bridal details for the photographer— garters, shoes, wedding bands, bouquet.

Then she was on the phone checking in with the brides and bridesmaids. Next, she called the groom and his groomsmen, making sure everyone had picked up their tuxedoes the previous day. After that, she gave Pamela her list of duties for the church since The Tie representative would be taking over those chores while Noelle went for hair and makeup appointments with the other wedding party members.

Finally, before leaving for the salon, she dropped by the Windmill. The place was empty, and she felt disappointed that Gil wasn't there. Part of her hoped he might be, but it was Christmas Eve, and his parents were in town, so she really didn't expect it.

But, to her joy, she saw that at some point he and his crew had set up the auditorium for the reception just as she'd outlined on the chart she'd drawn up for him. The tables and chairs matched the floor plan. The linens hung evenly. The chairs were flush with the table linens as they should be. He'd set up and decorated the cake tables, put out the place cards, table numbers, seating chart, signage, and the photo booth, everything she'd asked him to do and more.

Gil was a man she could depend on.

But Noelle already knew that.

She went to the salon, feeling far less stressed than she normally would have and in fact, actually had a good time listening to the other women talk, laugh, and tease. Gil had her back. She wasn't in this alone.

The salon appointment was over by two and she hurried back to the B&B to get dressed. The burgundy dress fit like it had been tailored just for her and the style suited her figure. The church was just a few blocks over and she didn't mind walking.

This was it.

She touched up her lipstick, picked up the emergency bridal kits, and walked out the door. To find Gil coming out of the B&B at the exact same time.

Noelle stepped off the last step of the stairs as Gil moved across the lawn toward her. His jaw had unhinged. Gil snapped it closed, but he couldn't take his eyes off Noelle. She was drop-dead gorgeous.

She was in high heels that elevated her height. She held her shoulders back, chin squared, and moved like a dancer. Her hair was upswept, showing off her elegant, swanlike neck and diamond studs glittered at her earlobes. A prism necklace on a crystal chain nestled at her world-class cleavage and the pendant reflected a rainbow of light all around her like an angelic halo.

But what struck him speechless was the dazzling smile on her face. He heard a soft gasp, then realized it came from his own mouth.

"Are you all right?"

"Um . . . Pamela called. She said you would need a ride to the church."

"It's okay. I can walk."

"Not in those shoes." Gil shook his head. "What, you're afraid to ride with me?"

"No." She laughed, but it was a nervous sound. "I just didn't want to make any extra work for you."

"Bookworm, it would be my honor."

He couldn't stop staring at her. How did she get her eyes to look so wide and lustrous? And her lips! They were perfectly outlined with a pink pencil liner and filled in with an even glossier pink that made him think of cotton candy.

How sweet it is.

She smelled as good as she looked. Like cinnamon-sugar Christmas cookies and vanilla buttercream icing.

"Thank you," she said. "For getting the Windmill set up so far in advance. You were a godsend."

"Couldn't sleep last night," he said. "Figured I might as well make myself useful."

"I appreciate it so much."

"Anytime." He stuck out his elbow for her to take.

She slipped her arm through his and a puff of pride passed through him at having her on his arm.

"You look amazing," Gil said as they got in the truck.

It was only a four-block drive, but Pamela was right. Noelle couldn't walk to the church dressed like the Sugar Plum Fairy. But then it struck him that she deserved a carriage fit for a princess, and all she'd gotten was his scruffy old work truck. Gil wished he'd had time to wash and vacuum out his vehicle.

"Thank you." Noelle grinned. "Apparently, I clean up well."

"That's the understatement of the decade." Yikes. That sounded rude. "I mean . . . It's just that . . . I'm used to you looking official and efficient or tousled in bed—"

"I know what you mean."

"It's just . . . wow . . . I've never seen you so gussied up."

"The magic of a professional makeup job." She rested her hands in her lap and stared out the windshield.

"Hey," he said, his chest tightened with all the emotions he hadn't had a chance to talk to her about.

She turned to look at him, her expression mild.

"I *am* sorry."

"For what?" She seemed surprised.

"The way I acted the other night at the ice rink."

"You did nothing wrong. I understand. Your daughter comes first."

"I overreacted. I was too harsh."

"You weren't."

"I was and I'm sorry. Can you forgive me?"

"There's nothing to forgive. Please don't give it a second thought. I've moved on from it. You should too."

He had a horrible feeling that he'd blown whatever chance he might have had with her. He wanted to say more, but they were already at the church, and he was slipping into the reserved parking spot behind the building.

Before he had a chance to get out of the truck and hurry around to open the door for her, she was already out and smoothing down the folds of her dress. The wedding party was collecting outside before entering. Pamela Landry, clipboard in hand, directed people how to line up. Pamela spied Noelle and waved her over and Gil's moment was gone.

Noelle went over to the woman and Gil trailed behind her, uncertain what he should be doing.

"We've got a huge problem," Pamela said, drawing her off to one side so the wedding party wouldn't overhear their conversation. "Huge. If we can't find a solution, we might even have to cut your segment from the show."

That statement would have defeated most people, but instead of shrinking back, Noelle sprang forward, body alert and at the ready to tackle any and all problems. Gil admired her resilience.

"What's wrong?" she asked, knotting her hands

into fists and rising up on the balls of her feet. "What's happened?"

"There was an accident." Pamela shook her head.

Noelle gasped and her hand flew to her mouth. "When? Where? Who?"

"The bus carrying the band for the reception was involved in a twenty-car pileup on the interstate just east of Dallas. There was an eighteen-wheeler that turned over and spilled its contents on the road. The bus flipped."

"Was anyone hurt?"

"No one was seriously injured, but two of the band members have concussions and one has a broken arm. They won't be able to play tonight. We've got to beat the bushes for a DJ and get all that set up ASAP."

"Oh dear." Noelle's brow knitted as she massaged the bridge of her nose.

Pamela swung her gaze to Gil. "Is finding a last-minute DJ something you can help with, Mr. Thomas?"

"I can do better than that," Gil said. "I can put together a replacement band that'll be just as good as the band you hired."

"Really?" Noelle's eyes widened.

"Cash Colton is a good friend of mine," he said, referring to one of country music's hottest stars. "He and his family just happen to be in town for the holidays. They own a ranch on the outskirts of Twilight."

"Oh my gosh, you are a lifesaver," Pamela said. "That's amazing."

"I'll get right on it." Gil pulled out his phone to start calling in the local musicians he knew.

"Thank you. You saved my fanny." Noelle leaned over to plant a kiss on his cheek, leaving her sweet scent lingering on his skin.

As he walked away, he heard Pamela say, "Curry, you need to hold on to that guy. He's one in a million."

CHAPTER 26

The wedding went off without a hitch.

Considering all the fires Noelle had doused over the course of the last six weeks, she was surprised by how smoothly things worked once Gil managed to round up a spur-of-the-moment replacement band. He'd be playing at the reception along with his friends and he'd gone home to grab his bass guitar.

Neither she nor Pamela risked telling the brides about the band snafu. They didn't want the twins distracted. It turned out to be the right decision. The twin brides and grooms had eyes only for one another. And everyone else thought she'd managed to coax Cash Colton to headline the band all along.

Noelle was so busy in her role as wedding planner/maid of honor, that she lost track of Gil during the ceremony. He had his role to perform, she had hers, but they'd still never had the conversation they so desperately needed to have.

But she thought about him. A lot.

He'd been a hero. He'd rescued the show. Without him, the wedding reception would have fallen apart.

Beyond his invaluable help, she appreciated his apology for his curtness on the night of the snow globe ice rink incident, even though it had been unnecessary. His compliments about her appearance brought a lump to her throat and a tenderness to her heart, although part of her couldn't help discounting his praise. She knew she'd just been wrapped up in a pretty package. The Noelle underneath the makeup and fancy dress was nothing particularly special.

"Is everything okay?" Noelle asked Pamela.

Pamela stuck her thumb in the air. "All I had to do was following your wedding planning bible. Great job, Curry."

"If you need anything—"

"I won't bug you. You've got a toast to give. Now go on, shoo."

Noelle turned to follow the others.

"Oh, by the way," Pamela called after her. "You look fantastic!"

Okay, from now on, she was wearing burgundy as often as possible. Grinning, Noelle hurried to help Sienna manage her train.

The meal of prime rib was fantastic. The Tie videographer went from table to table recording the conversations. The toasts were heartfelt, and no one messed up. The dual first dance between brides and grooms was as cinematic as it was sentimental.

Noelle danced with Cody's best man, but her eyes were on Gil as the band played "Can't Stop the Feeling." Too bad he was playing with the musicians. She would have enjoyed dancing with him.

A few minutes later, the song ended, and Gil took the microphone. "I wrote this song as a Christmas present to someone special and I have the brides' and grooms' permission to play it here for you now."

He began to play unaccompanied. Just Gil and an acoustic guitar. The song had a similar tone and mood to Fleetwood Mac's "Landslide." It was soft, gentle, and so very sweet.

"She was a shy girl, kept to herself, but across the street, there was a boy who caught her eye. She watched him from afar, as he grew into a man, dreaming of a day when she could take him by the hand." Gil crooned into the microphone. His gaze was locked on Noelle.

Her heart started pounding and her chest tightened, and she found it hard to draw in a breath. Gil had written a song about her. She was so stunned, she missed a few of the lines. Noelle blinked as he sang the bridge.

"They laughed, they loved, they grew together. They faced the world, hand in hand forever. They were the perfect match, two hearts beating as one."

She brought both hands to her mouth, overwhelmed and overcome. He was telling her that he loved her.

In a song.

In front of two hundred witnesses.

Someone swung the spotlight her way and suddenly she was bathed in hot white light. Everyone was staring. She was not a center stage kind of woman. She moved her hands from her mouth to clutch her stomach. Her knees trembled uncontrollably.

"She's not the girl she used to be." Gil's eyes were shiny, but she could barely see past the tears in her own eyes. "She's a woman in love, standing brave and tall. And she'll continue to bloom, oh, she'll continue to bloom. Into an exceptional woman, with the love of her life by her side."

Her brain couldn't absorb it. It was too much. This wasn't right. She was taking the limelight from the brides. She felt faint, dizzy. She had to get out of there.

Turning, Noelle flew out of the room.

He'd screwed up.

Badly.

Deep down, she was still that shy girl from across the street, no matter all the wonderful things she'd accomplished.

How inconsiderate he'd been. Even though the Buckhorns and Maxwells had been behind him singing the song at their wedding reception, it had been too much for Noelle.

Had he completely ruined things with her?

Gil set down the guitar and left the stage, running after Noelle. Behind him, he heard Cash Colton say, "Now that was a love song, people. Give it up for Gil Thomas. I'm gonna ask him if he'll let me record that song."

Thunderous applause from the audience.

His song for Noelle would be a hit if Cash recorded it, but that didn't matter. Nothing mattered without Noelle.

He needed to tell her how proud he was of her. How he wanted to be there to support her every step on her journey. How he was willing to do whatever it took to work things out with her. If that meant packing up and moving to LA, then that's what he'd do. Josie might even thrive in a bigger city where she would have more opportunities.

Now, in order to have a relationship with Noelle, he was open to change.

He had to find her. Had to tell her that he loved her. Had to ask her if she felt the same way. He couldn't go another minute without knowing the answer.

The band was playing Cash's number one hit, the sound pouring out into the corridor. He looked left, then right. Which way had Noelle gone? Had she left the building altogether?

The auditorium door closed behind him, blocking out some of the sound. He took a few deep breaths to slow his pounding pulse. *Chill.* He heard muffled voices coming from his office. Was it Noelle? If so, who was she with?

The door was open. Not a private conversation, he assumed, or else why not close the door? He moved toward his office, intending to just briefly poke his head inside and see if Noelle was in there when he heard Pamela's voice.

"Noelle," Pamela said. "This is an amazing opportunity. You can't let it pass you by. Say yes. Say you'll move to New York and become The Tie's new creative director."

Gil froze. He didn't mean to eavesdrop. That was certainly not his intention, but he couldn't seem to make himself back away.

Or even move.

"But what about my own wedding planning business?"

"You can hire someone to run Once Upon a Wedding. If you take our offer, you can write your own ticket. With your organizational and people skills, you can be so much more than a wedding planner."

"I—I . . ." Noelle stammered. "I don't know what to say. This is so unexpected."

"Say yes."

Gil pulled a palm down his face. How he wished he hadn't overheard this conversation. He couldn't tell Noelle what he'd come to tell her. That he loved her and wanted to be with her.

Not now. Not when she had such a huge opportunity in front of her. He couldn't hold her back. He couldn't be the reason Noelle didn't live up to her full potential.

He had no choice. He had to step aside. Keep his mouth shut and let her go. With his pitiful heart barely pumping in his chest, Gil turned and walked away.

Noelle was blown over by The Tie's lucrative offer. It was an honor to be asked, but she simply didn't want the job. What she wanted was to find Gil and have that long overdue talk.

"Thanks for your offer, Pamela. I'll take it under consideration."

"I can up the salary a bit if that'll nudge you in the right direction."

"The money isn't the issue."

"What is?"

"It's a personal matter."

"Aww," Pamela said. "The musician. I've got contacts in the New York music scene. Bring him with you."

"I'll give it some thought. For now, I need to get back to the wedding."

"It's almost over. Go get some rest. You've done an outstanding job and it's Christmas Eve."

"Merry Christmas, Pamela."

"You're not going to take the job, are you?"

Noelle shook her head.

"Giving it all up for love?"

"If I have that opportunity."

"Fine." Pamela laughed. "Go find him and tell him just how much you're giving up for him."

"Thank you for the offer—I'm very flattered."

"Yeah, yeah." Pamela waved her away.

Noelle returned to the reception. She found Benji and Spencer at the open bar. "Have you seen Gil?"

"He left right after you did. We all assumed, after that romantic song, he went looking for you and you two were smooching up a storm."

"No. He didn't."

Noelle pulled out her phone. She was just about to text Gil when the doors to the auditorium burst open with a loud *bang*.

Everyone jumped and all eyes swung to the entrance . . .

As Crescenda, dripping in diamonds and wearing a designer gown, sashayed into the room.

The second she saw her mother, Noelle started grinning as everyone else gawked.

Crescenda might be a showy, over-the-top attention-seeker, but she was here! She'd come to spend Christmas with her daughter.

Noelle zoomed across the room like a bee to a flower. "Mom!"

"Darling!" Crescenda threw her arms open wide.

"I'm thrilled you're here, but why?" Noelle asked, vaguely aware of her mother's bodyguards positioning themselves at the doors and the spectators gawking at the spectacle of Crescenda Hardwick in full bloom. "You told me you were spending Christmas with Basil in Kent."

Crescenda rolled her eyes and waved a hand. "I'm so over Oregano."

"The engagement is off?"

"When I told him I was going to spend Christmas with you, he gave me an ultimatum. Stay in England or lose the part. You know how I am with ultimatums."

"So, no Agatha Christie biopic?"

"Seriously, other than the mysterious disappearing act that the woman pulled, she was *so* dull. All she did was write."

"Well, she was a writer. What did you expect?"

"Something more exciting than one mere disappearing act. I mean seriously, what was the fuss all about? I've disappeared three times."

"With you it's a pattern. With Agatha it was an anomaly. But *why* did you decide to come spend Christmas with me?"

"Well, here's the thing . . ." Crescenda reached

up to toy with a lock of Noelle's hair that had escaped her updo. "That young man of yours called me and told me in no uncertain terms that I needed to be here with you for the holidays."

"When did Gil call you?"

"Oh, I don't know . . . Thursday? You know how I am with time."

"Well, I'm thrilled you're here."

"Any man who has the guts to call your mother up and yell at her must love you very much," Crescenda said. "Do not let him get away."

"I think you're right. And we'll spend Christmas Day together tomorrow, but I didn't know you were coming and for tonight, I've made other plans."

"You're running out on me? And after I came all this way and broke up with Oregano over you?"

"Nope, I'm leaving you to your adoring public." She pointed at Sierra and Sienna, who were practically drooling. "I'll introduce you around and then I'll be on my way. Tomorrow we'll have brunch and spend the whole rest of the day together. But for now, I'm leaving."

Crescenda frowned. "What's happening?"

"I'm setting boundaries with you, Mom."

"It doesn't feel like a good thing."

"You'll get used to it," Noelle said. "It's part of the new me."

It was almost midnight by the time Noelle got to Gil's place. She was breathless and a little shaky when she knocked on the door.

A few minutes passed and when Gil didn't answer,

her shoulders slumped. He must have already gone to bed. But of course. It was Christmas Eve. Josie would have him up by dawn.

Sighing, she turned for the stairs.

The door opened and Gil poked his head out.

He looked so sexy with his mussed hair and puzzled expression that she lost the words that had been on the tip of her tongue. His eyes rounded in surprise.

"Oh, hey," she said.

"Hey."

"You still awake?"

"Sort of." He wore gray sweatpants and a navy blue Twilight, Texas, T-shirt. His feet were bare.

"What are you doing?"

"Putting together a bicycle."

"Where's Josie?"

"At the B&B with my folks. They took her over there for the night so I could do the Santa Claus thing here."

"Do you need any help putting the bicycle together?"

"Know your way around a socket wrench, do you?"

"I could read the instructions."

Smiling, he held the door wide. "C'mon in."

She followed him inside and he closed the door.

"You called my mother."

"Are you mad?" he asked.

"No. She showed up at the reception."

"Hey, what do you know? Miracles *do* happen."

"She broke up with her sixth fiancé over me."

His eyebrows shot up on his forehead. "Really?"

"Well, in a totally Crescenda kind of way, but yeah. Thank you for calling her on the carpet."

"You're welcome."

"She said only a man who loved me would have the guts to call her out."

"You don't say."

"Does this mean you love me?" She lowered her lashes and cast him a sidelong glance.

"Noelle, I'm over the moon for you. I tried to tell you that in the song I wrote."

"Yeah, I was a little overwhelmed."

"Why is that?"

"No one's ever professed his love for me in a song."

"Good. I'm glad. I want to be special."

"Oh," she said. "You are, but why did you wait so long to tell me?"

"Because you're headed for the stars and I'm just plain old Gil."

"I'm not headed for the stars. I like keeping my feet planted firmly on the ground."

He winced.

"What is it?"

"I gotta confess. I overheard you and Pamela talking in my office."

She lightly swatted his shoulder. "That's why you ran off without saying anything?"

"You should take that job with The Tie. I don't ever want to be the thing that stands in the way of your happiness."

"You already are standing in my way," she said.

"What are you talking about?" He angled his head as if he couldn't figure her out.

"I don't want to move to New York."

"No?"

"Not in the least. In fact, I put in an offer on my grandparents' old house yesterday."

"What?" A huge grin broke across his face. "Are you serious?"

"It's on the market again and I love Twilight. It's always felt like home."

"What about your wedding planning business?"

"They have weddings to plan right here in Twilight. I can fly back and forth to take care of the weddings I already have scheduled in LA."

"Really?" His eyes were shiny again like they'd been at the reception.

"Really. I want to be here. I want to be with you." With other relationships, she'd thought about how much she'd have to give up for a commitment, but with Gil, she found herself thinking about how much she would get.

He came closer and settled his arms around her waist. "I love you, Noelle. I've been running scared, afraid of change, afraid to take a chance, but I can't run the risk of losing you. I know it's too soon to talk about marriage, but maybe, one day?"

"I love you too, Gil. You're my one and only. I've never loved any man but you."

He kissed her then, long and deep, and then he let her go.

Letting out a shaky breath, she said, "Maybe we better finishing putting that bicycle together before this starts to get spicy."

"It's almost done," he said. "Just need to put on the training wheels. I can do that in the morning."

"Are all the rest of the presents wrapped?"

"Uh-huh."

"Well, come here then, cowboy. I've always wanted to make love underneath a Christmas tree."

Dawn roused them just before seven as the rosy glow crept through the curtains. Noelle opened her eyes, barely able to believe she was here with Gil, and they'd finally sorted everything out between them and found the courage to confess their true feelings.

"How are you this morning?" He grinned, pulling the lap blanket over them.

"It feels like I got run over by Santa and his reindeer." She laughed, reaching up to touch a bow that was stuck in her hair.

"Mmm," he said. "Now, that's a package I'd definitely want to unwrap."

"Don't get too frisky. There's a seven-year-old who'll be coming through that door any minute."

"One kiss?"

"Are you absolutely sure I'm the one you want?"

"Noelle Curry, I love every single thing about you."

She gasped, breathless with joy. Noelle met his dear gaze, stared into the eyes of the man she'd loved for a decade and a half. "Are you absolutely sure, Gil?"

"It is the only sure thing I know, Bookworm." Gil started humming the song he'd written for her, the melody weaving around her soul.

A helpless smile overtook her face as she traced his lips with her fingertip. The warmth of his skin melted away all her doubts and fears and in the empty space left behind, a sweet, unshakable faith filled her up.

For indeed, she had truly found her home in Gil's arms.

At that moment, the door burst open, and Josie came tumbling in. "Daddy, Daddy, did Santa—"

Josie stopped in her tracks. Her eyes went wide, and her jaw flapped open as she stared at the big red bow on Noelle's head.

Feeling self-conscious, Noelle pulled the blanket all the way up to her chin, happy that in the middle of the night she'd gotten cold and put her clothes back on.

"Daddy," Josie whispered. "Did it happen? Did Santa Claus bring me a mommy for Christmas?"

"Yes," Noelle said. "He did."

"Oh boy." Josie jumped around the room. "Good thing I threw that coin in the fountain to make sure. Just wait until Silvey Zucker hears about this!"

EPILOGUE

One year later . . .

The morning sunlight glimmered off Lake Twilight as a rippling banner stretching across Ruby Street announced: Special Polar Plunge This Year, December 24!

That was today, Christmas Eve.

Their wedding day.

At the marina beach, Gil, dressed in a resplendent black tuxedo, and Noelle, in her wedding dress, gazed into each other's eyes as they said their "I dos" while family and friends watched.

Josie, Ebby, and Silvey were flower girls. Sienna, Sierra, and Benji her bridesmaids.

So much had happened in one short year. Noelle had closed on her grandparents' house. They'd renovated it and moved in together. Noelle flew back and forth to LA until all her wedding obligations there had been fulfilled, then bolstered by her connection to The Tie, she sold the business for a ridiculous amount of money and opened another wedding planning business in Twilight that she operated out of the Windmill.

Cash Colton recorded Gil's song about their romance and titled it "Noelle." It shot to number three on the Billboard charts and stayed there for seven weeks. Gretchen married Tyler and Ebby became Josie's cousin and they were inseparable. On Thanksgiving, Gretchen announced she and Tyler were pregnant with twins. Gil's parents decided with more grandchildren on the way, they wanted to be closer and left Costa Rica for Twilight.

While Josie and Silvey would never be the best of friends—they were both too competitive for that—they had learned how to get along and that was good enough. Noelle had hit it off with Joe Cheek's wife, Gabi, and they were in a knitting club together that met every Wednesday night. Gabi had introduced her to other women around town and Noelle had more friends in Twilight than she'd ever had in LA.

Crescenda was still Crescenda. Some things never changed. But at least she hadn't gotten married again.

Everything was coming up roses for the Thomases and after so many lean years, they embraced their new abundance with gratitude and love.

"I now pronounce you man and wife," the minister said. "You may take the plunge."

As the band played "Noelle" they stripped off down to their Santa Claus–themed swimsuits and, laughing, ran hand in hand into Lake Twilight. Gil had gotten Noelle used to cold showers and they had fun splashing the members of the wedding party brave enough to join them in the water.

While everyone else hopped out and quickly ran back to shore, Gil and Noelle stood in the water, kissing in the circle of each other's arms, ablaze with jubilant happiness as the sweet sound of Gil's love song to his wife and the thumping of their hearts blended into the most perfect melody of Christmas joy.

MORE FROM
LORI WILDE

Twilight Texas Series

Cupid Texas Series

Jubilee Texas Series

Moonglow Cove Series

Stardust Texas Series